PAPA

ON THE MOON

a novel in stories

MARCO NORTH

BITTERSWEETeditions

First printing, 2022.

ISBN: 978-0-9897153-3-1 (Paperback)

Library of Congress Control Number: 2022939442

Cover design by Bittersweet Content

Printed by Bittersweet Editions in the United States of America

www.bittersweeteditions.com

for The Ragged Lion, Jack Micheline

contents

Percheron

Some frogs had gotten into the well.

Walter stood waist-deep in the fragrant water, naked except for his beaten leather hat. Long strands of their eggs wove around him, sticky gray pearls with tadpoles inside them. Two of the dogs leaned over the opening and barked down at the strange noise of the buckets as he filled them.

Walter climbed up the homemade ladder and shivered in the noon sun. He sneezed a few times, looking down at his thick white legs and the brown tan that stopped half way up his arms. The dogs barked again at the naked man and his odd chore. Walter pulled up the buckets and dumped their contents into the field. The dogs sniffed them to satisfy their curiosity. He moved quickly, trying to dry off before he put on his pants and his boots.

He started up the mountain, through the thicket of raspberries that were still hard and yellow. The path led through a canopy of giant maple trees, their leaves bigger than a man's hand. Walter stopped and took a leak. The dogs were in the field below him, talking to a groundhog.

A soft whirring sifted through the trees, which made him think of a swarm of black flies, or a family of hummingbirds.

Walter found his way to the upper field, where the whirring grew deeper. He shivered once and blamed it on the cold well water, on a cloud passing over the pale autumn sun. A strange moment passed as Walter stood still, staring at his feet.

The sound was from a machine.

He ran as the low branches whipped his cheeks, a stiff lump rising in his stomach.

The tractor lay on its side, the combine blades behind it singing in the cool air. The machines were dappled with blood.

His father lay in pieces on the ground.

A small voice spoke from the back of Walter's throat as he nudged the old man's body with his boot and positioned the legs so that they were straight in the tall grass. He dragged the back of his hand along the wrinkled face, closing the eyes. He turned off the tractor and the noise was gone.

The horses thundered toward him. They were Percherons, black beasts taller than a man at the shoulder. They nuzzled his hair, their breath hot on his vest. He stood between them, blocking out the sky and the dogs and the blood on his hands. They stood, magnificent and tame, waiting for him to tell them what to do.

wild asparagus

They are silent, crawling down the walls. They are smothering him inside his pajamas. Lightning cracks silver. Blue-green hides flicker in the darkness. Little brother sleeps under blue eyes, a tiny O at his lips, whispering his sleep dreams of fresh-cut grass and bubbles, of seashells and broken shoelaces.

Thunder lifts the curtains. Hot raindrops spatter the windows. They ooze long lines through the monsters. The rain dissects them, drawing them into the corners. Paul bites his lip. Thunder crashes. The dogs are barking. The shadows are not scared. The taste of thin blood on his tongue. A wet piece of gum stuck in his hair. A record playing, skipping—

Where are the lovely straw-berr-ies?

He rushes outside. The leaves are down. The world is a lopsided color wheel. He fills his pockets with red ones. He rushes through piles, his cowboy boots kicking them high into the air. The moist scent of toads and mud pies tickle his nose.

He climbs to the top of an evergreen as sap runs into his eyebrows and covers his palms. They turn gray and sticky with bark.

A little red plastic cowboy is tied to a branch with white thread.

One of the dogs
is licking a greasy spot of egg
from the floor.

Paul is pocketing
a soup spoon
from its kitchen drawer.

The wild-eyed boy is digging under the bare stalks of a blackberry bush. Their limbs swat his face as he spoons the dirt into a neat pile.

He pulls the red plastic man from the back pocket of his Toughskins. The cowboy is buried in a shallow grave. He carefully refills the hole, pressing the mound with his palms. He sits on it, rocking back and forth.

He hides the spoon in the chicken coop, between the corner and the last nest. The hens roll their eyes, clucking to each other.

The wild-eyed boy runs out to the road and starts laughing.

He slaps his knees.

He sits in the garden, watching the tiny clouds of his breath.

After recess, the sleds were rolled up and returned to their shelves under the stairs. The red ones were cracking, unfurling in uneven rolls. The blue ones were new this year. They did not seem to move.

The children pulled their jackets over their heads, where they got stuck. They wandered around in a fleece darkness, mumbling.

Teacher. Teacher.

Paul came in last, staring at the fluorescent lights in the dark hallway. His eyes wobbled inside their sockets. Green flares bloomed through his heavy eyelashes. He did not blink as the world became neon, as children without heads under jacket torsos moved in slow-motion, as giant teachers pulled sweaters down, as bright blue boots looked black in the murk of the hall.

The shirts were tucked in. The coats hung in cubbies.

The slush-covered boots dripped in a row as sneakers were tied with bunny ears around bunny ears.

Paul could not move.

I am digging a tunnel in the snow with my pinky. I am building a miniature playground for the field mice. They will play here in the middle of the night. Under the microscope of my thumb I build a tiny igloo, a slide, a drive-in movie show.

And we can run around naked
in a summer storm.
Mom makes us wear cutoffs,
but we take them off under the splintery picnic table.
We race from the swing
to the barn,
the green grass hiding dollops
of goose shit
that will disappear from between our toes
soon enough.
I shiver in the afternoon air,
my heart beating through my thin ribs,
visible to the naked eye.
I want some watermelon.

I spy a wild asparagus.
I am seven.
I want to pull it from the earth
and show it to my father.

On the side porch, under the slanted piles of faded lawn chairs, half-complete encyclopedia sets, and a broken bicycle, is the piano. The air is cool and never moves. In autumn the squirrels rattle above the ceiling, clicking nuts into a dark niche under the low roof.

Only the black ones for a week. What can I make with the black ones? Ray Charles. I can make a little of him. Only the top keys—a cartoon. A man is peeing on his foot.

Ping. Ping. Ping.

A safe falls on him—hit the open strings with a stick.

I draw hearts on the broken keys with a blue crayon. I spend all afternoon playing the three lowest ones that work.

Wo ho ho! I yell.

Wo ho ho - a lowlo!

I stomp my feet on the pedals. The notes ring a long time. I wait for them to fade away, frozen at my makeshift chair.

Lowlo lowlo. I whisper.

I take a little nap.

In the black lamp of a no-mooned night, the chickens were killed in a silent flurry. The headless carcasses were strewn in lopsided circles. Death had come quickly, with autumn's first frost.

In the morning we poked them with our toes. They rolled easily in the crisp grass, in the lavender hour before eight.

Two nights later, the owl returned.

It swooped down from the oak tree, blurring past the tire swing. The wings went on farther than my eyes could see. They were white, radiant, lighting up the entire backyard.

It circled.

My father shot it once, twice.

In the morning we found it bleeding, hiding in a crevice under the barn. The field was covered in feathers and droplets of blood.

It was dead by noon.

Paul sat with his chin on his palms in the corner. The cigarettes curled smoke toward the stained-glass lamp over the dinner table. Their coffee cups half empty, the odd crusts of pie were smeared between the tines of a fork and eaten in nimble bites.

The strange laughter from his father—so loud, so taken. His mother's half caught smiles—trying to hide her teeth. The dinner guests—the droll professor, his carefully dressed wife. An eccentric from down the road—a refugee from Manhattan hiding in a pair of faded overalls.

Paul approached the table with quiet steps, his bare feet anticipating the noise of the floorboards.

He reaches for his father's wine glass.

His father nods.

"Don't bite it," he says.

Paul sips quickly, holding the glass with both hands.

His eyes are wide. He stands very still.

His father pulls the thin triangles of glass from behind his trembling lips. He places them in a pile on one of the good linen napkins, a pale pink stain of blood forming beneath them.

The trees are full of apples.
They are so red
the insides are pink.
We put on
football helmets
and shake them
and rain apples on our shoulders
to make a pie
or sauce
but not cider
because that gives me a stomachache.

dad is taking
a bath
in the stream
the oatmeal soap
sits on a rock
no one can
see his white ass
from the road
as he sings
and hollers
to a turtle
in the sun

It is a late afternoon in September. I am home from school, reading a King Arthur book in my room. The house is empty. I click my tongue against the roof of my mouth to fill the silence. I go to the top of the stairs. I have a habit of leaning forward until I am going to fall down them. My heart leaps. I go blind for a second. I fall backward.

My mother comes out of the bathroom. She is naked. She sees me and tries to cover herself with tiny hands. She is angry. She is swearing. She is slamming the bathroom door behind her.

She tells me to go outside.

I am braiding my sister's hair.
I am whispering to myself
one two and three.
I am looking for a bobby pin.
The party
downstairs
is full of adults.

Paul's orange kite
rattles furiously
tearing apart
cutting the thin line
in his grasp.

A hawk circles
and approaches
the orange paper
glue
and sticks.

Paul lets go
of the string
hoping the kite will be able
to hide
behind a cloud.

Paul walked along the dirt road, whispering secret words to the crickets and the trees. He thought about the long days of August, and how he hated the color blue at the bottom of the swimming pool. He held a hand over one of his eyes and tried not to hate the color so much.

We are eating dinner—barbecued chicken, potato salad, corn on the cob, lemonade. I jump up and run outside. Someone is calling my name. I run around the backyard, past the tire swing to the open field.

"What?" I whisper.

I turn in circles.

I look for a camel in the clouds.

A mountain calls my name.

My parents are telling me to come back inside.

I sit down in the tall grass and hide.

albino

PART I.

I.

Hitch left with his guitar.

She was in the kitchen, chopping parsley for soup.

He had been sitting in the living room, watching *Hollywood Squares*. The dog looked up at him. She nosed her leash once and barked as he carefully closed the door.

He walked quickly, pulling the collar of his jean jacket to his neck and hunching his shoulders against the clammy air that blew in from the water. The case thumped against his leg as he followed the double lines of the narrow, wet road.

He closed his eyes for a while, seeing how straight he could walk.

Hitch bought a loaf of bread and a jar of peanut butter at Stewart's.

He spread the slices across a bench in the bus station and made sandwiches.

Hitch put them in the bag and went outside, where a woman smoked a cigarette, blowing plumes of smoke into the night air.

Once he had put the guitar over his head, he took one of the sandwiches out of the bag. The bus labored onto the highway and he started eating.

A baby began to cry behind him. A woman made hushing sounds.

"Next stop—Chicago. It'll be about six hours," the driver announced, then clicked off the intercom.

Hitch leaned back into the seat and folded his hands together. The baby started to cry again.

Hitch closed his eyes and thought of her face and tiny hands. He started to imagine what she was doing, who she might be calling. He tried to swallow some of the sandwich and it stuck in his throat.

Hitch began to feel a strange form of vertigo.

His eyes opened once, seeing a Shell station he had been to countless times.

A young man he didn't recognize was washing someone's windshield.

He finished the sandwich.

They had met when he was fifteen, just after his father died.

His mother was slowly coming unhinged, talking with strangers in the supermarket about how good a man he had been. Hitch came home from school each day to find her sitting in the passenger seat of the Cadillac, staring past the edge of the driveway into the backyard.

She began sleepwalking, wandering through the house every night after he had gone to bed. She rearranged couch pillows, made up the beds, and counted silverware. After this, she stood in front of the refrigerator with the door open.

He would find her at the kitchen table in the morning, sipping black coffee.

Martha sat next to him in biology. She wore sweater sets

and smelled like vanilla soap. She let him borrow her notes when Hitch missed his classes, arranging the funeral.

One afternoon, she made a point of dropping them off.

His mother had taken to putting on perfume every twenty minutes, and he was trying to hide the bottles from her. Martha helped him, finding an empty shelf in the garage.

She stayed for dinner when he asked.

They sat in the kitchen, quietly munching canned corn and the last box of fish sticks, dipping them methodically into mounds of tartar sauce. His mother gripped the edges of the table, nearly falling back in her chair, sneezing violently, again and again.

Hitch wore one of his father's suits to the funeral. Martha stood next to him the entire time, holding his hand behind their backs so no one could see them. She ran her pinky along the inside of his palm, counting out the moments of the service until it was over.

They buried his father under cherry trees, as he had wished. Blossoms littered the moist earth and stuck to everyone's shoes.

His mother was medicated now, and sat quietly in a chair. She nodded slowly to each person as they paid their respects.

He began shopping for the house, buying an assortment of TV dinners and frozen vegetables. Martha found some recipes for him and showed him how to make eggs with biscuits and sausage gravy.

Once a week, they made pancakes. He ate his with molasses. She ate hers with powdered sugar and syrup.

They took naps on the front porch together, fumbling through their clothing as cars went by. She would leave him asleep in the swing, making her way home before midnight.

He dreamt of lizards that turned black in the desert sun.

A wind covered them with sand in the afternoon, until their eyes opened and they emerged, crawling toward a playground.

Summer came, with small-town baseball games under bright lights.

Hitch brought his father's guitar down from the attic and sat it on his bed. He read the Chet Atkins chord book and bought a new set of strings.

One morning, he strummed it quietly and did not leave his room until the sun went down.

He wrote his first song for her, about cherry trees and kissing her on the riverbank. He wrote about how she kissed with her eyes open and how this scared him a little.

She wanted to hear the song, but Hitch wouldn't play it for her. It was full of forced rhymes and had two chords. He offered to hum the best parts to her when she was driving, or when he tickled the back of her neck.

Hitch ate cherries with cream and sugar almost every night.

He saved the pits, lining them up across the edges of the windows, a backward count to the first day of school.

Martha got him to skip their afternoon classes, drinking coffee and eating doughnuts in a diner off of the highway. She kept her sunglasses on, and he hunched down in his seat with his hand on her leg, under the table.

Martha took her bra off under her shirt and passed it to

him, covered by a pile of paper napkins.

The Safeway parking lot was empty.

They explored shoulders and hip bones, breasts and thighs, the sun making bright triangles on their skin.

He fantasized about her with long black hair, driving a fast car, not the tiny Honda. They robbed small-town banks and slept in motor lodges. He ordered an entire Chinese menu and ate three bites from each white box. She bit him when she kissed, leaving tooth marks on his mouth, and walked around in nothing but a pair of black panties.

"Chicago, ten minutes," the driver said over the intercom. "Chicago."

Hitch stretched, looking out at the dark and empty station. The woman with the baby made her way down the aisle and outside. He moved his hand around over his head, feeling for the guitar.

It was still there.

He went outside, his hands deep in his pockets, his breath making little clouds in the wet air. The woman cooed to the crying child.

Hitch chewed the insides of his cheeks as he started toward them.

"If you like, I could play your baby a song," he said in a quiet voice.

The woman stared at him.

"Could make him go to sleep," he said, looking away from her eyes.

"No thanks," she said, turning away from him.

"Alrighty," he said, kicking something with the toe of his boot and following it back to the bus.

He sat down, looking out at them.

He thought of writing a lullaby for the baby. It would be about streetlights that never went out, about the click-clack of windshield wipers and the hum of tires on a wet road, about the soft hush of cars as they passed them, about how they would be in New York before they knew it.

If he could just close his eyes, he would be there when he got up.

II.

When they had just moved in together, she was always in the bathtub when he left for work.

He would reach into the water and grab her ankles. The dog would start barking as she screamed and laughed with her hands over her breasts, making one of her shy faces. After they kissed, she would talk to him before he left, about buying milk or detergent.

Hitch remembered washing the dog on the front lawn and how it took all afternoon. He remembered the way her feet curled up inside her flip-flops when she read the Sunday newspaper.

Hitch rolled his jacket into a ball and leaned against the window as the gentle wiggling of the bus began to tickle his ears.

He thought of his mother sitting in the dark living room, waiting for him to come home from school and make her dinner.

She lived in her nightgown, not bathing for days. He begged her to go outside, even to the front porch. She said that the medication had made her sensitive to light. She told him that the sun burned her skin, even through her shirt.

An ambulance passed on the highway, its lights flashing into the bus. Hitch looked past his reflection in the window, watching the driver holding the steering wheel with both hands. The man in the passenger seat sipped from a Styrofoam cup and stared at the road with the same empty expression.

Hitch tried to imagine whom they were taking to the hospital.

He thought about the day he saw the plate of butter gone soft and the overturned bowl of fruit.

A prickle riding along the back of his hands, he called her name.

"Mom?" he said, leaning to see if she was in the living room.

A rolling pin traveled across the kitchen floor as he moved to the dining room.

She was not there.

He went to the downstairs bathroom, walking across a pile of stationery strewn across the floor.

She lay in the corner, covered in vomit. One of her hands rested on the toilet bowl. She was perfectly still.

Hitch turned the light on and felt her neck for a pulse.

A day passed.

Morning came.

The low hum of the bus tires gave way to the sound of children playing in the spray of fire hydrants. There were mufflers left on the side of the road, and the fragrance of beer bottles sitting in sun-drenched parking lots.

Neon liquor store signs sputtered in the afternoon as they passed rows of empty stores. Everyone looked out the windows at the neighborhood passing silently.

The AC came on, making Hitch shiver once and sneeze.

A stranger said, "Bless you."

He nodded a quick thanks and sneezed once more.

The dark station gave way to the smell of pizza slices under heat lamps, to escalators and chain stores.

The flat sun on Eighth Avenue showed steps that led to Brooklyn. He peed for a long time in a corner of a parking lot, beyond the car alarms and the windows full of shoes.

PART II.

I.

Hitch rolled onto his side on the bare mattress. He pushed his clothes into a tight ball and rested his head on them.

People were running up and down the hallway.

He struggled to his feet, searching for the pull cord as he wobbled around the tiny room. Finding it, Hitch saw a collection of cockroaches crawling across his guitar case. He started swatting them to the floor, then caught himself and felt all that he had been drinking.

He ran into the hallway and to the bathroom.

Hitch threw up into the dark, lidless toilet.

Clem and Eugene heard him, and watched from the doorway. The short chubby man and the tall quiet one traded expressions.

"You don't look so good," Eugene said. "You look like you kissed the wrong end of a baby."

"Come on," Clem said, shoving Eugene.

"You look uglier than a mud fence, buddy!" Eugene said, waving his pudgy hands in the air.

Eugene scratched the insides of his nostrils.

"This ain't a traffic accident," Hitch said. "Keep driving."

"Do you want some water?" he asked.

"Yeah," Hitch said.

Eugene went to his room. Clem put his hands in his pockets and leaned against the doorway.

Hitch heaved, and nothing came up.

"Did you play a show tonight?" Clem asked.

"Yeah," he said.

"Did they pay you with drinks?" Clem asked.

"Basically," Hitch said.

Clem rubbed the toe of his shoe on a worn spot in the

carpet.

"You need a manager," Clem said.

"I need to get the cockroaches out of my guitar," Hitch said, slumping to the floor.

"This place was a roach hotel way before it was a people hotel," Clem said, wiggling his pinky in one of his ears.

Eugene returned.

"Here we go," he said, leaning over Hitch and waiting for the water to run cold.

He handed him the paper cup.

"Thanks," Hitch said, staying on the floor.

"Okay. Let's race," Eugene said. "Will you be the judge?"

"As long as I can sit here," Hitch said.

"He ain't gonna see nothin'," Maryanne mumbled.

Hitch kept his eyes closed, feeling the cold tile wall against his back.

"Just keep the motherfucking door open," Larry said from down the hall.

"Lighten the fuck up," she said, leaving the door open a few inches.

Hitch sensed Maryanne's boots bumping against his knees, and listened to her pants unzipping. She began to pee, breathing heavily through her nose.

"Larry," she called. "Bring me a napkin or something."

"What?" he said, after a moment.

"Tissues," she said. "Whatever—you know there's no fucking toilet paper in here!"

Hitch opened one of his eyes slightly and saw the marks of the elastic from her underwear which drew a red line below her belly button.

"Larry!" she called.

"There's a roll in my room," Hitch whispered to her. "The

door should be open."

"Never mind," she said, wiggling quickly and zipping her pants up.

She stood over him, and he opened his eyes all the way.

"Show's over," she said, under her breath.

Hitch tried to smile, and suddenly felt sick again. He threw up clear fluid into the toilet as she left the bathroom.

"Feel better," she said from the hallway.

He waved a hand at her and threw up again.

II.

Hitch sipped from a sweaty bottle of Corona in a dark, narrow bar. The afternoon sun came through the dirty windows and cracked glass bricks, exposing a patina of cigarettes and fingerprints and poster glue.

A Johnny Cash song began to play on the jukebox as an old man rested his forehead on the bar and went to sleep. A mechanic in a Mobil station uniform worked his way through a takeout burrito and his second Dos Equis.

The bartender made her way down the bar and placed a whiskey glass upside down in front of him.

"Buyback," she said. "Sorry I didn't get you before."

"Thanks," he said, pulling an extra dollar from his pocket and pushing it toward her.

"Do a shot with me?" she asked.

"Okay," he said.

She poured two shots of Jameson, alternating between the glasses until some spilled over their tops. He made a face to himself and chuckled.

"I'm bored," she said, downing half of hers.

Hitch sipped at his, cautiously.

She popped the cap off another Corona and slid it toward

him, taking the upside-down glass and putting it away.

"Not too much going on, hunh?" he said, trying not to stare at her tattoos or her torn black T-shirt.

"Day shift sucks," she said. "But Richie won't put me on nights, until I can handle … this."

"Hunh," he said, finishing the first Corona.

"It's sort of like babysitting first graders before you get the real problem kids," she said as she pushed the dollar on the bar back to him.

"Play something besides Johnny Cash and Tom Waits, would you?" she asked.

Hitch went to the jukebox and coaxed the crumpled bill inside it, adding another from his pocket. He chose some Coltrane, some Howling Wolf, and a song by the Shangri-Las.

"Nice," she said after a moment.

"Those are the biggest shot glasses I've ever seen in my life," he said.

"Welcome to the Mars Bar," she said. "I'm Lucy."

"Hitch," he said as they toasted.

She sat down on a cooler, and began flipping through the sports section.

He went back to staring out the dirty windows.

A woman stood on the far corner.

She grabbed randomly at the edge of her coat and a shopping bag as her face turned in on itself. She shouted at the traffic light and stopped at the curb.

She ran back along the sidewalk and stopped, shouting at herself, her fingers stretching away from her palms.

He watched her throw the shopping bag into a garbage can, then run toward the corner. He saw her stop at the curb once more, her face frozen in fear.

Hitch left the bar and walked toward her.

"You okay?" he asked.

She stared at her feet.

"Need a hand crossing the street?" he asked.

"No," she said.

"I'm just gonna buy some gum over there, and then I'm gonna cross back that way," he said, watching the woman rub her hands against her thighs and count under her breath.

"I need at least twelve," she said.

Hitch went to the Mobil station and bought a handful of mini Reese's Peanut Butter Cups with the remaining change in his pocket.

"Want one?" he asked, showing her one of the candies.

"It ain't fuckin' Halloween yet," she said.

She stared at him and smiled defiantly, her eyes rolling around, her teeth a jumbled, yellow mess.

He dropped one of the candies into her coat pocket and waited for the light to change.

Hitch went back to the bar and paused in the doorway. He thought of giving Lucy a candy too.

She gave him a small wave as he started back to his room.

Maryanne sat on a milk crate as Larry stood over her. Hitch leaned away from his door, peeking into their room as quickly as he could.

Larry snipped at her bangs with a large pair of scissors. He looked up as Hitch jabbed his key into the wobbly lock and cleared his throat.

"Hey ho, it's puking cowboy Joe," he said.

"Just trying to get my dumb door open," Hitch said.

"Doors ain't dumb," Larry said, snipping randomly at the tips of Maryanne's hair. She let out a deep breath as she stared at an invisible spot on the floor.

"Does it look okay?" she asked.

Hitch caught himself.

"Well?" Larry asked.

"I think so," Hitch said, and tried his key again.

"It looks fucking great," Larry said, squinting and stepping away from her.

Hitch closed his door and sat on the mattress, pulling his boots off. He lay down with his hands crossed over his chest and closed his eyes.

He woke up to the dark blue sky outside his window. The edges of the buildings glowed yellow as the lights came on in apartments. A siren gurgled as a police car pulled away.

The bed in the next room creaked in steady rhythm, then stopped.

He heard Larry say something.

There was no response.

Larry repeated himself, louder.

Hitch closed his eyes and tried to go back to sleep. He rested one of his feet on the floor, as he had done on the porch swing to keep it still. Hitch listened very carefully and heard Larry say, "You know, I cut your fucking hair. I kiss your pussy sometimes."

Maryanne spoke quietly to him.

Hitch opened his eyes, concentrating on the edges of the sky.

The creaking stopped abruptly and there was silence in the next room.

Hitch watched a man unpacking his groceries in an apartment across the street.

He opened his guitar case and saw no cockroaches.

Hitch tuned the guitar quietly, then fingered a B^7 chord as he began to learn a moving bass line.

Larry groaned.

Hitch played louder.

Something began thumping against the wall.

Hitch fished a pick from his pocket and began playing louder. He closed his eyes, seeing if he could visualize his fingers as they counted out the bass line.

The thumping grew slower.

Maryanne said something.

Hitch realized he had stopped playing the guitar. He put it away and pulled his boots on. As he opened the door, he heard a heavy thump and both of them shouting at the same time.

He went down the hall and to the stairs.

Maryanne screamed in pain, and then there was silence.

He went out into the street.

Hitch went to three pay phones until he found one that worked.

"Collect call from Herbert," he said when the operator asked.

There was no answer. The machine picked up and he heard the beginning of the greeting, realizing how strange it was to hear his own voice before the operator disconnected him.

A man with yellow-white hair sat on a milk crate. His eyes darted back to the sidewalk from inside his red face. He sipped noisily from a beer wrapped in brown paper.

Hitch went inside the bodega on the corner and bought a forty-ounce Ballantine. As he unscrewed the cap and took the first sip, he began to feel clammy under his shirt.

"You know what time it is?" the man on the crate asked him.

"About eight," Hitch said.

"You got any matches?" the man asked.

"Nope," Hitch said, looking into the man's tiny black eyes.

"Can you get me some matches?" the man asked. "My leg ain't right."

Hitch went into the bodega and got some for him.

"I didn't hurt it around here, you know," the man said, lighting a cigarette. "It was in the war."

"Which war?" Hitch asked.

The man sucked hard on his cigarette, pausing dramatically and staring off into the distance. He studied one of his fingernails.

"'Nam," he said.

"My dad was there," Hitch said, sipping from his beer.

The man on the crate raised his can.

"Victor."

Hitch held out his beer in a toast.

"Hitch."

"Sit down," Victor said. "You ain't goin' nowhere."

Hitch paused, looking down the street. He made a tiny nod to himself and pulled up an empty crate.

"I like Hershey Bars," Victor said. "Do you like Hershey Bars?"

"They're okay," Hitch said.

Three Puerto Rican girls walked past them, shouting and widening their eyes.

One of them dropped her purse and the other girls said she was drunk already, and that she had a nice ass.

"I don't think her ass is so nice. She has a fucking pear ass," Victor said under his breath. "I like an ass like a tomato, so you can just sink your teeth in there."

Hitch stayed quiet.

"You got a girlfriend?" Victor asked.

"Sort of," Hitch said.

"Well, where the hell is she?" Victor asked.

Hitch cleared his throat, and began to form a response.

"You can't trust her?" Victor interrupted, flicking the last stub of his cigarette toward the gutter. "Is that it?"

Hitch nodded once.

"She did lie sometimes," he said.

"Come on," Victor said, "we all lie sometimes."

"So, did you really hurt your leg in Vietnam?" Hitch asked.

Victor nodded once.

"I tell you something—I would bite that bitch's pear ass 'til she screamed if she sat on my face!" Victor said.

They laughed and drank.

"I got nooooooooooo problem with a little pear ass on a Saturday night," Victor shouted to a truck that rumbled past them.

"I gotta pee," Hitch said, standing up and looking up and down the street.

"You're good around that corner," Victor said, pointing down the block.

"Watch my beer?" Hitch asked.

Victor nodded yes and lit up another cigarette.

"Thanks again for the matches," he said.

Hitch began to undo his belt as he turned the corner. He peed behind a dumpster, watching a cat sniffing though some garbage bags.

When he returned, Victor was gone, and there was no bottle of Ballantine.

His elbows jumped strangely, and he forced his hands into the pockets of his jean jacket.

Hitch tried to call again, but she wasn't there.

III.

He went to the club early, and ate two slices of pizza at the bar. Hitch rationed out his complimentary beer, deciding to perform as soon as possible.

"What's your name again?" the bartender asked, as he began washing pint glasses.

"Hitch," he said.

"Are you playing the same stuff as last night?" he asked.

"I haven't really thought about it too much," Hitch said, twisting his glass around on the coaster.

"A little advice—and you can take it or leave it," the bartender said, waiting until Hitch made eye contact with him. "Just play something quiet. They're gonna talk no matter who the hell you are. Play a loud song and they just talk louder."

"Hunh," Hitch said, nodding reluctantly.

The bartender refilled his glass.

Hitch went back to eating his pizza.

"You save the crust too?" the bartender asked.

"Yeah," Hitch said.

"It's like the dessert," he said.

"Yeah," Hitch said, smiling a little. "I guess so."

The first band didn't show up.

Hitch set up slowly, moving the stool into different spots on the worn carpet, practicing fingerings and fitting the capo onto the head of the guitar so he wouldn't have to reach for it.

He put a pick in each of his pockets.

It was a warm Saturday night. The tables were littered with thin girls that wore barrettes in their long dark hair and men in jeans wearing shirts with no sleeves. Hitch watched a woman putting her cigarette out and the man who lit her new one.

He made his way to the bar.

"Water, no ice," Hitch said.

"You should start," the bartender said.

Hitch made a pistol with his fingers and pointed it at him.

"Right on, man," he said.

The bartender laughed to himself, suddenly uncomfortable.

"Okay, Cowboy," he said. "You go get em'."

"You wanna introduce me?" Hitch asked.

The bartender looked up and down the bar and made a face.

"Just go on," he said. "Nobody listens to me anyways."

Hitch made his way through the tables and chairs as people leaned forward to let him pass.

In one swift motion he tapped the mic, placed his water on the floor, and pulled the guitar to his lap. He cleared his throat, nervously.

"This one is for my cherry blossom girl," he said as loud as he could. "If any of you have a cherry blossom girl, then you'll know what I'm talking about."

The bartender made a face at him to play quieter. Hitch nodded, and broke into the song.

He strummed wildly sometimes, changing the tempo in mid-measure.

Finishing the intro, he paused dramatically and stared at the first person who was listening. Squeezing his eyes shut, he sang as quietly as he could.

Someone laughed nervously. A few faces smiled.

Hitch picked a short arpeggio and strummed dramatically, letting the resolving chord ring out before he sang again.

He looked up and saw that no one was looking at him.

Finishing the song, Hitch looked down at the carpet as sparse applause gave way to people continuing their conversations.

He sipped some water and retuned his E string, waiting for the room to grow quiet. He tried to get the bartender's attention.

Hitch began playing "Old Susannah," and the room grew so loud he could hardly hear the guitar.

He stopped in the middle of the song, leaning into the microphone.

"Thank you," he said, as sincerely as he could. "You've been a wonderful audience."

He packed his things quickly and left through a side door.

Outside, he smelled gasoline and garbage.
He fake-yawned and walked west, toward the Mars Bar.

A woman with tattoos across her arms, depicting poker hands and bulldogs, stood behind the counter in a tank top. Hitch paused in the doorway for a moment, then went in.

He sat at the dogleg corner of the bar.

"Hey there," she said to him.

"Howdy," he said with his best Southern accent.

She raised her eyebrows and waited.

"Corona, please," he said.

He studied the names scratched into the top of the bar, and listened to the jukebox.

Clem and Eugene came in, spying him in the corner.

"You look a lot better," Eugene said.

Clem ordered two rum and Cokes.

"How was your show?" Clem asked him.

"Okay, I guess," Hitch said, shrugging his shoulders

"Did you ever write a song about a dog?" Eugene asked.

Hitch shook his head.

"People love songs about dogs," Eugene said.

"Yeah, like *Old Yeller,*" Clem said.

A Louis Prima song came on the jukebox. Eugene began dancing up and down the bar, making up words and singing along.

Clem leaned into Hitch's ear.

"Maryanne was looking for you," he whispered.

"How come?" Hitch asked him, quietly.

"No idea," Clem said.

They sipped their drinks.

Hitch began to speak, then stayed quiet.

"What," Clem said, not looking at him.

"Maryanne," Hitch said. "Tell me something about her."

Clem shrugged his shoulders.

"What's her deal?" Hitch asked.

"What do you mean?" Clem said.

"Where's she from?" Hitch said.

"I know her dad is a high school principal or something like that," Clem said after a moment.

"How old is she?" Hitch asked.

"Twenty-two?" Clem said. "Yeah, we had a birthday party for her. She's born in December."

"Virgo?" Hitch asked.

"Pisces," Clem said. "Pisces, I think."

Eugene finished his sing-along and came back to them, wiping the sweat from his face.

"Why don't you ask her yourself?" Clem whispered to him.

"Don't talk about my big ass behind my back," Eugene said.

"Lighten up," Clem said. "*Eugenious.*"

Eugene finished his drink in one long gulp.

"Aaaaaahhhhhhhhh," he said, and burped.

Clem and Eugene danced in the tiny space between the pinball machine and the front window. Hitch kept one of his knees against the guitar case, making sure it didn't get stolen.

He nursed the rum and Coke they had bought him.

As the bar filled, the bartender turned up the volume of the jukebox from beneath the cash register. A girl with earrings in her cheeks lit cigarettes and left them in an ashtray. Hitch turned sideways to avoid the smoke curling into his eyes. He stared at her dirty fingernails and the game she was playing with a book of matches.

Hitch began to feel sick, and saw that his hands were shaking.

He caught Clem's attention.

"Can you watch my guitar for a second?" he asked.

"No problem," Clem said, letting Hitch squeeze past him.

He made his way to the murky twin bathrooms in the back, feeling waves of heat rippling along the back of his neck. Hitch kept one of his hands on his stomach, trying to calm himself.

Inside the left bathroom, he felt a cool draft, and a sudden sense of helplessness. Hitch leaned against the door and closed his eyes.

The door thumped once.

"In a minute!" Hitch said as loud as he could.

The door pushed open and two women slid into the tiny bathroom. Their glossy eyes rested on his throat. Their hands moved gently in the air between them.

"Is your name Mike?" one of them asked, speaking in an eerie, slow-motion lisp.

"Excuse me," Hitch said, moving to open the door.

He slipped outside, and saw Larry talking to Clem and Eugene at the end of the bar. Clem made a face at him and Hitch ducked into the second bathroom.

He unzipped his fly and listened to the slow, steady stream, feeling a strange satisfaction with how much had been inside him.

He heard the door open.

"Hold on," he said.

"Hitch?" the voice asked.

"Who's that?" he said.

"It's Maryanne," she said. "Let me in."

"Alrighty," Hitch said, resisting the impulse to stop peeing.

"Thanks," she said. "You're a lifesaver."

"What do you mean?" he asked, wondering how much longer he would pee.

"What do you think I mean?" she asked.

"Won't Larry find you here?" Hitch asked her after a moment.

"I didn't think so," she said. "He was eighty-sixed a while ago, but it's a new bartender tonight."

"Oh," Hitch said, shaking once.

He zipped up and turned to her, feeling the dark walls of the tiny room.

"Do you need to go?" he asked.

"Where?" she asked, nervously.

He motioned to the toilet.

She produced a half-hearted laugh while Hitch reached out and flushed.

"Actually, we should go to the storage room for a bit," she said.

Maryanne opened the door slightly and pushed him in front of her.

"It's the door to the right," she said, waiting for the bartender to look away.

They entered the dark room, sensing the cool air from the ice machine and then a sudden silence.

"Buy you a warm beer?" she asked, opening two Budweisers that she pulled from a case.

They touched the bottles in a quiet toast and sipped.

"Warm beer, cold women," she said.

"Hunh?" Hitch asked.

"You never heard that song?" she asked.

He fixed his gaze on her arms, avoiding her face.

Maryanne hummed a little, her voice scratchy and out of tune.

She pressed her index finger under his chin and pulled his face up to hers.

"I should tell you something," she said.

"What?" he asked, his voice suddenly nervous and loud at the same time.

"This is not gonna end up with me fucking you," she whispered.

Hitch's elbows jumped, as he laughed awkwardly.

They stared at each other as the sound of the bar seeped through the door.

Hitch forced his mouth into a lopsided smile.

Maryanne let out a long breath.

They both stood motionless for some time.

Maryanne's fingers danced against the sides of her legs as she said his name under her breath.

She set her teeth together and shook her head once, then again.

"We should just go," she said. "He was banned. He won't see me."

Hitch shifted his weight from one foot to the other.

"You know, Larry is really not a bad guy," she said. "He's got a kid, and the court won't even let him see her. He's just angry. I mean—you'd be angry, right?"

Maryanne pulled from her beer.

"This tastes like shit," she said, and threw the bottle into a corner. It made a small breaking sound, as if it was now in three pieces.

"What the fuck are you doing here anyways?" she asked him, suddenly.

Hitch drew a slow breath.

"Did you come here looking for pussy or something?" she asked, almost talking to the air next to his cheek.

Maryanne began to laugh angrily.

"You came to New York for some solid gold pussy, right?" she said, laughing and snorting. "Well, you gotta have some kinda platinum dick for that … Puking Cowboy Joe."

She turned around and peered through the crack of the door, giggling to herself.

"Oh man, he was pissed," she said.

"How come?" Hitch asked, hovering behind her.

"Larry likes to know where I am at all times," she said. "It makes him nervous when we aren't together."

Hitch drank the warm beer.

Maryanne felt around behind her and touched Hitch's wrist. She brought his hand to her hip. Squeezing it once, she returned to looking through the crack of the door.

"He is so hammered," she said.

"So early?" Hitch asked.

"Every time he tries to call her, he gets drunk," she said. "They won't even let them talk on the phone."

"How old is she?" he asked.

"Four," she said, running her finger along the back of his hand.

Hitch pressed his hand into her hip.

"Do you have twenty bucks?" she asked him.

"For what?" he asked.

"A six-pack, a fifth of whiskey and some cheeseburgers," she said. "Deluxe cheeseburgers."

"I got ten," he said.

"Screw the burgers," she said, opening the door and wiggling away from him in one motion.

Hitch stepped back into the darkness of the storage room.

"Don't worry, he's gone," she said.

The bartender eyed Hitch and Maryanne as they made their way toward the pinball machine.

Maryanne leaned into Clem's ear and whispered to him. Hitch retrieved his guitar from under the bar.

"I kept it warm," Eugene said. "Like it was an egg."

His room smelled of sawdust and wet clothing.

Maryanne kicked off her shoes, unbuttoned the top of her jeans and curled up on the bed. She held a hand out to him, silently directing him to give her a beer.

He did, and went to the window. Looking down at the street, he cleared his throat twice. Sipping at the cold, sweaty can, he turned to her.

"Don't worry," he said. "I'm not gonna play you any of my songs."

She made a funny face.

"Oh no," she said. "That would be okay."

He went straight for the guitar case.

She cleared her throat.

"Maybe a little later," she said.

Maryanne patted the empty spot next to her on the mattress.

Hitch pulled his boots off and sat next to her.

They drank in silence.

A plump, gray-pink pigeon sat on the windowsill. It marched back and forth along the splintered wood and peeling paint.

Maryanne sighed and closed her eyes.

A second bird landed on the sill and stood still.

Hitch made soft noises to them as he sipped his beer. Maryanne opened her eyes, and began to make cat noises.

They cooed and whistled and meowed in the near darkness of the room.

Their empty beer cans were lined up on a makeshift shelf.

An ambulance siren called out, as it approached and stopped. A red-and-yellow pattern splashed faintly on the ceiling.

The last two beers in their hands, Maryanne cracked the

seal on the pint of Old Crow. She sent her pinky into the bottle, then touched it to the tip of her tongue. She returned her pinky to the bottle and touched it to Hitch's lip.

"You can play me one of your fancy love songs in a little bit," she said, letting her face rest on his knees. Hitch leaned against the wall as she slid one of her hands under his thigh.

Putting his beer on the precarious nightstand, he rested a hand on her cheek.

The lights on the ceiling changed slowly as a police car arrived, interspersing white bursts within the red and yellow ones.

Walkie-talkie voices filtered up from the street, uninterpretable.

The birds flew from the windowsill.

Maryanne began to snore lightly.

Hitch looked at the dark shape of his guitar case in the shadows. At one point, a white spot emerged from inside it. Hitch squinted into the darkness and saw the white spot moving down the length of the case and along the windowsill.

He saw its legs and a pair of antennae. The white insect made its way to the shelf of empties and disappeared inside one of them.

Hitch began to consider the possibility of an albino cockroach, and if there were more of them inside his guitar case.

Maryanne shifted her cheek against the warmth of his lap, and he closed his eyes.

PART III.

I.

The muffler rattled violently for three days, until it fell off in the outskirts of Greater Cleveland.

Immersed in the near dawn fog, Hitch felt the telltale thud and then a sudden sense of relief as they made their way west. He looked back and watched Maryanne turn to a more comfortable position in the back seat.

Following a series of service roads after the off-ramp, Hitch found a place to pull over. The deep throated rumble of the mufflerless Chevrolet gave way to silence as he turned off the ignition.

Hitch wandered into a clump of trees and peed.

Returning to the car, he tried to decide how hungry he was. Leaning inside, he touched Maryanne's elbow.

"Are you hungry?" he whispered.

She turned her face into the seat.

"I just want some eggs or something," he said.

She pulled her coat over her face.

They ate and drove, stopping to sleep when Hitch grew tired. Maryanne took the wheel very little, and spoke less. She made the deafening rumble of the engine her excuse. Even when they stopped, she spoke one-word sentences.

She asked him to guard the bathroom door at a rest stop as she took a towel bath.

The car grew capable of less and less, topping out at thirty-five miles an hour on the level highway. Hitch decided to take the old roads that ran parallel to the interstate.

On the fourth day, they both slept in the back seat.

Maryanne's empty stomach gurgled, with Hitch's hand resting on it, underneath her T-shirt.

A pale sky hung low outside the dirty windows.

Hitch listened to the cars passing when he woke up. He tried to decide what time it was by their patterns, then closed his eyes for half an hour, working his hand deep under Maryanne's shirt.

The sky grew dark, and long thin clouds stood against the dark spaces between them.

"Hitch," Maryanne said in a low whisper when she woke up.

He pretended to be asleep.

"Hitch, just tell me one thing," she said, moving his hand to her nipple.

Hitch pretended to wake up.

"Seriously, just tell me—does this haircut look like shit or what?" she asked, rolling onto him.

A moment passed as Hitch lay beneath her, looking up into the shadows. She undid his belt buckle.

"Honestly," he said, "I'm no judge of haircuts, but—"

"Shhh," she said, her face moving out of the darkness through an oncoming headlight, and then her lips were against his, dry and salty, tasting of cigarettes and stomach acid.

She took his hands and pressed them to her breasts. Hitch felt around beneath her shirt, trying not to let her breath distract him from kissing her again.

"Listen," she said. "After this, can you buy me some breakfast?"

She began unbuttoning his jeans.

"I don't—" he said. "We can just eat. I mean—we can just eat if that's what you want."

She stopped moving against him, her eyes hovering over his.

"Let's just do this," she said, "and then eat."

Hitch lay still, looking at her.

Maryanne undid the remaining buttons.

Her naked torso hovered above him as a truck passed and honked.

"C'mon, Cowboy Joe," she said.

She began to take his jeans off.

"Sing!" she shouted, pressing her palms against the roof of the car.

Hitch thought of a front lawn littered with five-dollar bills, and broken radios. Dead grass began to grow between the cracks of the sidewalk.

The moon rose into the windshield, resting on the edge of the dashboard.

Maryanne whistled a quiet melody to herself, running Hitch's hand along the curve of her stomach. Hitch shivered once, and pressed his fingers into her hip. He dragged them along her pelvis, and she shivered with him.

Maryanne laughed once, and pushed his hand away.

"That tickles," she whispered.

Hitch rested his hand on her thigh, stretching his fingers as far as they would go.

"Your hands are so warm," she said.

Hitch stopped for a moment, realizing he had left his capo in New York.

The diner was almost empty.

Maryanne and Hitch ordered a pair of number three breakfast specials. She nibbled on her bacon for a few seconds, then placed the scraps on the edge of his plate.

She took a triangle of toast from him, spreading butter and grape jelly on it.

Hitch sipped from an overfull coffee cup, working milk into it.

A Beatles song played from somewhere in the kitchen.

Hitch rolled his sleeves up, fishing an ice cube from his water glass and dropping it in the coffee. Maryanne leaned forward, blowing on the surface for him. He pulled the yellow cup from her and drank cautiously.

"So—do I have a solid gold pussy or what?" she asked, her eyes wide.

Hitch searched for the right words.

"I mean, come on—I'm not a sandwich," she said, stifling a giggle. "I'm a meal!"

"It greased my gears," he said quietly.

Maryanne laughed dramatically and took another piece of his toast.

"You know, Larry owed me money," she said, turning abruptly to look at the rusting red car in the parking lot.

"How much do you think that piece of shit is worth?" she asked.

Hitch shrugged his shoulders, scooping some egg yolk onto his remaining toast and chewing methodically.

"Between the blowjobs and the bullshit and the shitty haircut and more fucking blowjobs, I think I'm even with him now," she said.

Maryanne took one of her pieces of bacon back from Hitch's plate and split it lengthwise, eating half of it.

"Remind me to never get on your bad side," he said.

Maryanne moved from her side of the booth and sat next to him. She kissed him quickly on the cheek.

"You're such a sweetie," she said. "You're gonna make some girl very happy one of these days."

Maryanne walked off, toward the bathrooms.

He ate his eggs, and then the rest.

He had a refill of coffee.

Hitch stared at the tiny, empty juice glass, wondering how long she would be in the bathroom. He thought she was cleaning herself and imagined her half-naked body in the bright, cramped room, washing his semen from her leg, her mismatched socks in the sink.

Twenty minutes passed, and the waitress returned with the check.

"Where's your friend?" she asked.

"Bathroom," he said.

"Nuh-uh," she said. "I was just in there."

Hitch got up slowly and went to the men's room. Switching the light on, he saw that no one was there either.

He paid the check and made his way through the wet parking lot.

In the sulfur half-light of the streetlights he read the greasy fingerprint message she had left on the driver's side window.

Thanks Cowboy Joe.

Hitch sat behind the wheel, the keys still in his pocket. He watched the cars and trucks lurching along the interstate.

The leftover funk of her cigarettes grew heavy in the night air as it mixed with the smell of jam and bacon.

He put the keys in the ignition, and turned on the radio. Checking the rearview mirror, he saw something crumpled under the back window. Leaning back, he found her underwear.

Hitch absently stuffed them into his pocket and pulled away from the quiet chrome and neon glow of the truck stop.

II.

He studied the lush green that passed slowly outside the windows. There were wet piles of stovewood, and hollow shells of old cars. There were long stone walls that bent with age, somehow staying intact.

He tasted pollen on his lips, dry and sweet.

The white noise of the mufflerless car had become invisible.

Hitch made a series of right turns, then bought a loaf of bread and a jar of no-name peanut butter. Making a pile of sandwiches on the hood, he watched a swarm of birds flying in patterns above him.

The radio played a love song from the '70's.

There were homemade signs with pink and white balloons tied to them that read "Hepner Reunion."

Station wagons full of families dressed in their Sunday clothes drove all around him. The children stared out the back windows as they passed the slow-moving Chevrolet.

A man asked him for directions.

A truck pulled over to the side of the road with smoke rolling from beneath its hood.

He saw the birds again, and decided they were flying north.

Two boys wearing hip waders walked by the side of the road.

A beer ball that had been made into a wind toy spun loose in the late morning breeze.

Later that day, the heater began to give out a dark and foul stream of air. Hitch stopped using it, despite the hacking cough he was developing. His eyes watering, his stomach full of salt and acid, he followed the birds.

An eerie buzzing grew in his ears, and even the loudest trucks did not block it out as they passed him.

It rained now.

Giant drops splashed on the windshield as the remaining wiper pushed them around, jerking randomly back and forth.

He could not see the birds anymore.

Sneezing violently, then coughing up a mouthful of peanut butter and phlegm, Hitch tried to find a safe place to pull over.

The highway glistened in the late morning. He dug his hand into his pocket, grabbing at the panties that were still there.

He chewed the insides of his cheeks and thought of her slanted teeth and her terrible haircut. He thought of Clem and Eugene and the white-haired veteran that shouted at Puerto Rican girls and stole his beer.

PART IV.

I.

When he tried to start the car later, nothing happened. There was no dry electric click, no smoke from the heater.

The Chevrolet had gone completely mute.

Hitch massaged the dashboard with the heels of his palms, and tried the radio a few times. He pumped the gas gently, trying to remember the last time he had filled the tank.

Curling up in the back seat, he ate the last of the sandwiches and fell asleep.

He dreamt of taking Martha to the hospital.

The nurses moved in slow-motion, taking her blood pressure, and then her temperature.

They held hands, the same way they did at his father's funeral. During one of their visits, he realized it was how she measured time.

In the waiting room, he developed a habit of buying a cherry soda from the machine, which he tried not to finish before she was wheeled out.

She slept in the car as he drove home.

The dog greeted them in silence as he carried her to their bed.

He drank a beer and then a second one in the kitchen, looking out at the rooftops as the dog nudged her forehead into his free hand, listening to Martha's thick and measured breathing in the next room.

When he woke up, he crawled into the driver's seat and tried the ignition.

Hearing nothing but the raindrops pattering on the roof, he stared out into the night.

He saw a post office, a shack with a sign that read "night crawlers," a general store that was closed, and a tiny diner with most of its lights turned off.

Pulling his jacket close to his chest and turning the collar up, he ran to the little sign that read "home cooking."

Inside, an old man was organizing piles of coins next to the cash register.

"Is it alright if I use your bathroom?" Hitch asked him.

The man nodded yes and motioned beyond the end of the counter with his elbow, counting quietly to himself.

Hitch sat in the tiny wood-paneled space, feeling the warmth of the electric heater blowing on his knees. Although nothing came out, he flushed without thinking about it and washed his face and the back of his neck.

The soap smelled of lilac.

Walking back into the room, he watched the old man sliding the coins into paper sleeves.

"Was wondering if you'd come in," the old man said, carefully taping a flap of red paper closed.

Hitch cleared his throat as he thought about of what to say.

"Are you a churchgoing man?" the old man asked him.

"Yes sir," Hitch said, standing in the middle of the room with his fingers tucked into his back pockets.

"Don't stand there with Bette Davis-hands and tell me that," the man said.

Confused, Hitch folded them in front of him.

"Pour us some coffee and sit down," the man said.

Hitch made his way behind the counter, pulling two white cups from a shelf and pouring.

"One sugar and a drop of milk in mine," the old man said.

Hitch told him about his father's funeral, about his mother's suicide attempts and the heart attack that eventually claimed her life. He talked about traveling to New York, and about Clem and Eugene's races.

The old man listened without interruption as his clear gray eyes studied Hitch's face. Sometimes he scratched inside his ear with his pinky to see if anything interesting would come out.

Martin offered him a small room above the diner.

Hitch learned how to make eggs and hamburgers on the giant grill.

Martin's wife Ellen went to church every other day. He drove her in their Ford pickup, recognizing the unnamed roads quickly, and finding the tiny church with no problem. He went inside with her, but sat in the last row. The parishioners sang with ancient voices as the organist hammered the keys. The ones who didn't have the words memorized followed along in their prayer books.

Hitch couldn't listen to the services for longer than ten minutes. Instead, he found himself studying the dark-colored glass of the windows, and the oily face of Christ that hung above him.

The old went to their knees, standing and sitting in unison as candles of remembrance dripped onto the floor tiles below.

Ellen would wait for him after the service was over, preferring his arm to her cane. She directed him to a series of roadside stands on their way back, buying sugar corn and zucchini, cut flowers and strawberry rhubarb pies.

The songs began to come out above the murmur of the miniature black-and-white TV that sat in the corner.

Martin and Ellen never mentioned the sounds Hitch made in the tiny room with his door open. They kept a steady list of chores for him, providing three meals a day and some tip money.

The trees were starting to turn, and the open window allowed a permanent breeze. He kept it open, watching the sky grow a dark clear blue each night before he fell asleep.

Hitch began to write a song about distance.

He made random notes in a small book about his first day of school, about leaving his parents for the first time, about how it was easy to lose someone in the supermarket or a large department store. He thought of the friends he had made in grade school, trying to remember more than their first names and birthday parties.

He wrote about being far from home, about the way some people were like seeds spread across rows and rows of tilled earth where nothing seemed to grow.

He watched a young woman in a red-and-white-checkered dress putting wet laundry on a clothesline from his window.

Hitch decided she was the returned daughter of the woman who ran the post office. He studied her movements while she made her way back and forth across the backyard as the clothesline sagged lower and lower.

She pushed her hair from her eyes whenever the wind whipped around her.

Hitch strummed an E minor chord each time she clipped a clothespin to the line. He played a G chord when she pushed her hair back. He waited for words to come in the silence between them.

The dry rumble of a motorcycle surfaced, and the woman looked toward the road. She craned her neck and saw no one, then Hitch at his window as he watched her.

She stared up at him, the wind flapping her dress against her knees.

Hitch pulled back from the curtains, knocking the guitar

hard against the dresser as he receded into the darkness of the room.

He imagined her eyes might be blue, as bright as robin's eggs.

Hitch scrubbed the grill down, and flipped a grilled cheese sandwich with mustard and sliced tomato for the man who drove the motorcycle. Martin made small talk with the customers as Hitch prepared two chopped salads and reheated some meatloaf in the oven.

He fantasized about the young woman in the red-and-white-checkered dress coming into the diner, a barrette holding her hair back. He named her Rosie, short for Rosalyn. She would sit at the counter and order a tuna melt on whole wheat and a Diet Coke, or maybe some tea with lemon because it had gotten colder tonight.

She would wear a light-blue cardigan that was a little old, and concentrate on Hitch in the kitchen, trying to see if her tuna melt was ready, twirling the straw in her Diet Coke. Hitch would move to her, stopping at the window that separated them.

"Miss, do you want Swiss or American on that?" he would ask her quietly.

She would think for a second.

"American," she would say.

Hitch would make himself a matching tuna melt with American cheese and eat it quietly in the kitchen, waiting for her to ask what kind of pies they had.

II.

There was a light knock on the door.

"Yes?" he said, turning down the radio on the bedside table.

"Good morning dear," Ellen said.

"Morning," Hitch said. "I'll be down in a minute."

He heard her shuffling down the stairs.

Martin was filling the toothpick dispenser next to the cash register.

"Gonna get an order of kielbasa," he said to Hitch. "Ellen is going to church today."

Hitch nodded and took the truck keys from him.

Ellen sang quietly to herself as Martin helped her put her jacket on.

The front door opened, and the young woman came into the diner. She wore a blue dress and her hair was pulled back with two barrettes.

"Hello," she said.

"This is Hitch," Ellen said.

He cleared his throat and shook her hand as gently as he could.

"Betty," she said, looking down at the floor.

"Alright," Ellen said. "Let's go."

Betty sat between Ellen and Hitch with her hands pressed against the dashboard.

"Sorry there's only two seatbelts," he said. "I'll take it easy on the potholes."

"It's okay," Betty said, under her breath.

She sat with Ellen during the service, as Hitch found a place in the last row. The clouds moved quickly above them, changing the colors of the stained-glass windows so often they made him feel like he was inside a kaleidoscope. Hitch closed his eyes and tried to remember her smell.

He awoke as the final hymn was being sung.

Betty stared back at him for a brief moment, and his cheeks flushed with sudden anger.

Hitch drove them home in silence, as Betty and Ellen talked about the sermon and which people sat where in the church.

Helping Ellen out of the truck and to the diner, he watched Betty fixing her lipstick in the rearview mirror.

"Hitch, dear," Ellen said. "Betty needs to go to town for a few things."

"No problem," he said.

"I thought so," Ellen said, patting his elbow twice.

He pulled his jacket closed and returned to the truck.

"Excuse me," Betty said, after clearing her throat.

"Seatbelt on?" Hitch asked without looking at her, as he turned the ignition key.

She closed her eyes and rested her head against the window.

Hitch drove her to a pharmacy, then a department store.

Betty got directions for a bookstore, and disappeared inside for almost half an hour. He sat behind the steering wheel and listened to the radio, tapping drum solos with his index fingers. The collection of shopping bags stood crisply beside him, and he could see tissue paper and smaller bags inside them.

Betty bought him a roast beef sandwich and some potato salad.

They ate on the way back, with the radio on.

"Sure you got everything you needed?" he asked her at one point.

"What do you mean?" she asked, defensively.

"I didn't see your list," he said. "I could never go to that many places without a list."

Betty tapped a finger to her temple.

"This is my list," she said, and then looked in the side-view mirror to see if she had gotten any mayonnaise on herself.

"Have you lived here your whole life?" he asked her a few minutes later.

"Oh no," she said, laughing a little.

Hitch eased them past a collection of potholes.

"We used to live near Cleveland," she said.

"Did you go to school there?" he asked.

"High school," she said.

Hitch thought for a moment, trying to decide how old she was.

"So, you're probably done with college?" he asked.

She frowned for a second and turned to look out the passenger window. She pulled her sweater closed and began to chew the insides of her cheeks.

Hitch sighed, trying to breathe her smell in as deeply as he could.

Lilac, he decided.

Lilac and mayonnaise.

III.

The trees that lined the road to the church turned yellow, then orange. Bloodred leaves fell and stirred in the cushion of air that trailed behind the pickup truck.

He worked on the Chevrolet sometimes, replacing the alternator, then the sparkplugs. He removed the entire steering wheel assembly, as the mess of wires it contained spilled out across the seat. While Hitch experimented with switches and toggles, the car sat in front of the post office, slowly growing gray with sparrow shit and highway dust.

Thanksgiving came and went.

Martin and Ellen were consistently kind and generous, yet kept a conscious distance from him. He had only been inside their part of the house a handful of times, either carrying something or taking something away.

Betty spoke to him as if her speeches had been rehearsed, waiting for him to ask how she was, or comment on her hair, or a new shade of lipstick.

The songs continued to come out, some terrible, some promising. The pile of good lyrics had grown, divided into categories titled "love," "memory," and "story". The guitar seemed more familiar to him, and he felt strange if his forearms were not resting on its body.

Sometimes he took long walks along the highway while the cars whipped past him. He wandered through cornfields and into clusters of trees, looking for old bottles to decorate his room.

It snowed early, well before Christmas.

Outside his window, he could see white covering the back fields as they extended to a line of trees. In the warmth of his room, he watched *Gunsmoke* and *Jeopardy* on the tiny TV in the corner.

The moon rose, full and cold, as strong weeds and burdocks poked through the snow's luminous crust of ice.

The pink-orange lights of the house next door flickered when the neighbors moved from the kitchen to the pantry. Blurry shadows extended into the night, hypnotizing him for minutes, sometimes hours, as he sat with a beer in his lap, loosely strumming difficult chords.

She walked out to the back porch.

He turned his light off, so she would not see him.

He watched her blowing lazy plumes of smoke into the air.

He felt a sudden shiver, and pulled the top blanket from the bed around his shoulders. Hitch glanced at the clock and saw it was late, almost three.

Her silhouette was drawn perfectly by the light behind her. Hitch studied her movements, thinking Betty had changed during the past months and had grown brittle.

Swigging twice from his beer, he leaned the guitar in the corner. Carefully placing his favorite pick on the dresser, he saw her begin to dance.

Betty turned in slow-motion circles, close to the stairs that led to the fields. She coughed once, and then could not stop, tossing the remains of her cigarette into the shadows.

He watched her throw her jacket into the air, and then her sweater. She twirled in the backyard in nothing but her nightgown. He saw her approaching the fields, remaining tall as she skated across the icy crust and did not fall through it, moving in figure eights and flat-footed ballet moves.

Her hair looked darker against her bright pink skin. She looked heavier than he had imagined, and her eyes were still terribly far apart.

A week passed as Hitch tried to write a song about Betty's mysterious habit. He collected his thoughts about dancing and what it might mean.

After church, he was alone with her in the truck as they drove to town for her monthly errands. They had taken the trip in silence the last few times, sparing each other from manufactured small talk. Just before they reached the bookstore, Hitch turned to her as he stopped for a red light.

"You're a terribly good dancer," he said.

Her face flushed with embarrassment. She chewed the insides of her cheeks, then began mumbling to herself.

The light changed.

"Does this have anything to do with innocence?" he asked her.

"What?" she said.

"Do you wish you were a little girl again?" he asked her, half apologizing.

A dog chased a squirrel into the street, and Hitch stopped the truck in the middle of the block. Instinctively holding his hand out, he kept her from hitting the dashboard.

Betty burst into laughter.

Hitch stared at her, suddenly terrified.

She tried to stop, but broke into a series of tearful, laughing fits as he circled the block, eventually finding a parking space.

He turned off the ignition.

"What is so funny?" he asked her.

She reached out and tapped the back of his hand with her finger once, then again.

"I'm just really stoned," she said. "And really bored, which is a dangerous combination."

Hitch's hand jumped away from hers.

"Maybe you are writing some interesting songs up in that room," she said, as she got out of the truck.

Walking around to his door, she opened it.

"Come on," she said.

Hitch got out and locked the doors.

"How did you learn to dance like that?" he asked her when they were inside.

"Mrs. Lehtonen's School of Dance," she said, making her way to the sociology section. "From when I was seven until I was twelve."

Hitch nodded and began to walk behind her with his hands in his back pockets.

They ate lunch in a tiny Chinese restaurant.

Betty spoke vaguely about different parts of her life, dipping the corners of her dumplings into a pool of soy sauce, then blowing on them until they cooled. She talked about how helpless everyone seemed to her.

Hitch listened carefully, thinking of writing a song about a woman with regrets, about fortune cookies and freshly fallen snow.

She spoke for two hours, about the choices life makes for people, about the places she had been.

Betty told Hitch a story about a polka-dot underwear set and a long train ride from Paris to Berlin. He felt like she was trying to shake him, maybe exaggerating the details of her story to sound more impressive. He didn't finish his lunch, hoping this would keep them from returning to the tiny clump of houses and his broken Chevrolet.

As the sky grew dark, he drove them back.

She sat close to him, without a seatbelt on. Betty found an oldies station on the radio and they sang along to the Fleetwoods and Frankie Avalon while the highway clicked by.

At one point, she leaned into his ear.

"Put your guitar in the truck next time we go to town," she said, her breath warm and sweet on him. "We could get a motel room for the afternoon and you could play a concert for me."

He dreamt of her.

Betty carried the Chevrolet on giant shoulders while he danced in the palm of her hand. He played a miniature guitar and sang falsetto as she held him next to her mammoth ear, trying to understand the lyrics.

Hitch dreamt of rain gutters clogged with leaves, of grapefruits rolling across the floor of his tiny room.

He woke up early, trying to get it all down on paper,

searching for chords that matched the way he felt.

Hitch worked on the Chevrolet with a sudden sense of urgency. With a thermos of hot coffee, he spent hours rebuilding the electrical system, sure the ignition key would eventually turn the engine over if he was patient enough.

He turned off the grill, scrubbing it down with a wire brush after the dinner shift. Martin counted the money from the register. Ellen returned clean plates to their places on the shelves.

Betty came in, closing the door quietly behind her.

"Hitch?" she called to him, from the center of the room.

Everyone turned to her.

"One of our storm windows won't close, and Maggie is at her sister's house," she said. "It's just freezing in there. Can you come over in a bit?"

Ellen winked at Martin.

"No girl should be stuck with her windows open tonight," she said, poking Martin's elbow and stifling a laugh.

He snorted once as he nodded at Hitch, and then toward the door.

Hitch pulled his coat on over his apron, feeling their eyes on him.

"You are too kind to let me borrow him," Betty called to them as he shut the door.

Crunching through the snow, he tried to picture the color of her eyes and suddenly could not.

Inside, she led him upstairs after touching a finger to his lips. The house was dark and smelled of cinnamon and apples. She brought him to a bedroom and closed the door behind them.

Betty pressed him toward the edge of the bed until he sat on it.

Disappearing into the bathroom, Hitch heard her running water. He laughed once to himself, and stretched his arms behind his head. Hitch studied a pile of books on the floor, wondering if she had actually read all of them.

Betty returned in a white bathrobe with a basin of water. Placing it next to his feet, she shrugged the robe from her shoulders and stood naked in front of him, except for a pair of white tube socks. He looked into her eyes as much as he could, trying not to fixate on the mismatched play of her breasts and the cockeyed triangle of her pubic hair.

"Surprise," Betty whispered.

She began dancing slowly, making her way past him and then hopping onto the bed like a schoolgirl.

She leaned into his ear and whispered, "Take your shoes off."

He did.

She tried to jump gracefully to the floor, but collided with the dresser.

Betty pulled his socks off and rolled up his jeans. She washed his feet with her long dark hair and recited prayers over them.

He lay back onto the bed.

"No," she said suddenly. "Sit up."

He did, and touched her wet hair for a moment. She pushed his hand away from her.

"No touching," she said.

Betty bathed his feet for another few minutes.

"Alright, you can lay down," she said.

He slid back into the sheets, and she curled up next to him.

"I had an abortion, and I swore never to have sex again," she said. "So I might still get a chance to go to heaven."

Hitch took a deep breath and let it out slowly.

The house creaked, as the wind rattled the windows.

"Life is hard," he said.

She ran one of her fingers across his chest.

"I was in an accident, you know," she said. "A terrible one."

"What do you mean?" he asked her.

"When I was little, I lost my thumbs," she said.

Hitch wondered if she was telling the truth. He tried to picture her hands, and began to sense a strange metallic taste in the back of his throat.

"But——" he said.

"They took my big toes, and made them into thumbs," she said.

"Really?" he asked, thinking of the tube socks she was still wearing.

She ran her hand under his shirt, across his stomach.

"Really," she said.

They lay halfway under the sheets as giant snowflakes began to fall outside the window.

Hitch hummed a melody to himself. Betty rested her face on his shoulder, pressing her body against his.

"You know what?" she said to him in the middle of the night.

Hitch looked into her eyes in the near darkness of her room.

"You're probably not as screwy as you think you are," she said.

"What do you mean by that?" he asked her.

"I don't know," she said, her cheek warm against his shoulder. "It's like you're a David that thinks he's supposed to be Jesus."

Betty pursed her lips and went back to sleep.

Hitch watched the snow falling as the taste came back, thick and heavy on the back of his tongue.

PART V.

I.

The dog toy rattled around in his bag. Its twin bells jumped every other step as he made his way along the river. A handful of flowers hung moist and green in his free hand.

He closed his eyes as a sneeze approached, then passed. The mud on his boots made clicking sounds on the shoulder of the highway.

She was not home.

Hitch thought to wait inside, then wandered into the backyard.

A garden was marked out with yellow string tied to stakes in the wet grass. There were rows of plastic markers in the earth, describing flowers and herbs and a few vegetables. A pair of work gloves and some tools sat on the back stairs. He sat down, and twirled a spade around for a few minutes.

A cloud passed in front of the pale white sun.

A car approached and stopped. The gravel in the driveway crunched beneath its tires. The ignition went off and there was a sudden stillness in the air around him.

His stomach gurgled.

Hitch stood up.

"Martha?" he said quietly, but loud enough for her to hear him. A car door slammed shut and another one opened.

He walked out into the driveway and saw her.

Martha turned to him, then slumped against the open door. A bag of groceries slowly turned over as eggs and a glass bottle of milk splashed onto the ground.

She stared at him for a moment, then cleared her throat.

"Where's your guitar?" she said quietly.

He began to speak, then shook his head to himself. Hitch

took a step toward her and stopped.

She pushed some of her hair behind her ear, and looked him up and down.

"It got long," he said. "It looks nice."

"It's a wig," she said, after picking an imaginary hair from her sweater.

Hitch shifted his weight from one foot to the other.

"You lost weight," she said.

"Yeah," he said, forcing half of a grin.

Martha kneeled down to the ground and began picking up the eggshells, piling them in one of her hands.

"Sorry if I startled you," he said, putting his hands in his back pockets.

"You could never startle me," she said, looking up at him.

Her eyes stayed on him and did not blink.

The dog began to bark from inside, and scratched against the door.

"Mama's coming, honey!" Martha called out.

Hitch cleared his throat and took his hands from his pockets. The sun emerged from behind a cloud as two sparrows flew past their heads, then landed in a tree.

Martha handed the car keys to him.

"We need milk, and eggs," she said, and went inside.

II.

Hitch sat behind the wheel for some time before going to the grocery store.

The lights turned on, one by one, while he watched Martha opening the curtains and the windows.

the golden macaroni

I.

Beyond the fallen rocks and the tall grass, in a green hollow that stretches away from the road, sits a tiny white house. A patio chair rests upside down, the once white set littered with crab apple blossoms and wet leaves. Two spiderwebs crisscross along some firewood left in a mildewy pile beside the front porch.

A farmer passes slowly on his tractor, its tire chains jangling against the asphalt and then breaking into the soft shoulder of the road. The weeping willow tree that marks the edge of the front lawn moves in a breeze. A row of lilies of the valley bend low beneath the dew collected on them as a handful of yellow jackets circle the garbage cans.

Trish turned once, then again, under the twisted sheets and comforter, pulling her feet into their concentrated warmth. Two angry blue jays that circled below her window woke her.

Wiping the sand from her eyes, she felt her throat and sat up. Feeling underneath the pillows, Trish found the thin gold chain and the tiny cross that hung against the broken clasp. Pulling the covers up to her chin, she rested back in bed and turned sideways, wedging a pillow between her knees.

She thought of the sink full of plates crusted with egg yolk, and the empty tins of cat food on the counter. Trish imagined a tiny square of light making its way through the kitchen to the toaster, growing brighter as it traveled across the avocado-colored linoleum floor.

She went back to sleep.

Charlie's soft, translucent hands brushed a fly from his face. He snorted once into his fingers and rubbed them against the blanket. He stared at the ceiling for a short time, then at his fingertips as he turned them over. Charlie rolled his face into the pillow and blew his nose, muffling his giggles as he blew again.

He went to the kitchen, tiptoeing through the piles of dirty laundry and old newspapers. Pulling a fresh brick of cream cheese from the refrigerator, he sliced himself a piece and ate it. Clicking his tongue against the roof of his mouth, he went back to bed.

The fly was still in his room.

Trish pulled a bathrobe around her long white nightgown. She twirled once and then again in front of the tall mirror that hung from the back of her bedroom door. Running a finger along her eyebrows, she went to the kitchen.

Trish pulled two paper plates and a pair of plastic forks from a closet. Digging into the back of the freezer, she pulled out a store-bought ice-cream cake and rested it on an open space on the counter. At the back of the silverware drawer she found a tiny box of candles. She placed three together, and then five together. Trish lit them as quickly as she could with the lighter from her purse.

"Charlie!" she shouted.

Trish shuffled toward his bedroom and knocked twice with her knee against the door.

"What?" he said, quietly.

"I'm coming in," she said. "So, please be decent."

Charlie flipped his pillow over, smoothing out the clean side.

"Happy birthday to you," she sang as she came in. "Happy birthday to you. Happy birthday, dear Charlie. Happy birthday to you."

Charlie laughed and clapped his hands. He blew out the candles quickly.

"Did you make a wish?" she asked him, already pulling the candles out and laying them in a pile on the nightstand.

"Yeah," he said.

"I forgot the knife," she mumbled, and went to the kitchen.

Charlie stared at the cake, then pressed his thumb into the frosting. He tasted it.

"Chocolate," he said, with a sense of satisfaction. He counted the candles to himself once, and then again.

She returned with a bread knife and started to cut the cake.

"Wow!" she announced in a booming voice. "This is one solid cake."

"Maybe we should put it in the sun," he said.

Trish smiled and rested her hand on his chin.

"How old am I this year?" he asked her.

She cleared her throat.

"Thirty-five, sweetheart," she replied, collecting the paper plates and the cake and taking them to the kitchen.

The cat emerged from one of his hiding places. Trish cleared a space on the kitchen table and found a half-empty can of Friskies on the top shelf of the refrigerator.

"Charlie!" she called out. "You know, while you're eating cream cheese in the middle of the night, maybe you could feed Ralph too."

She turned the can upside down on a dessert plate and rested it on the floor.

Ralph sniffed it twice and began to eat.

Trish found her cigarettes in her purse and lit one, leaning against the counter and staring at the dirty dishes.

"How about a soda, honey?" she called to him.

"Okay," he said from his room.

Trish filled two tumblers with ice and topped them off with Dr. Pepper, taking hers outside.

Stepping onto the front lawn, she shivered once as her bare feet adjusted to the cold, wet grass between her toes. She made her way to the overturned patio set.

"Charlie!" she shouted. "Bring some newspapers!"

She heard a thud from inside.

"I'm okay," he said, after a moment.

Trish smelled the smoke curling away from her cigarette as it mixed with the scent of wet earth and rotting flowers.

They ate outside in their pajamas, sitting on a layer of newspapers, breaking the cake into pieces and eating it with their fingers. Ralph came and sat on the table, watching them with a lazy expression on his face. Trish tickled Charlie's elbows, asking him what he wanted for his birthday dinner.

Trish and Charlie wiped their hands on the grass to clean them and rested their heads back as they tried to see the sun through their eyelids.

"I want to go fishing all by myself," Charlie announced after they had gotten dressed.

Trish said nothing.

"Behind the house," he added.

"Charlie, you've never caught a fish in your life," she said.

Charlie sat down in the darkness of the living room and rested his hands on his knees.

"I didn't say I want to catch a fish," he explained. "I want to go fishing."

Trish let out a short breath.

"Just behind the house?" she asked.

Charlie nodded yes.

"Okay," she said. "But you're going to call me at the store every half hour, so I know you're okay."

Charlie smiled.

"And don't tell Ralph or he'll never eat his Friskies again!" she shouted as she smiled.

Charlie pushed his hair from his forehead.

"Alright," he said. "I won't tell Ralph anything."

Trish found the kitchen timer and placed it on the coffee table. She turned the dial to thirty minutes and showed it to Charlie.

"I know how," he whispered.

II.

A dead earthworm lay bloated in a puddle in front of the IGA that reflected the faded American flag above the parking lot entrance. Trish pulled in fast, parking across two spaces. She went inside, her purse jangling noisily at her elbow.

She bought canned pineapple chunks, bacon, milk, Strawberry Quik powder, a half-gallon of chocolate ice cream, and two frozen chicken pot pies. At the checkout counter Trish stared at the collection of cigarettes, suddenly forgetting what brand was hers.

"Salem 100 Lights?" the cashier asked her after a moment.

"Two packs, please," Trish replied.

"It's Saturday," the cashier said. "Why the rush?"

Trish smiled secretly and wrote a check.

"Thanks!" she shouted over her shoulder, grabbing the grocery bag and churning toward the parking lot.

She unlocked the door to the store and made her way past the rocking chairs and trunks full of old photographs. Trish flipped the light switch behind a collection of particularly wide ties.

Dialing the phone next to the register, she waited for Charlie to pick up.

"Hi sweetheart," she said. "Okay, time to go fishing."

She listened to him describing the fish he thought he might catch and how big it would be.

"Alright, it's 11:30. I'm calling back at noon. That's thirty minutes from now," she explained. "There's cream cheese in the fridge, and keep an eye on Ralph. Don't let him near the road."

Charlie promised everything would be fine.

She hung up, and began dusting the store. Trish went to the front window and repositioned some dolls. The once white paint job had deteriorated to a consistent gray, with each crack revealed in perfect detail by the grit that came in from the street.

Trish opened the door, looking both ways to see if any shoppers were out.

She reversed the sign in the front window so it read "open."

Trish crossed the street and knocked lightly on the glass door of the luncheonette counter. A waitress waved at her and raised one finger. Trish nodded yes and went back across the street.

The sun had come out and the three-block downtown felt much warmer. She sat on the front steps, letting the suddenly balmy air surround her. The smell of fresh cut grass mingled with car exhaust and the rosewater perfume she wore.

The waitress emerged from the luncheonette in her robin's-egg-blue uniform. She crossed the street carefully, placing the egg salad on rye and a Coke with lemon on the stair next to Trish.

"Put this on my tab," Trish said, sliding two singles into the waitress's pocket.

"Sure," she replied.

Trish ate two bites, then suddenly ran to her car. She pulled the groceries from the passenger seat and put them in a tiny refrigerator in the back of the store.

Charlie called.

Ralph was sleeping and he had seen no fish.

Trish finished her lunch and rearranged the board games by box size instead of alphabetically.

An old woman came in and examined almost everything in the store, turning things over to see what might be hidden underneath them. She bought an empty picture frame and two German Christmas ornaments.

After she left, Trish turned the radio on and listened to an oldies station. She checked her watch. It was almost one.

She watched the occasional car passing as she sat on the crooked stool behind the register. She arranged the coins in their tiny compartments and closed the register.

Trish called home.

Charlie answered.

Ralph was eating some of his soft food now, and Charlie still hadn't seen a fish.

"I'm just waiting for one good customer," Trish told him, "and then I'll come right home."

Charlie went back outside, sliding into the sneakers that sat outside the kitchen door. He walked carefully to the stream and sat down on the tiny wooden bridge that crossed it.

Shielding his eyes, he tried to see beneath the surface of the water. A gray fish moved quickly beneath him, nearly the same color as the rocks. Charlie pulled out the broomstick with the piece of white string tied to one end. He smeared his fingers into the sweaty chunk of cream cheese in his pocket and pasted some of it to the end of the line.

Lowering his bait into the water, he found a comfortable position to wait in.

Ralph watched from inside the kitchen door.

III.

Trish worked on the word jumble from the daily paper. While listing the alphabet along the edge of the page, her pen ran out. Searching around the register, she did not see another one. Trish dug deep inside her purse, below the cigarettes and her wallet, beyond her change purse and a compact umbrella. Past her house keys and the store keys and another set of keys, she found an object wrapped in paper.

Trish stopped abruptly and made a strange face.

She slowly pulled the parcel from her purse.

A round, heavy circle was wrapped in newspaper, with a web of cellophane tape wrapped around it.

Taking a pair of scissors in a drawer, she also saw a new box of ballpoint pens. Trish cut the paper away and found a lopsided, ceramic plate that had been spray-painted gold. A lattice of elbow macaroni decorated its edges in a series of rings. At the center, a glittery swirl of macaroni stars spelled out "mom" in crooked letters.

Trish sighed and bit her lip.

She thought she might cry a little, but one small laugh came out instead.

A giant sound rumbled in the distance, like thunder. The lights dimmed, then surged brightly, then went out entirely as the radio murmured into silence. Trish sat in the dark afternoon light with one hand on the golden dish. She cleared her throat once and again.

She lit a cigarette, waiting for the lights to come back on.

Going to the window, she could see a handful of people filing out of the luncheonette across the street.

"You too?" Trish called to them, from the door.

"Yeah," the waitress called back to her, while everyone else remained silent.

The waitress crossed the street to her.

"Can I bum one?" she asked, quietly.

Trish gestured toward the door with a tilt of her head.

The waitress followed her inside.

"I'll try not to knock anything over." The waitress giggled.

Trish laughed through her nose.

"There's nothing that valuable in here," she announced. "Unless Trivial Pursuit gets you juiced up."

Trish lit the waitress's cigarette.

"What's that?" the waitress said, motioning toward the golden plate.

"It's a present from my son," Trish replied.

"Is it an ashtray?" she asked.

"Kind of," Trish began. "But more like something… ornamental."

"Like a trophy?" the waitress asked.

Trish smiled.

"Something like that," she murmured.

"Well, I think we're closed for the day," the waitress announced.

"Me too," Trish said, quickly rewrapping the dish and placing it in her pocketbook. "Let's go."

They made their way to the front door.

"Christ!" Trish shouted to herself, running back to the tiny refrigerator.

She pulled the bag of groceries from inside it.

"Do you like chocolate ice cream?" Trish asked the waitress after she had locked the front door.

The waitress nodded yes.

"We're having a little birthday party today for my son Charlie," Trish said, flipping the end of her cigarette into the street. "Want to come over for a while?"

"Okay," the waitress said.

The two of them waved at the cook across the street.

"See you later, Phil!" the waitress shouted as she untied her apron, rolled it into a ball, and tossed it into the back seat of Trish's lime-green Impala.

Phil waved at her long after they had turned onto Main Street, heading east.

Trish switched the radio on, trying to find a station that was working.

Classical music spurted through the old speakers as they passed the IGA.

She wondered if Charlie had gotten a nibble today.

Trish promised herself she would put all of the dishes in the dishwasher tonight after they ate ice cream and chicken pot pies, after Charlie had gone to sleep with his hands crossed on his chest.

She remembered when she had first bought the dishwasher and how its mechanical hum seemed to disturb the peaceful sounds of night in the countryside, and then how it eventually became a comforting lullaby to her that she had missed for some time now.

the radio hour

PART I.

I.

I heard a bowl clattering to the floor, and silverware ricochet against the side of a metal chair. A baby cried in one long straight wail, then sucked in deeply.

"How fucking hard is it to cook oatmeal?" I heard a man say.

A woman mumbled something.

"Not so fucking hard," he continued, knocking a chair to its side.

The baby coughed and cried as if its head was being squeezed in a vise.

I opened my eyes, staring up at pale green wallpaper.

The room smelled of mold and rosewater. My window shade was up, but I could not see any of them.

An insect buzzed around one of my ears.

"Jesus Christ," he said, "it's instant!"

A door slammed.

A screen door flipped around on its hinges.

I heard her putting the chair back on its feet, then hushing the baby as she sang something that sounded like "Twinkle, Twinkle, Little Star."

The front lawns of the neighborhood were littered with empty beer cans and dirty plastic toys.

I drank coffee on the porch steps, resting the cup on my knees.

The sun was burning off the last bits of fog in the damp, sour air that hovered in the motionless street.

Bud came downstairs, wiping his face with a hand towel.

"Hey Paul," he mumbled.

I had noticed that he shaved every day before anyone saw him. The craterlike burn scars that covered his face and neck allowed tiny patches of hair to grow between them the way weeds grow through the cracks in the sidewalk. At first I thought it was a compulsion, and now I understood it was something he did to feel less conspicuous.

He cracked a can of beer open and sucked at the foam coming out.

"This fridge just doesn't get cold enough," he announced, and sat cross-legged next me.

I might have made an excuse and avoided anyone else in the house, but Bud usually respected my privacy. We had more in common than the midlife loners and doe-eyed interns who filled the rest of the place.

"Are you going to do laundry today?" he asked me.

I hesitated.

"I wasn't gonna ask you to wash my guys," he said, laughing at me. "I was gonna go with you."

I nodded okay.

"If I smell that bad, you can just tell me," I said.

Bud snorted, sucking from his beer.

"Paul—" he said, after he swallowed. "You smell awesome."

Sari came out from the women's half of the house with a folding chair and a tumbler of iced coffee. She tied her hair in a ponytail and eyed us.

Bud stared at Sari's black, zippered halter top, and whatever cleavage she was revealing.

"Morning," I said.

She nodded as she stared out at the street.

A handful of children churned past us on dirt bikes, all of them shirtless and with crew cuts. One of them stayed behind, stopping to ogle her.

Bud stood up and gave him the finger.

The kid gave him the finger back, then flicked his tongue at Sari.

He pedaled off.

Upstairs, I crammed my dirty clothes into a garbage bag.

The windows in the next house were open, but I could not see inside the dark kitchen.

The baby started crying again, a normal sort of crying. The woman's silhouette passed, and I could hear a television set come on. She was watching a game show.

Bud knocked on my door.

"I'm ready," I said, opening it and seeing that he wore a ruffled blue tuxedo shirt and some plaid pants.

"Laundry day means you gotta wear the clothes you never wear—so the rest gets clean!" he said.

II.

Everyone had gone to the mall for steam table Chinese food and the multiplex. I stayed behind and brought my manual Olivetti down to the kitchen. After I fed a fresh piece of paper into the machine, I poured myself a half glass of bourbon and dropped some ice cubes into it.

I didn't have a very clear idea about what I was working on. Maybe something about this kid I was friends with in third grade who always wore Superman T-shirts. His mother was scared he would jump off their roof because he thought he could fly, so she took all of the Superman shirts from him. Then, he just drew an S on all of his regular T-shirts. When his mother took them too, he walked around naked and drew an S on his chest.

They moved away about a month later.

Unwrapping a soft pack of Marlboros and lighting one, I tried to inhale but thought, better to puff on them and just give the illusion of actually smoking.

The kitchen was dead hot as I stared at the mismatched glasses and the cracked dishes. There was no backyard, just a slab of concrete where we kept our garbage and Sari's dirty white Chevette which didn't work.

I saw the family in the next house, eating dinner on their back porch.

Raising my hand once, I waved at them, but they did not see me. They were the only Black people I had seen in Glens Falls.

Pouring a second drink, I typed the alphabet a few times, then some names of potential characters. The kitchen was just boiling.

I made some ham and swiss sandwiches with extra mustard and took them out to the porch.

Next door, the father was teaching his teenage daughter how to drive. They chugged up and down their driveway in a giant Lincoln for half an hour. Eventually she pulled into the street. I waved again and he nodded at me this time before cautiously pulling away.

It was getting dark, and I wandered into the lawn of our other neighbor's house, staring up at the second-floor apartment, trying to see if the young couple was home.

All of their rooms were dark.

I wondered what their names were, coming up with imaginary ones, and then suddenly trying to put them out of my mind.

Sari came out to the front porch and sat on the steps, hugging her knees against her.

"The bartender is in!" I said dramatically, waving both of my hands in the air.

Sari stared at the toys in the lawn across the street.

"Drink?" I asked her.

She nodded.

I went inside and made her a whiskey and Coke.

"Thanks," she murmured, taking it from me and sipping from it.

"I think the soda's kind of flat," I said. "It was from Albert's shelf."

I sat down next to her.

She wiped the backs of her hands across her face, catching a tear that dangled from her chin.

"I know he's cheating," she said.

I nodded, and started in on my second sandwich.

"Paul, please don't tell anyone," she said, after a moment. "I've got enough guys trying to get into my pants."

The street had grown dark and the lights sputtered on, one at a time.

"Maybe it'll work out," I said, breaking the near half hour of silence we had shared.

I sighed, and stood up, patting her gently on the shoulder, realizing I had touched her without thinking about it first.

III.

Eventually, there was work to do at the theater.

I unloaded platforms from a semi with Bud for the better part of two days, stacking them and testing the mechanisms that locked them together, putting aside the ones that didn't work. The electricians rolled around at the tops of thirty-foot A-frame ladders, sending buckets up and down with gel-frame holders and replacement parts for the rented lights.

Sari arranged the props for the new production on a series of tables, outlining each object's proper place with white tape.

She paused sometimes, staring off into space.

I had kept the long-distance fight with her boyfriend a secret, not even telling Bud about it.

We worked on the catwalks next, high above the stage floor.

Our tools were tied to us with wires as we laid out the rigging for a mechanical peacock's tail to open. Bud kept quiet, holding nuts, bolts, and lock washers in his palms for me, the way a nurse hands operating tools to a surgeon. Neither of us wore gloves, and our hands were covered with calluses and tiny scratches from the sharp ends of the aircraft cable we had to thread through the various pieces of hardware.

I thought about the scars on his face while we worked in the near darkness, seeing if I could remember their shapes.

IV.

There was only one TV channel that worked.

I smoked Bud's skunk weed with him when he watched the *Morton Downey Junior Show*. We took turns screaming at the people he had on.

One afternoon, Sari and her amazon-sized roommate Ellen joined us on the sagging cushions of the mustard-colored couch set. I was baking instant brownies.

Declining the whiskey and the joint we offered her, Ellen sat and stared alternately at the TV, then at us as we jumped around on the cheap furniture. Next came Albert, who read books in his room when we had time off. He was in his forties, drove an ancient blue Desoto, and usually delivered pizza for a living. Albert often talked about getting as far as he could from his father, who was an elementary school principal somewhere in Iowa. He decided to sit with us, running his fingers through his beard as he repeated Morton's commentary to himself.

During a commercial, he admitted to me that he didn't really know what anchovies were.

The show was about something like cross-dressing Republicans and their secret lovers, but all I noticed was the mammoth ashtray Morton rested his cigarettes on, the way his pants were hiked up to his armpits, and how every once in a while, he seemed to say something terrifyingly true.

Ellen and Albert didn't make it through the entire show before they excused themselves.

Mike dropped by later, parking his noisy RX-7 in front. He was one of those halfway good-looking actors who worked as a stagehand to be around the theater at any cost. The first time we met him, he told us that everyone in Wisconsin called him

"Snake," and that was what we should call him. Sometimes, I tried to decide if he really needed the wire-framed glasses he wore, or if they were just a prop to make him look smarter.

My trays of instant brownies were ready, and we ate them on the front porch.

Bud found a deck of cards and dragged a big cardboard box up from the basement to use as a table, teaching us how to play Euchre as the sun set on the neighborhood. We all took a lot of wild chances, because we didn't really understand the rules.

A fat, longhaired teenager coasted past us on an old bicycle.

"Was that a guy or a girl?" Bud asked, as we chuckled into our cards.

"It was a girl with sideburns," Mike said.

"She's so big, she can't even pedal," Sari said, squeezing together some brownie crumbs and tossing them into her mouth.

"She just coasts," I said, finishing out the hand.

"We win again," Bud said triumphantly.

He coaxed me into a messy high five.

"One more like that and Sari takes her shirt off," Bud said.

Sari laughed to herself as Mike eyed her.

"Not on your life," she said, dropping her cards on the cardboard box.

Bud leered at her, grinning and laughing. Suddenly, he seemed unfamiliar to me.

"Oh, please baby, please," Bud cooed to her, getting down on his knees.

"Enough!" she said, crossing her arms across her chest.

"Are you cold?" Mike said in a sweet voice.

"Fuck off," Sari said, as she stalked off into the street.

Mike stared angrily at Bud.

"You guys gotta lay off," I said, "or she's just gonna stay in her room the rest of the summer."

"He's the one," Mike said, pointing at Bud.

"Come on, Mike, I said.

He bristled.

"What do you think you've got—X-ray vision?" I said. "It isn't her fucking fault she's the only girl."

Mike wandered into the neighbor's front yard, kicking some empty beer cans into the gutter.

"You're an animal, Mike!" Bud called out to the empty street.

For some reason, a streetlight clicked off as he started his car and drove away.

"We should go get her," Bud said quietly.

I felt like I knew him again, as if he were a house cat that had attacked me and was curled back up at my feet now.

I went inside the door and slid my sneakers on.

"Maybe we think she looks hot because she's the only girl," he said, as we started toward the main road that skirted the neighborhood.

"C'mon—she's got some mystery boyfriend, she drinks like one of us," I said at one point. "And that's one serious pair of sugar tits."

"I suspect she's a real blonde," Bud said, peering at the 24-hour supermarket in the distance which stood empty and bright.

V.

"No," I heard her tell him. "I'm not taking the baby to church with me."

"Why the fuck not?" he said.

"Because, it's too far to walk," she said. "And she just cries."

"She cries here too," he said.

I heard a can open, thinking it was a beer but then thinking it was a soda.

"I ain't gonna watch her," he said.

"I can't take her," she said. "I just can't."

"You can't?" he asked. "Or you won't?"

There was a sudden silence as I heard a chair slide across the floor.

I smelled the cigarette smoke on my fingers, and tasted the heartburn in the back of my throat from another dinner of instant brownies.

"You better fucking pray," he shouted. "Leaving your own child alone to sit around in her own shit?"

The baby coughed and began to cry.

He leaned out of their kitchen into the narrow space between the two houses, inches from my shade that flipped against the windowsill in a sudden breeze.

"Leaving her hungry?" he shouted. "You better ask God about that."

I felt a bug crawling across my legs and jumped around in the bed, trying to swat it off of me.

The man stomped around the apartment for a few minutes and then I heard him leave. The baby stopped crying just after his truck churned on and rattled away. I raised the window shade and looked into their kitchen.

The baby glanced at me, now quiet.

I tried to play peek-a-boo with her.

She stared at me.

Her cheeks were red and glistening wet. She had a spoon clenched in her hand, and she dropped it on her tray.

It was almost noon when I realized I was late to go to the theater. We had to prepare the stage for the matinee.

VI.

We took Dan, the assistant technical director, to Sandy's Clam Bar off the interstate for his birthday. He hid at a table in the corner of the big room while we took turns buying rounds of Miller Genuine Draft and jabbed at selections on the jukebox.

"Why the hell do they call it a clam bar?" Mike announced in a dramatic voice. "I don't see any clams!"

Sari and Big Ellen were just walking in, and it seemed like they had heard him, but they didn't let on.

Bud pulled Mike back toward the jukebox.

Dan looked up at the two women, rolling his lips into his mouth nervously.

Sari extended a small, quickly wrapped gift to him.

"Here," she said, nudging my elbow to make sure I took some credit. "It's from all of us at 93 Chestnut."

"Open it!" Bud shouted at him from the back of the room.

Dan saw it was a deck of Elvis Presley playing cards.

Sari pushed Ellen toward him a few steps.

"We wanted to invite you to come and play Euchre on the porch sometime," she said so quietly he could not hear her.

He thought to ask her to repeat herself, but Sari shook her head behind Ellen and then telegraphed a big smile to him.

Dan managed a laugh, making sure to show his teeth as he waved the cards above his head.

"Thanks, you guys," he said.

The beer was cheap, and the place filled quickly.

We ordered above people's heads, two or three deep at the bar. It was difficult to really hear what people were saying to me over the classic rock that pumped out of the jukebox, so I just watched their expressions while their hands moved around, smiling and nodding and saying "yeah" every once in a while.

Everyone from the theater seemed to snap into happier,

more outgoing versions of themselves on payday.

A song by the Who came on.

Bud got the bartender to give him a pint glass. He emptied his beer into it and waited until he had a few people's attention. Leaning his face in as far as it would fit, he bit down and tipped his head back all the way. Downing the beer, he waved his arms around.

"Look Ma," he said, returning the empty glass to the bar. "No hands!"

Sari came up next to me and whispered into my ear.

I nodded and smiled.

"I said, why the fuck does he have to do that?" she shouted, rabbit-punching me in the back.

Before I could say anything, Bud had refilled his glass and was doing the trick again.

Some strangers turned to watch him.

As the glass broke, he dropped his head, pulling the pieces from inside his mouth and placing them on the bar.

"Let's go," Sari said, grabbing the back of his T-shirt and pulling him through the crowd.

Mike started after them.

I held his elbow.

"She'll get him home," I said.

"Was he bleeding?" Mike asked me.

I nodded yes, and watched the bartender sweeping the broken glass onto a piece of cardboard.

Mike mumbled to himself, trying to speak through three hours of cold beers.

"He's just embarrassed," I said. "I broke a whole bunch of glasses like that."

He stared at me, trying to make a decision.

"But I was just a kid," I added.

"You think you know everything, Paul," he said, after a minute. "Don't you."

I shifted my weight from foot to foot, staring at him without blinking.

"Some stuff is pretty easy to figure out," I said. "Aren't we just kids pretending to be grownups?"

Mike waved at the bartender behind me and ordered another beer.

VII.

Dan came in his pickup truck the next afternoon, and we all went to a gorge. Sari made sure that Ellen sat in the front with him.

Albert slathered himself with suntan lotion and read from a giant book about World War I. Bud was more quiet than usual, but he was hungover. Sari wore her perennial tight, black, zippered tank top and a pair of cutoffs. She was the first to walk into the water, raising her hands high into the air.

"Whew!" she shouted. "It's fucking cold!"

Mike kept back from us, as if he was taking notes while squatting behind some trees.

Dan and Ellen found a pair of big rocks to sit on, and drank some of the Dr. Peppers we had stopped to pick up.

I waded in, toward Sari.

"We all look like a bunch of townies," I said, so that only she could hear me.

"Well," she said quietly, "we sort of are townies—at least until August."

I tried to find some footing where the riverbed was not so slippery.

"This is one freaky summer job," I said. "We never have to work."

"For us, it's a summer job," she said, and then motioned toward Dan and Ellen. "This is their whole life."

I pulled my T-shirt off and tossed it to Bud at the water's edge.

"Man, you are white," Sari said.

"Townie tan," I said, correcting her.

Later, we moved closer to the falls.

The water ran strong and noisy over the rocks. Clumps of moss grew between them, which we ripped up and tossed to each other, playing an improvised game of pepper. Sari threw one of the clumps to Bud, but he wasn't looking, and it smacked against his neck.

"What the fuck!" he shouted at her, grabbing the moss from the ground and whipping it back at her. I pulled a clump from the rocks at my feet and threw it at him, hitting him square in the chest.

"Quit it!" he shouted, and for some reason I began to laugh.

I reached for more, and pegged him on the forehead.

"Quit it!" he shouted at me, his voice wobbling inside of him.

I laughed, almost cackling with pleasure, with the ease it took to hit him.

Sari got him next, on the leg.

Bud stalked the water's edge, not giving an inch as he told us to stop.

We calmed down, suppressing our laughter by breathing deeply and grinning at each other.

Mike and Albert were skipping stones where we had first gotten in. Dan and Ellen were holding hands on the giant rocks.

"Why don't you come in the water with us?" she asked Bud.

"I can't swim," he said.

"It's not even three feet deep," she said, kneeling down until just her head was above the water's surface.

The gorge thundered below us, as the water crashed more than one hundred feet down to the basin. I was hungry and hungover, and the cold, sweet water felt like medicine. I dunked my head in and looked for the tiny fish that I knew were swimming past my feet.

PART II.

I.

Mike and Bud drove to New York for July Fourth. They had half-offered for me to go with them, but I would have had to squeeze myself behind their seats in the space under the back window.

I gave them some addresses of places to go, and then outlined the best route on a map they had bought at a gas station that morning. They didn't really listen to me, even when I told them that it would be difficult to buy their own fireworks unless they went to Chinatown, which would be a war zone.

Finishing their late-morning beers, they drove off toward the interstate.

I lit a cigarette and fake-smoked on the front steps.

I thought about how I could have caught up with my college roommate and his girlfriend if I had gone with them. I was sure they would be very interested in the young couple that lived next door, outside my window. They would have laughed when I told them about the waitress I had dated earlier that summer. She turned out to be a Jew for Jesus, and had a habit of confessing odd things to me in the middle of the night, like her obsession with Guns N' Roses.

Sari stuck her head out of her window above the porch.

"Want to go to the river?" she asked.

I made a face, half surprised.

"But your car doesn't work," I said.

"It's supposed to be about a fifteen-minute walk that way," she said, pointing away from the interstate.

I made some ham and swiss sandwiches with extra mustard

and took three of Bud's beers, putting them in a paper grocery bag with a few books I had intended to read before going back to school.

Waiting on the front steps, I thought about Sari in her room. Maybe she was pulling herself into a bathing suit, trying to decide if she really needed to shave her bikini line. I wondered if she kept herself trimmed for her boyfriend, even though she wouldn't see him for at least another month.

In my imagination, she had a big pimple in the middle of her back that she couldn't see.

Cracking one of Bud's beers, I closed my eyes.

The neighborhood was quiet.

Cars were shuffling along the interstate in the distance. Someone turned on a lawn mower, or maybe a chainsaw.

The screen door opened.

Sari was ready, wearing just her bikini and some cutoffs. I looked up at her, unable to stop myself from drinking in the boxlike shape of her knees, the short curves that marked her hips. Part of me realized what I was doing, and how it did not seem to bother her.

"Are you okay?" she asked.

"Just hungover," I said, rubbing the backs of my hands against my face.

We walked through the neighborhood without talking.

The mysterious fat teenager on the bicycle coasted past us.

"Still think that's a girl?" I asked her.

"Absolutely," she said.

There was a long bend in the river, surrounded by sand.

Pickup trucks and old cars were parked randomly alongside

the road and in the tall grass. We made our way through the people dozing on bed sheets and towels in the afternoon sun.

Finding an empty spot close to the water, we dropped our things in the sand, kicking off our shoes. I rolled my T-shirt and shorts into a makeshift pillow, placing them on my beach towel.

Sari stared out at the water, motionless.

She took off her shorts all at once, slipping into the water almost noiselessly as she pulled herself forward with a few quick strokes.

The riverbed was littered with people from the neighborhood. Sluggish men with army tattoos rested their hands on women's hips, standing waist-deep in the water, smoking cigarettes and staring off at the horizon.

Sari's head appeared from beneath the water's surface as she flipped her hair back from her face and checked the bikini knot at the back of her neck.

I suddenly felt very small, as if I was surrounded by twelve-foot people. Sari looked like she was very far from me. The sun came out from behind some clouds and bright flares cut through my eyelashes.

I put my T-shirt over my head and lay back into the towel and the warm sand beneath it.

Ideas came to me, swerving in my ears. I felt the sun pushing through the skin of my eyelids. Rolling onto my stomach, I took slow, calculated breaths, pushing images of nightlights and ants and the naked waitress from my mind.

I opened one of the beers in the paper bag and gulped it down, thinking I would fall asleep when I rested my head back into the sand this time.

Sari stood over me, intentionally letting the water drip off of her goose-bumped legs onto my feet. She breathed noisily. I imagined her hands on her hips, and some of the river people staring at us as I woke up.

I did not move.

"Hey," she said quietly.

I stayed still, as I sensed her lowering herself to the sand next to my ear. Sari's wet hair smelled of algae and her bubblegum scented shampoo.

"I still have a boyfriend," she said.

She waited for me to say something.

I pushed my hands into the cool sand, looking for something smart or funny to say.

She gave me a peck on the cheek.

"Not that I don't mind the company," she whispered.

I turned my neck toward the warmth of the sun, pretending to move in my sleep.

"Sweet dreams," she said, standing up and kicking a little sand on me.

In the afternoon, Sari bought us some ice-cream sandwiches from a concession stand which we ate slowly, and then quickly when they began to drip down our arms.

We washed our hands at the water's edge, cracked the two remaining beers, and studied the couples around us. Some of them were sleeping with their hands resting gently on their pelvises or over their breasts. Some were staring fiercely at the river and the children, covered with muck, who pranced at the water's edge.

"God," she said.

"What?" I asked.

"That guy is creeping me out," she said, pulling my T-shirt on over her bikini.

A skinny man was staring at her, rubbing his penis inside his shorts.

He stood up quickly and ran into the water.

"Sari—" I said, and then stopped myself.

"What?" she said.

"Every guy is into you," I said. "Jesus Christ, I try so hard not to stare at you."

Her face turned in on itself.

"Look at this place," I said, motioning toward the people standing in the river. "It's a human cesspool."

She rolled her lips inside her mouth.

"It just makes me feel so ugly," she said, under her breath.

"Maybe we all stink," I said, my hand waving around in the air. "Every last one of us."

I sipped from the beer and stayed quiet.

She sighed and sort of shook herself.

Raindrops scattered around us. Thunder boomed in the distance.

"No fireworks tonight," I said quietly.

"What?" she said.

"It's the Fourth of July." I said.

"Oh," she said. "I totally forgot."

We packed our things quickly and started home.

The rain caught us halfway.

I had the instinct to run, and then a sudden realization that there was no reason to. Sari flashed a little smile, then made a face that said something like "who cares?" I thought to share the random thoughts I was having with her. Editing them together and trying to leave out the religious waitress, they began to take a simpler shape.

The pack of kids on their dirt bikes churned past us, shouting to each other. A pickup truck followed them. I looked at the children in the back as they stopped at a red light. They sat motionless, looking past us at the darkening sky with their towels draped over their shoulders.

The giant teenager wheezed past us next, her face contorting as she managed to pedal the bike. The rear tire sprayed a stripe of mud up the back of her pants and shirt.

We were getting soaked, walking slowly. Sari shivered once, and stifled a sneeze.

"Four more weeks," she said.

"Yeah, I know," I said.

"That was kind of fun," I said, just before we got back to the house.

"I'm going in," Sari announced.

She moved quickly, and the screen door flipped around behind her. I stood on the front porch, noticing that the upstairs neighbors had left their windows open.

Crawling under the covers, naked and wet, I watched the light slowly fade from the room.

II.

I dreamt of a dark sky that loomed through my windshield. The white lights of oncoming cars and the red ones blooming in front of me were one connected object, something like the legs of a centipede. Clouds hung low over power lines and smokestacks as the windshield wipers did their business. Giant trucks thundered past me as the highway lights sputtered on and off, orange and sulfurous.

There were road signs for places I had never heard of, like "Honey Road" and "East John Pruitt Drive."

The rain grew heavier as the car tires in front of me drew crisscrossing lines in the slick road.

Someone honked, looking to pass me.

I thought I smelled gasoline as I stared at the power lines, suddenly realizing they reminded me of the string game children play called Cat's Cradle.

The pinprick sensation of raindrops on my feet woke me. My room was dark.

I went to the bathroom, and then wandered through the house, eventually going downstairs.

Standing outside on the porch, I saw Albert's Desoto parked at the curb. It looked somehow heroic in the dramatic shadows made by the streetlights.

I began to feel terribly lonely.

III.

Mike and Bud didn't make it back for the next performance, so it fell to me to run the lighting board.

It looked like a fake computer from an old science fiction film. The cream-colored plastic was filthy, and smelled like barbecue potato chips.

All I had to do was press the enter key when the stage manager told me to, over the headset.

I felt a perverse sense of power, and began to fantasize about hitting the escape key or one of the red ones, like F12, at some high point in the show to inspire some kind of community opera chaos.

There were four cues right after each other.

The orchestra was actually all right. I liked the overture at the start of Act Two.

The curtain rose.

Everything outside of my mind seemed to lurch into slow-motion, with the color slowly sucked out of it. At the same time I had a flurry of ideas all at once, a thousand cars driving like mad down a thousand roads at the very same time.

I heard the stage manager call the next cue. I saw my finger hit the enter button, sure I was late.

When I was a boy and this happened all of the time, I thought of raisins at this point and it seemed to help. Raisins, and taking the dishes from the dishwasher and putting them in the kitchen cabinets.

The stage manager called the next cue.

I hit the enter key.

I smelled gasoline again.

The soprano went into the first aria.

I took a deep breath and let it out as slowly as I could.

"Raisins," I said to myself.

PART III.

I.

August came, and Mike and Bud were still missing. Sari had disappeared into her room, studying for some test that would get her into graduate school. The husband in the apartment across from my window had bought a big black motorcycle. His pickup truck was in pieces scattered across the driveway. Somehow I never saw him, just his tools and empty beer cans.

Big Dan had started sleeping with Big Ellen. They came down to the porch sometimes after they had sex. Her in his shirt, him bare-chested. Once, I thought I could see his semen leaking from her underwear and down her big white leg.

The kitchen was just too hot to work in, so I began taking the Olivetti out to the porch with an AM clock radio. The country station was okay. I was still coming up with imaginary names for the young couple next door, still wondering about that kid who thought he was Superman and drew the S on his chest, and how he scared his mother.

One night I took pictures of Albert's blue Desoto under the orange streetlights. Mosquitoes circled my ears as I made long exposures with my trusty Olympus.

Afterward, I sat on the porch steps, sipping on the next-to-last beer as the sounds of motorcycles and bug zappers punctuated the evening. Dan came downstairs in his underwear, breathing in the night air with a dramatic flourish.

"You still up?" he asked.

I nodded yes, not really interested in making conversation.

"It's so fucking hot in there," he said, "Plus, Ellen snores."

I forced a small smile for him.

The sound of dishes breaking came from the upstairs apartment next door.

"What the hell is that?" Dan asked, under his breath.

The woman screamed.

"They're right next to my window," I said. "And they have a baby."

Dan nodded, starting to think.

"He'll come downstairs in a second," I said. "He hits her, and then he leaves."

"We should do something," Dan said.

"I don't even know what he looks like," I said. "We could be drinking next to him when we go to Sandy's and we wouldn't even know it."

"Why doesn't she call the cops?" Dan asked.

We stared at the street for a moment, listening to him stomp down the stairs on the other side of the house, and pulling away on his motorcycle.

"I don't know," I said, breaking the silence. "It's really hard for some people to take a step like that."

"What do you mean?" Dan asked.

"For instance—I'm really into some girl, and I just get really nervous around her. It's impossible for me to ask her out," I said. "Now, you take some girl who's just kind of interesting. I can ask her out no problem."

"You don't want her so much," Dan said, half to himself.

He shrank into the corner, and crossed his legs.

I went back to the story about the Superman kid, and finished my beer.

The radio was playing a whole set of songs by the Shangri-Las. I tapped my foot in time, and felt that Dan was copying me from his corner of the porch.

"Paul, you're right about something," Dan said.

"Seriously?" I said.

"You are," Dan said.

"You don't know me very well then," I said, opening the last can.

"Well," Dan said, from the shadows, "I sort of tried to kill myself last summer."

I looked at him and tried to decide if he was joking with me.

"But if I was doing anything like what you said—" he added, his voice growing steadier. "I screwed it up, because I didn't really want to."

I nodded, and extended the last beer for him.

"Let's split it," he said, and poured half of it into one of my empties, spilling foam all over my papers.

"Fuck, I'm sorry," he said. "I screwed up your masterpiece."

I laughed really hard.

"My masterpiece?" I said, passing some of the pages to him.

He looked at them, full of the alphabet and occasional names.

"Actually you are pretty nuts," he said, after a moment. "I would not show that to too many people."

II.

I dialed my father up a few nights later. They didn't trust us to pay the phone bill, so I had to call collect.

He wouldn't accept the charges. It was our way of saying hello without actually talking. If I told the operator I was making a collect call from Roy Rodgers, then he would know I really needed to talk to him.

He was breathing on the other end of the line, then spoke slowly and methodically to the operator.

I really wanted to talk to my little brother, but I did not have the phone number. I decided to write him a letter instead. I had the address to the hippie hospital they had him in. He might be ready to come home in a few months. It was hard to tell.

PART IV.

I.

I wandered in a small forest. The trees were heavy with leaves that reminded me of the human hand as their veins bobbed randomly in the breeze. The stretch of sand by the river was clogged with people. Sari had come with her boyfriend and then they left after giving me a little nod. He was tall and quiet.

Breathing in the warm, wet air, I held it inside me for as long as I could. The low afternoon sun was pushing into the forest and across my bare feet.

Mike and Bud had gotten into a massive car accident on the way back from New York. Everyone was visiting them in the hospital but us. I didn't know what to say to them without sounding like their father.

I exhaled slowly, letting my breath whistle inside my nose. Mosquitoes were circling my arms.

I thought to push myself deep into the woods, between the birch trees that rustled above me now. Maybe there was a forgotten tree house, or hunter's stand that I could stay in for my last week in Glens Falls. Red berries dangled from the bushes around me. They were poison, and I think they are called wolf's fruit.

I squished some of them in my palms and painted my name on one of the white trees.

As I turned the corner, I saw fishing poles on the front lawn of the house next door. They lay split and broken, connected by a tangle of monofilament. T-shirts and *Hustler* magazines were flipping out of the upstairs windows.

Climbing up the stairs to my room, I saw the young mother passing her kitchen window. She was in her underwear. I heard a needle dropping onto a record, and then an ABBA song from their apartment. She turned the volume up and the baby started crying.

The vacuum cleaner churned on.

I sat on my bed, staring at their window.

She appeared for a moment, holding the baby tight to her breasts as she shoved the vacuum cleaner back and forth. Her singing was terrible, and grew louder.

"Dancing Queen" was on now.

I knew she had seen me. I waited for her to see the sympathetic face I was making for her but she kept her eyes down, sometimes shoving a chair out of her way.

I thought of finding my way up the stairs to the woman and her baby, of holding both of them tight in my arms so they could cry into my T-shirt. I thought of whispering to them that everything would be ok, now that I was there. Her husband might come home then, and I would be waiting for him on the front steps with a baseball bat in my right hand. Staring at him, my head would shake slowly back and forth. I would crack one of his beers and slurp it all the way down.

Mike and Bud were not there to back me up. Albert was watching from his window. Sari and her boyfriend were taking a nap, naked in the afternoon, their perfect bodies sticky and wet like half-sucked candies.

Big Dan would pull up in his pickup, waving at me to back off.

The guy never saw him coming, the lead pipe in Dan's thick hands and the dull wet thud against the back of his head.

The woman from upstairs stood behind the screen door now, holding the baby in one arm. She smoked a cigarette, pulling on it with her free hand.

"Where's he from?" I would ask her.

"Trenton," she said. "New Jersey."

I would put some of his fishing lures in a paper bag as Big Dan threw him into the back of the truck.

I could even hear the wind whistling in our ears as we drove down the interstate with the windows down and the radio blasting.

We eventually bought a ticket at the Greyhound station, propping it perfectly in his scraped hand, leaving him sitting in a plush blue seat in the back of the bus, blood running along the side of his head.

I went downstairs and poured myself a glass of Bud's whiskey and dropped an ice cube in it.

The kitchen was full of pizza crusts and cereal bowls.

It didn't take too long to clean.

I rolled a fresh sheet of paper into my turquoise Olivetti and sat for a while.

Sari and her boyfriend were working on her car in the back alleyway, swearing at her socket wrenches and the metric system.

I started typing.

Cooper's farm

PART I.

I.

Aaron kissed her once between the shoulder blades, then dressed quietly in the dark. Iris slept easily, her face turned into the pillow as her fingers dangled past the edge of the bed.

The rooster began to crow.

Aaron went downstairs, making the flypapers spin as he passed them.

He drank the cold coffee from the bottom of the percolator, and munched on a heel of black bread. The night's frost had drawn a lacelike pattern across the kitchen windows. The compost pot smelled of orange peels and eggshells.

He drew a deep breath, pressing his palms against the giant oak table as one of the dogs' collars began to clink against itself.

It was Cooper.

Aaron sat back into the chair and held his hand out. The horselike Chesapeake licked his fingers, then stopped abruptly, looking up at him with his sad yellow eyes.

Aaron gave the dog a strong petting as he massaged his forehead and the velvety corners of his ears. Cooper rested his wet mouth on Aaron's jeans.

"Big day, Butch," he said.

They went to the mudroom with the compost pail, and he pulled his tall rubber boots on.

Aaron fed the chickens.

The hens made nervous clucks as he lifted them one at a time, checking their nests. He filled his felt hat with a collection of their warm eggs, walking carefully to the front steps of the farmhouse, where he rested them. Cooper gave the hat a quick sniff, then followed with his loose-boned walk.

Aaron spread corn on the ground for the ducks and geese as their noisy pack surrounded him.

Patches got fresh water, and a bucket of sweet oats. Aaron felt the pony's swollen belly with his hand, chuckling to himself and shaking his head.

One of the pigs walked alongside him and the dog, on her side of the electric fence. Aaron stopped and pulled a piece of fabric that had been caught in it. The pig waited, drooling a thin line from her snout. It landed on the barbed wire, which sent a short jolt through her.

Cooper barked once, as she squealed and sneezed.

The herd moved cautiously, eyeing Aaron as he turned off the fence and entered the pen. He spread feed and old vegetables into the troughs.

A clump of giant zucchinis had grown in the corner. He pulled a yellow pocketknife from his pocket and cut the largest one free from its vine.

Breaking it open with his hands, he dropped the pieces in between the pigs as they nosed each other and found empty spaces along the trough.

Smoke curled slowly from the chimney, and he could see the warm glow of the lights in the kitchen as they blinked on.

Pulling some late, withered green beans from the vegetable garden, he ate them one at a time as his boots made sucking noises in the mud.

Aaron walked the long oval of the driveway that set the farmhouse back from the main road. He smelled the dead hay and the fallen apples, which had begun to rot. The stream was running high and noisy.

A handful of deer walked gingerly through the front cornfield, looking for something to eat among the broken stalks that littered the ground.

Cooper stood still, watching them. His body grew tense, as his eyes seemed to make calculations of distance and probability. He rose slowly, preparing to launch after them.

"Cooper," Aaron said. "Come."

The dog turned, and walked alongside him as they made their way back to the house.

Paul and Adam were at the kitchen table, putting butter and syrup on their pancakes. Iris sat away from them, nursing the baby.

"Leave some for your father," she said to the boys, and watched them put some of the pancakes back on the empty plate.

"Two is fine," Aaron said to them.

Iris looked up at him, frowning.

"I already ate a little," he said to her, quietly. "And I don't want them complaining in the car."

The baby finished nursing with a noisy smack of her lips.

"Is she better?" he asked.

"I think so," Iris said. "She got her appetite back."

Cooper nosed his leg.

"Everybody's hungry," he said, and went to fill Cooper's bowl.

The boys wrestled with the orange juice container and some spilled onto the floor. Cooper quickly licked it up.

"Quit fucking around," Aaron said, and they shrunk into their chairs.

"Not today, boys," Iris said. "Not today."

Cooper barked once, at the window.

Paul jumped to the side of his chair. Adam dropped his fork on the floor.

Aaron laughed at them, eating the pancakes with his fingers and standing over them.

"Okay," Iris said. "Get dressed."

The boys went upstairs.

"And wear undershirts," she said. "It might get cold."

Aaron looked out the window at the pigs as they ate.

Iris thumped the baby's back for a while, until she burped.

"You need to get dressed too," she said. "We might hit traffic."

"You think?" he asked.

"We can't be late," she said, rebuttoning her shirt. "And you still need to shave."

Aaron did not leave the window.

She rested her hand on his shoulder, and rocked the baby in her other arm.

"You should think about—" she began.

"Remember when I grew a beard, and then I shaved it off and the boys didn't know who I was?" he asked.

"Yes," she said.

He smiled to himself as a tiny laugh came out of his nose. He felt the stubble on his cheeks.

"Alright," he said, and went to the downstairs bathroom.

"I can see him," Paul said, looking down at the front evergreen from the bedroom window.

Adam's face turned into itself.

"He's waving," Paul said.

"No," Adam said.

Paul buttoned his blue gingham shirt and tucked it into his new Toughskins. Adam sat on his bed and stared angrily at the floor.

"He can be my friend too," Paul said, walking over to Adam and standing over him.

Adam shoved one of his shoes against Paul's.

Paul pressed back, slowly.

Adam pushed back as hard as he could.

"He isn't even here today," Adam said, his chin quivering.

"But, I just saw him," Paul said, pushing his hands into the stiff pockets of his pants.

"You can't see him at all," Adam said, turning to the wall.

Paul waited for a moment, chewing the insides of his cheeks, then went downstairs.

Aaron started the big white Ford pickup truck and came around to help Iris and the baby into the front seat. Cooper followed him, waiting.

He barked once and Aaron opened the hatch door in the back.

"Cooper," he said. "Kennel."

The dog lunged into the dark bed of the truck.

"Cooper, don't glob on me," Paul said.

Aaron closed the hatch and put the truck into gear.

A few moments later, he stopped as everyone lurched forward in surprise.

He ran down the driveway to the corner of the barn.

Feeling for the switch, he turned the electric fence back on.

Walking back to the truck, he checked his white shirt and black pants for mud spots.

They pulled away from the farmhouse and the pair of evergreens.

Red and yellow leaves littered the dirt road and the way to the interstate. The sun flickered through the thick forest as Cooper began to bark at squirrels.

Aaron's face turned quickly, shouting incoherently through

the plastic window of the cab.

He stopped, and drove all of the way back to the farm in silence.

Inside, he checked the downstairs bathroom and the rooms upstairs.

He found Adam sitting on the toilet in the upstairs bathroom, his face wet with tears.

Aaron breathed quietly for a moment.

"Come on, Butch," he said, and watched the little boy pull up his underwear and tuck his red gingham shirt into his Toughskins.

Adam looked up, and waited.

Aaron pulled him into his arms and carried him downstairs. Adam curled his finger into his father's hair and closed his eyes as he waited to be put in the back of the truck.

Cooper began licking Adam's cheeks.

"Dad," he said, as he found a place to sit. "I forgot to flush."

Aaron stared down the long dirt driveway and started the truck again.

II.

Adam slept against Cooper's chest, with his hand wrapped around his ear.

Paul sat against the window, watching the road unwind behind them. He saw shopping malls and then giant bridges. Tall buildings in the distance reflected the afternoon sun in short flashes that filled the windows.

The truck made its way through a cemetery crammed with gravestones. Paul felt them surrounding him on all sides.

The truck stopped.

Paul leaned back and closed his eyes.

"C'mon, boys," Aaron said, getting out of the cab.

Adam woke up.

"Come on, Paul," Aaron said. "We don't have time."

Paul fake-yawned and crawled out.

"Cooper," Aaron said. "Stay."

Old couples stood in groups of three and four. A gray-haired man with a long, curved back approached them as they got out of the truck and stretched their legs.

"Aaron," he said. "So sorry."

Aaron nodded once, closing his eyes slowly.

"I brought these for the boys maybe," the old man said, pressing two white yarmulkes into his hand.

Aaron turned them slowly with his fingers.

"Thanks, Saul," he said, under his breath.

The old man studied his face, and spoke quietly to himself.

"What?" Aaron asked, growing tense.

"You never lookcd a bit like him. All I see is your mother," he said, and moved slowly back to the others.

The couples spoke among themselves and stared at the white truck covered in patterns of mud and rust. They left their hands on each other's shoulders as they watched.

"Boys—" Aaron said.

Paul and Adam stepped cautiously toward him.

Aaron held Paul's face for a moment, pulling his chin up with his finger. He smoothed his curly black hair and pinned a yarmulke on him. Paul kept quiet and waited until he was done.

Adam stepped forward, and Aaron pinned the remaining one on him.

"That was a hell of a piss you took this morning," he said.

The boy blushed as he walked back to the truck.

Iris touched his shoulder.

"And you?" she asked.

Aaron touched his pockets and frowned.

"I knew you would forget it," she said, pinning his yarmulke on him quickly.

"I haven't worn this since we got married," he said.

"Maybe you'll never have to wear it again," she said.

The baby opened her eyes and made a small noise.

"They're waiting for us," she said, tying a kerchief around her head.

They walked together toward the hearse and the open grave.

The clump of relatives stood to the side.

Aaron's family surrounded him in the dry grass.

Paul yawned, lost in the words that were being read. He watched his father's fingers tapping against his leg. He saw his face going stiff, then remembering to breathe, then falling slack.

The ground smelled like toads, he thought.

Aaron looked down at him, and put his hand on his shoulder. He began to smooth his hair and knocked the yarmulke to the powdery earth. Two of the women watched them, one frowning, one smiling at him.

Aaron pinned it back on his head, and they both stared at the long black coffin.

He had visited him with the boys, three years before.

The home was yellow, smelling of mint and paper cups.

An early summer sun spread a window pattern across the fuzzy green carpet. The boys sat on the edge of the bed, their legs dangling in space. Ezra wore a clean shirt with a monogram on the pocket.

"You know, Aaron, this one looks just like my mother, God rest her soul," he said, motioning at Paul.

"I think there's a lot of Iris in him," he said, looking into the old man's yellowing eyes.

Ezra stared at a corner of the room, his mouth half open.

"Aaron—show them the pictures from Niagara Falls," he said. "The vacation in Niagara Falls."

"Pop," Aaron said, getting up from his chair.

"Dad, you went to Niagara Falls?" Adam asked.

"No," Aaron said under his breath. "We never went."

The boys grew quiet, and pursed their lips.

"Cuba," Aaron whispered. "We went to Cuba."

"Yes," Ezra announced after a moment. "We did that too."

"Pop," Aaron said. "Pop, you're drooling."

He wiped the spit from Ezra's chin with a Kleenex, not seeing the drops on his pant leg. He looked for the wastebasket, but couldn't find it.

Aaron went to the bathroom and flushed the tissue down the toilet.

Ezra stared at the two boys, lost in thought. Adam sat quietly, half confused. Paul stared back at him, trying to finish his thought.

The old man went to his shirt pocket and pulled out two crisp twenties that had been folded in half.

"Aaron—take this for them," he said, as his hand began to shake.

"What?" Aaron said, from the bathroom door.

"Before you move away. Just put it into the bank," he said.

The boys stared at the money in his spotty, quivering hand.

Aaron came back into the room.

"Pop," he said. "Don't do this."

"Why can't I do this?" Ezra asked.

"It's no good," Aaron said.

"Why?" Ezra asked. "Everybody needs twenty bucks."

"Pop—just stop it," Aaron said. "Pop, you're drooling."

He wiped his father's mouth again, this time putting the Kleenex back into his pocket. He pushed Ezra's outstretched hand back to his shirt, and watched him stuffing the money back inside.

Ezra sighed, his eyes growing wide.

"Will you let me buy them ice cream?" he asked.

"Please, Dad?" Paul and Adam said.

"Always with the ice cream, Pop," Aaron said, as he nodded yes.

"I think they only have vanilla," Ezra said, motioning toward his cane in the corner.

Aaron went to get it.

"Oh, and maybe strawberry," Ezra said.

The boys waited in the doorway.

"Do you like strawberry?" he asked them.

"I like chocolate," Adam said, smiling and showing his missing front teeth.

The ceremony was over.

Paul watched Aaron crying.

Iris stood away from them, with Adam's face turned into her side.

The baby's face went red. Her wail seemed to hang in midair.

One of the women approached, her heels wobbling on the uneven ground.

"Aaron," she said, holding one hand toward him. "So sorry."

He nodded.

She stepped closer, and held him,

"We're all going," she whispered, squeezing him as tight as she could.

Aaron's arms stayed at his sides.

She pulled three twenties from her purse and slid them into his shirt pocket.

"For the children," she said. "They should have something nice from today."

Aaron began to prepare a rejection for her.

"Bup-bup-bup," she said, quickly putting her hand on his lips.

She left quietly.

Iris carried the baby to the truck as Adam followed them.

Aaron picked up a small rock and placed it on the headstone. Paul followed him, and placed a stone next to his.

The rock fell off and slid to the ground, and he carefully placed it again.

Aaron leaned down and kissed the top of his head.

"Come on, Butch," Aaron said, starting toward the truck. "It'll be a long time before you have to do this."

PART II.

I.

Elisa had fallen asleep in her chair.

Adam and Paul were watching *Hee Haw* on the tiny black-and-white television. The coffee table was strewn with dessert plates, a container of sour cream, and a jar of strawberry preserves.

"More?" Iris asked them, getting up.

"I could eat one more," Paul said.

"Me too," Adam said.

Iris headed for the kitchen, tucking a corner of a blanket closer to Elisa's chin.

One of the kitchen windows was open a crack, letting in a cool spring breeze. Iris looked out into the dark night, seeing nothing but her reflection.

Smoothing her hair away from her face, she lit the flame under the small pan and dropped a pat of butter into its center. As it melted and began to foam, she carefully placed three blintzes and slid them around once, making sure they didn't stick.

Iris looked into the window quickly, trying to picture her face with bangs.

She heard a small chirping noise.

Iris did not pay it much attention, but found herself walking toward it and saw nothing. She sighed, blowing her hair from her face and looking up at the ceiling.

A bat hid in one of the roof beams.

She ran to the living room, screaming. Scooping up Elisa, Iris went inside the closet under the stairs and closed the door.

"Mom," Paul said. "What happened?"

"A bat," she said. "There's a bat in the kitchen."

The boys thundered upstairs, returning in their garage-sale football helmets. Adam found their BB guns on the side porch and removed the long mechanisms from inside them. Paul dropped pieces of giant chalk down the barrels, and shook the guns furiously.

"Mom," Paul whispered to the door. "We'll get him."

The boys tiptoed into the kitchen and turned the lights on, one at a time.

Cooper came in and sat quietly in the corner. The blintzes were burning.

Paul turned the flame off, and spied an oily black spot on the ceiling.

"There!" he shouted.

They fired, producing a fine cloud of chalk dust.

"Did we get him?" Adam asked.

"Yeah." Paul said.

The chirping continued.

Cooper barked suddenly, and the boys jumped. Their helmets fell into their eyes, as they shook their guns and fired again.

"Did you kill it?" Iris shouted from inside the closet.

Cooper ran in circles, barking and jumping over chairs. The boys fired again and again. They did not see the truck lights outside, or hear the screen door slamming shut.

"What the fuck is going on in here?" Aaron said, standing in the doorway.

"There's a bat," Adam said, pointing at the ceiling.

"Where?" Aaron said.

Adam squinted for a moment, then showed him where it was.

Aaron looked around the kitchen, and found a brown paper bag.

Standing on a chair, he held the bag over the bat and waited patiently. The boys pushed the helmets back on their heads, and rested their BB guns on the floor.

Cooper sat next to them and waited.

After a minute, Aaron closed the bag and stepped down.

Outside the screen door, he placed the bag on the ground. The bat crawled out after a moment, and flew into the dark.

Cooper barked once, and nosed the screen door open. Adam and Paul ran their hands along his ears and the space between his eyes.

Aaron went inside.

II.

Paul pounded a nail into a piece of wood. Seeing it had gone through, he tried to pry it away from the dining room floor.

Iris came into the room.

He looked up at her.

"I'll get it out," he said.

"You'll what?" she asked, walking over to see what he had done.

"I'll fix it," he said, quietly.

"It's a perfect day outside. We have seventy-two acres of woods, and you're pounding nails into the dining room floor," she said. "I don't understand you."

"I said I'll fix it," he said.

"Just go outside," she said. "Your father will fix it."

He dropped the hammer and ran through the mudroom and out the garage.

A milk snake wove slowly through the grass, and he nearly stepped on it.

Paul froze as it passed his dirty sneakers.

He ran up the hill and into the woods.

Red squirrels ran along the low branches of maple trees. A blue jay flew past his head on its way to the barn.

Paul found a stick and walked slowly, prodding the grass to see if there were any more snakes.

He made his way to the junk pile with the rusting Model T and the half-full cans of hairspray. He poked them with sharp rocks, listening to their hissing sounds as they emptied in the quiet afternoon.

He sat in the car seat, and wiggled the ancient steering wheel from side to side in an imaginary car chase. He shook the Model T violently, rocking it back and forth as he tried to turn it on its side.

He made the stick into a gun and shot at the men who hid behind trees.

III.

Adam ran into the field, looking for the ball. The crickets had begun chirping early, and they jumped from one stalk of grass to the next.

"I think it went over there," Paul called to him, pointing to the right.

Adam went toward a hollow in the tall grass and found the soft red kickball.

He stopped, smelling something foul. He looked down at his sneakers, and turned slowly.

A dead groundhog lay in the grass, a swarm of white maggots streaming out of its bloated stomach. Adam breathed through his mouth and kneeled down, poking the carcass with his finger.

"Did you find it?" Paul called to him.

"Yeah," he said, standing quickly and returning to the backyard.

"I've got a ghostie on first and third," Adam said.

"Nuh-unh," Paul said. "First and second."

"No," Adam said. "He stole third."

"How?" Paul asked, coming toward him.

"He can steal third," Adam said, "because he tagged first."

"I called no tags," Paul said.

"But I found the ball," Adam said.

"So?" Paul said, his hands on his hips.

"So, it's a do-over," Adam said.

"I called no do-overs," Paul said.

"Go fetch," Adam said, and threw the ball as far as he could back into the field.

"But—" Paul said.

"Go find your own fucking ball," Adam said, as he walked away.

Paul watched him disappear inside the house. He sat down and retied his shoelaces.

He lay down in the grass, checking to see if any of the clover had four leaves.

He closed his eyes and tried to see the color of the sky through his eyelids. He opened them and saw a figure walking slowly down the driveway.

Paul stood up, seeing it wasn't Aaron.

He started toward the stranger, who could hardly walk.

Paul saw it was Mr. Lozinsky, and that he bled from a gash on his forehead. The white-haired man held his hands out in front of him, ready to fall down.

"Help me," he said.

Paul took his hand and led him toward the farmhouse.

"Goddamn Appaloosa," he said

"Your dog?" Paul asked.

"No, my horse," Mr. Lozinsky said.

Paul stared at Mr. Lozinsky's hand in his, and all of the blood. He hoped there would be no milk snakes in their way.

"Why did he hurt you?" Paul asked.

"I dunno," Mr. Lozinsky said.

Paul had him stand still as he opened the screen door for him.

"Okay," Paul said. "We're going inside now."

"Maybe he knew I was gonna cut his balls off soon," Mr. Lozinsky said, lifting his feet carefully and entering the dark mudroom.

"Mom!" Paul shouted. "Mr. Lozinsky is here!"

He listened, then heard her say something.

"He's bleeding a lot!" he shouted.

IV.

"Boxcar," Elisa said, sitting in her chair at the kitchen window.

"Dippit eggs?" Iris asked them.

Adam and Paul nodded.

"I want two," Paul said.

Iris carefully cracked three eggs into the cast-iron skillet.

"Boxcar," Elisa said, touching her hand to the window.

"Mom," Adam said. "Boxcar got out again."

"Christ," she said, and pulled the pan from the flame. She looked out at the giant boar as he stalked the pen of sows and then back to the half-cooked breakfast.

She scooped the eggs quickly onto their plates.

"Sunny side up today," she said, and went to pull her boots on.

Iris stood outside the farmhouse, looking at the yellow

patch of grass that showed where the truck was usually parked. She started toward the giant pig and looked back at the kitchen, and the children.

The boys came outside, with pots and pans and wooden spoons. They approached him, making as much noise as they could. The boys shouted and made up nonsense rhymes, banging the spoons in a steady rhythm.

Boxcar ignored them, and made his way into the muddy pen.

Cooper found them and began barking.

Boxcar chased one of the sows and cornered her. He mounted her in one swift motion, his corkscrew-shaped penis wiggling in the mud before it went inside her.

She squealed and coughed as he flattened her beneath him, lurching into her.

The boys stood still, staring at the young sow. Iris let the spoon hang by her side, and looked down at them.

Boxcar stepped off of her, his penis gradually returning inside his body. He made a single grunt after sniffing her ears.

"Will she be okay?" Adam asked.

She did not move.

Cooper barked once at Boxcar, who stalked back to his pen.

The sow stood up on trembling legs and went to the empty trough.

"Should we feed her?" Paul asked.

Iris stared off at the main road for a moment.

"No," she said. "Wait for your father to get back from the auction."

PART III.

I.

Selena snored in between Paul and Adam in the giant sleeping bag. Sparrows were chirping in the trees. A bee hummed in circles outside the blue tent in the backyard.

She woke up first, studying the way the sun made a strong blue light that wrapped around the boys' faces.

Outside, she could hear a ladder moving against the house and the sounds of hand tools.

"Mom?" Selena called.

She crawled from the tent and wrinkled her nose, smelling something sour.

"Mom?" she called again, looking at her bare feet and seeing the moist green paste she had stepped in.

Roberta began to scrape the paint from the highest point she could reach.

Selena made a face as she wiped her toes in the grass.

Cooper came to her, and licked her feet clean.

Selena began to laugh.

Roberta stopped scraping the farmhouse and looked down at her.

"Morning, hon," she said.

"Hey, Mom," Selena said, as she carefully zigzagged through the grass that led to the backdoor.

Selena stood in the doorway between the kitchen and the living room, watching Iris as she fed Elisa. The baby ate tiny helpings while she looked out at the birds pecking into the suet that hung from the feeder, grasping at the air with her tiny hands.

After breakfast, the children went upstairs to change out of their pajamas into play clothes. Paul and Adam stared at Selena's underwear and her long, black, curly hair.

"Do you know how to be a doctor?" Paul asked her.

"No," she said.

"I'm a good doctor," he said. "Do you feel okay?"

"No," Selena said, sitting on the edge of the bunk bed in her underwear.

"Where does it hurt?" Paul asked, pulling his T-shirt on.

Selena shrugged her shoulders.

"You should lie down," Adam said from behind Paul.

Selena lay back on the bed with her hands crossed on her stomach. Adam climbed into the bed above her and leaned his face over the edge.

Paul found a stethoscope in the back of one of his drawers.

He stood over her, warming the metal disc with his breath and rubbing it between his palms. Paul moved Selena's hands to her sides in one gentle motion. Resting the disc on her chest, he listened carefully. He moved the disc to her stomach, her knees, and then her shoulders with a very serious expression.

"Can you roll on your side please?" he asked her.

Selena did, and he listened to the sounds in the small of her back and behind her kneecaps.

"That tickles," she said, under her breath.

"Sorry," he whispered to her.

Paul pulled the stethoscope from his ears.

"Can you cough for me?" he asked her, as he pressed his ear to her shoulder and listened.

"Okay," he said. "You can lie on your back again."

Selena lay on her back and stared up at him, her giant green eyes studying the empty expression on his face.

"What's wrong with me, Doctor?" she asked.

Paul scratched his head and thought.

"Well, let's check one last thing," he said, tugging at her underwear.

Selena kicked her panties off and waited patiently.

Paul stared at her naked body.

Selena wiggled her knees slightly while Adam leaned farther over the edge of the upper bunk bed.

"I'm getting cold," she said.

Paul put his hand on her stomach and made his fingers into the shape of scissors. He cut an imaginary line across her abdomen.

"Okay," he said. "You can get dressed."

Selena pulled her clothes on quickly and sat on the edge of the bed.

"What was the operation?" she asked.

"I cut your tubes," he said. "My mom got the same operation and it made her feel better."

"Oh," Selena said.

Roberta rested the paint scraper at the foot of the ladder.

She went to the garage and pulled the heavy black bicycle from behind the snowplow. Roberta inspected the tires and saw they were plump with air. She tested the seat and the handlebars, making sure they would not twist.

Roberta stood on the dirt-and-gravel driveway and waited, holding the bike away from her.

In one motion, she pushed it forward and tried to sit on the seat. After a few wobbly adjustments, she fell off.

Pulling herself from the grass she heard the screen door open.

"Are you okay?" Iris asked her.

"Yes," she said, masking her anger with a small laugh.

"I'm almost done with dinner," Iris said. "Do you want some help?"

"I'm fine," Roberta said, as she wheeled the bicycle farther down the driveway, toward the road in the distance.

Selena and the boys walked toward the main road, then down to the stream. They stood and waited until Roberta arrived with a bucket full of apples. She sat down on the bank and produced a paring knife from her apron pocket.

As she cut the peels from them, the children took off their clothes and made them into neat piles on the rocks in front of her.

Adam splashed into the water, sliding across the mossy rocks beneath him.

"Careful," Roberta said.

Selena held Paul's hand as they made their way into the water. The three of them stood still, watching the minnows swim around their ankles, laughing when they nibbled their toes.

Paul searched for small, flat stones to throw, seeing if they would skip more than five times before they disappeared beneath the water's surface.

Adam showed Selena how to put her face in the water and blow bubbles.

Aaron rumbled down the driveway and stopped the big white pickup on the tiny bridge that spanned the stream.

He came down to them, a string of lake fish swinging from one hand. Aaron gutted them one by one with his yellow pen knife, letting their hearts and livers and intestines float downstream. The children watched his every movement until he cleaned the knife blade against his cutoffs and placed it back in his pocket.

Cooper appeared on the bank of the stream, sniffing the apple peels and then the water's edge.

Aaron pulled at the string that dangled from the ceiling in his attic studio. A dim light bulb clicked on as he made his way through a series of canvasses that leaned against each other in rows, leading into the small corners of the room.

He raised the window shade on a small window at the far end of the attic.

Afternoon light broke into the space, revealing tiny dust particles that floated slowly all around him.

Hanging three of the fish against a thick white card, he positioned them until he was satisfied.

He drew them quickly with a chunk of charcoal on rough gray paper, finding the slender highlights of their still-wet skins with the end of an eraser he kneaded into a point.

Tossing the sketch to a homemade countertop, he selected a small rectangle of Masonite. He ran his fingers across the milky-white base coat, testing its surface.

A cloud passed in front of the sun and the light streaming through the far window grew soft and dark, revealing a handful of dead flies on the bookshelves and a collection of gallery invitations tacked to the wall.

The light returned, warm and strong on the silvery fish. A wet line of diluted blood dripped against the white card behind them, slowly working its way to the floor.

Aaron drew a few shapes on the Masonite and pulled a box of oil paints toward him. He moved quickly, mixing three separate base colors, thinning them with turpentine and testing them on a clean corner of the palette.

Iris called from downstairs. Dinner was ready.

"Go ahead without me," he called to her.

There was a sudden silence in the already quiet room while he waited for her to respond.

Someone thumped methodically up the stairs.

Cooper stood in the doorway, his big eyes shining in the darkness. The dog came to him, weaving through the piles of finished canvasses.

Aaron inhaled the odor of fish and dust and turpentine and dog fur deep into his lungs, then closed his eyes and let his breath out slowly.

Cooper curled up next to his feet and he and went back to painting.

II.

The apple orchard sprawled across a few acres, the trees pressed tight against each other. The boys walked without conversation. Their silence was punctuated by birds suddenly flapping from their perches above the plush, jade-colored moss that covered the forest floor.

Cooper ambled close to them, pausing to inspect a collection of wild mushrooms and a rotten tree stump.

Selena called from beyond the tree line.

The boys hid behind a boulder big enough to brush against the lowest branches of the trees and listened to her approach. She waited next to Cooper for a little while, then went back toward the stream and the farmhouse.

Iris called for them, far in the distance.

"I see your friend," Paul whispered, pointing at a branch above them.

"He isn't there," Adam said.

"But I see him," Paul said.

"He's my friend," Adam said. "And he doesn't like you."

Paul shoved Adam into a pile of leaves and laughed at him.

"Asshole," Adam said, not getting up.

Selena found them.

"Where were you?" she asked, her hands on her hips.

"We were invisible," Paul said.

Selena wrinkled her nose at him.

"We'll show you how to do it sometime," he said.

Adam got up.

"Let's shake the trees," she said.

The three of them climbed the nearest apple tree and yanked it violently. The small pink fruit plopped gently to the forest floor.

Cooper barked and turned in circles below.

The children filled their shirts with them and made their way back to the farmhouse.

III.

The crickets were chirping early, and everyone sat on chairs in the backyard.

Iris ran her fingers through Paul's hair, then Adam's, then Selena's.

"They all have them," she said.

"Christ," Roberta said, lowering her chin to her chest.

Iris checked Roberta's hair, then Aaron's.

"You two are okay," she said.

Iris kneeled in front of Roberta, who studied her scalp while the children sat in nervous silence.

"Nothing," Roberta said.

Iris sighed.

She went inside the house.

The baby sat in Aaron's lap. He ran his fingers through her fine, short hair. Aaron made a face to himself and shrugged his shoulders.

Iris returned with a pair of clippers and an extension cord.

"Don't move," she said to Paul, and quickly clipped the hair from his head. She moved to Adam and did the same.

Iris paused over Selena, and her long dark hair.

"Don't worry honey," she said. "It'll grow back even prettier."

Selena began to whimper as her hair fell to the grass in giant chunks.

Iris left two long curls over each of her ears. She smiled at Aaron and Roberta.

"That's not funny," Aaron said.

She cut them off.

The mattresses and the sheets were made into a giant pile, past the barn. Aaron doused them with gasoline and lit them on fire.

They took turns washing their heads with the medicinal shampoo, then spread the rest on Cooper, washing themselves off with the garden hose before the soap burned their eyes.

IV.

The town pool was surrounded by a rusting chain-link fence. Iris, Roberta, and the children crawled out of the Dodge Dart and made their way to an empty spot of grass near the shallow end.

Iris and Roberta sat with their feet in the water as Elisa splashed herself in front of them.

The boys took turns seeing how long they could remain underwater, resting on the plastic rings at the six-foot section.

Selena wore just the bottoms of a leopard-spot bikini as she skipped along the asphalt, trying not to burn her feet on the hot tar.

"We're lucky she's so young," Roberta said. "A few more years and they wouldn't mistake her for a boy."

"I think they're too scared to ask if a boy is wearing a leopard-spot bikini," she said, slapping her legs.

Paul and Adam stared at the toilet bowl full of paper and shit, listening to the double sound of other people peeing. They stepped through sour chlorine puddles that reflected a pale blue sky in the roofless bathroom.

Returning to the pool, they slid into the water and stood still until vitamin-yellow urine spread through their suits.

A young woman screamed.

A lifeguard jumped into the water a few feet from them.

He emerged holding a man with red bubbling from his nose.

They laid him down on the asphalt as blood spurted across the lifeguard's face and into the clean, blue water.

"He dove in too shallow," Paul whispered to Adam.

V.

Mr. Lozinsky arrived just after ten in the morning, a long box slung across his shoulder. Aaron met him halfway down the driveway and brought him to the pigpens. They crossed the electric fence and walked among the year-olds that nuzzled their ankles.

One of the young boars was separated from the herd and into an empty pen.

Aaron went back to the farmhouse.

He pulled a wheelbarrow from the garage and rolled it to the electric fence.

The boys approached, their faces and chests decorated with stripes of white paint, wearing nothing but cutoffs.

They leaned against the tall sticks they carried.

"We are Indians," Paul announced.

Mr. Lozinsky gazed at them, not smiling, not frowning.

"Can we watch?" Adam asked.

Aaron shrugged his shoulders.

"I guess so," he said.

Selena caught up to them. She wore a red cowboy hat and a toy pistol set around her waist.

"You should go inside," Aaron said to her. "I don't think your mom wants you to see this."

Mr. Lozinsky nodded quietly, motioning for her to go back to the house with a flick of his head.

She stood still, growing angry.

"I know what you're going to do," she said through her teeth.

"There's a lot of people in our house this summer," Aaron said to her. "And they all need to eat."

Selena stared at him, defiant.

"I could eat just cucumbers," she said quietly.

She ran back to the house, her red felt hat flapping against her shoulder blades.

"Stand here," Aaron said to the boys, motioning toward the wheelbarrow.

Mr. Lozinsky pulled a long knife from his box, running it against the hairs on his forearm. He nodded in silence and returned it to a sheath that he threaded his belt through.

Aaron produced a pistol from his pocket and put two bullets in the chamber. Mr. Lozinsky pulled a noose from his box.

Paul watched them, gripping the wheelbarrow with both of his hands. A buzzing came into his ears and didn't go away.

He watched them put the noose over the young pig's neck, holding it still then shooting between the pig's eyes with the pistol pressed against its pink skin. He saw it wandering around the pen with the red dot growing slowly, and then Mr. Lozinsky running his sharp knife across its throat and the avalanche of blood that burst out.

The pig slumped to the ground and to its side.

They lifted him into the wheelbarrow and rolled him to the barn, where he was hoisted up. Cooper stood at a distance, then sat on his hind legs and watched their movements. The pig was cut open from his neck to his anus, and his insides dropped into the wheelbarrow. Mr. Lozinsky pulled out the heart and the liver and the kidneys. The rest was dumped in the woods behind them.

The boys studied the carcass as they began to cut the skin from the body.

The pig's mouth opened slowly, and then its eyes rolled toward them.

Paul and Adam ran screaming toward the farmhouse, sliding on grass wet with goose shit and falling down before they disappeared inside.

Aaron and Mr. Lozinsky sat at the kitchen table. The pig's heart had been sliced thin and was frying in the cast-iron skillet with some onions.

A bottle of cognac sat between them, next to two short glasses.

Aaron poured for them, and they toasted by silently nodding to each other. Mr. Lozinsky drank his in one slow gulp. Aaron sipped and coughed once.

"Someday, I teach you to drink," Mr. Lozinsky said.

Aaron laughed once to himself.

"Killing animal is more difficult," the old man said, standing up halfway to see if their lunch was ready.

VI.

A dark blue Plymouth decorated with white clouds made its way down the driveway and parked in front of the kitchen window.

Iris looked out at the car and then at the kitchen clock.

"He's early," she said to Aaron, who sat at the table sipping black coffee.

"Roberta's still in the tub," he said.

"What kind of person paints clouds on their car?" she asked him.

"It must be a Brooklyn thing," he said. "Since we left."

Stanley waved at them, staying in the front seat.

"Or, it could just be a Stanley thing," Aaron said.

Iris poured herself a cup of coffee and sat down next to him.

"Three years, and we're like strangers to these people," she said.

The boys came downstairs, looking to see who it was.

They ran through the mudroom and out the front door.

Stanley picked his nose quickly and inspected his finger. Sliding his feet into an ancient pair of flip-flops, he opened the door to meet Paul and Adam.

"Helllloooooooooo," he crowed to them, and pinched their chests.

The boys laughed and stood awkwardly.

"That's a tittie twist," he said. "Try it on a girl sometime. It's wild."

Adam rolled his eyes at Paul.

"I have to take such a shit," Stanley announced.

Stanley sat at the kitchen table with Aaron and Iris.

He swirled some ice in a glass and poured whiskey into it.

"Cheers," he said under his breath, and drank.

Selena came from the living room and leaned against the doorway.

"Hi Daddy," she said.

Stanley turned to her, unprepared.

He held his arms out, waiting for her to come to him. She approached cautiously and rested her face against his shoulder.

He held her.

"What the fuck happened to all your hair?" he asked at one point.

"Me and Paul and Adam got bugs in our hair," she said. "Iris had to cut it off and then we lit the beds on fire."

"Hunh," Stanley said. "So, that's what happens when you leave the city."

Iris and Aaron watched Stanley and Roberta walking next to each other, making their way down the driveway, past the stream and into the front fields.

Aaron reached for her hand and squeezed it.

Iris sighed.

"I'm going to check on the baby," she said.

Stanley left later the same day, his cloud-painted Plymouth leaving a trail of dust as it disappeared.

Roberta finished painting the house a few days later.

Selena got tired of playing doctor with Paul and Adam and read books at the kitchen table instead, helping Iris feed and bathe the baby.

One day in late August, everyone piled into the white Ford pickup. Roberta and Selena's bags sat in the back with the children.

Aaron drove them to the bus station.

On the way home, they stopped for ice cream at the Dairy Queen.

Paul and Adam ate their Dilly Bars in silence.

Aaron shoved Paul gently.

"It's okay, Butch," he said. "Don't throw your stethoscope away."

Iris dropped her jaw.

"Aaron!" she said.

The baby woke up.

Paul threw his half-eaten Dilly Bar into the trash and crawled into the back of the truck.

Adam laughed to himself quietly, then louder.

PART IV.

I.

Aaron took pictures of the three of them in the driveway on the first day of school.

Paul had been in the sun all summer, and looked almost Spanish with his dark skin and curly black hair. Extra teeth had sprouted on top of old ones, making his crooked smile seem innocent and wolflike at the same time.

Elisa stood behind him, holding his belt loops. Iris had braided green ribbons in her hair to match the calico dress. Her white socks were dirty from being chased by the old rooster.

Adam had tied his shirt around his waist and stood bare-chested. He stared into the camera without a smile. His blonde hair had begun to go brown, but his pale blue eyes had not changed.

Cooper stood behind them, looking lazily at a woodchuck hole. His tongue swung outside his pink mouth, as he seemed to wait for the camera to click.

Iris came out of the house with their lunch boxes, kissing each of them on the forehead as they took them. She stood close to Aaron, and kept her hand in the center of his back as the children walked down the long driveway to wait for the bus.

"Do you think she'll be okay?" Iris asked.

"She did alright in kindergarten," he said. "First grade will be fine."

"We should have driven them today," she said.

Aaron made a face.

"Then the bus driver would never pick them up," he said, walking toward the barn.

"Where are you going?" she asked.

"The tractor needs some work," he said. "Maybe new spark plugs."

Iris did not move.

"Are you going into town today?" he asked her.

"No," she said.

He stopped, a few steps from the barn.

"What are you doing today?" he asked her.

She made a small movement with her elbow.

He started toward her, shaking his head to himself.

"What are you going to do today?" he repeated, quietly.

"The boys stacked a lot of wood last week," she said. "There's still a pot of chili and some leftover chicken."

"And?" Aaron asked.

"And what?" she said.

"And the house is empty," he said.

Iris chewed the inside of her cheek and looked at the evergreens.

Aaron took a slow breath and let it out.

"Do you want to take a walk?" he asked her.

Iris looked at him and said nothing.

"Put some boots on," he said, giving her a nudge back to the house.

She went and found them.

Sitting on the steps, she took off her shoes and pulled on a pair of tall green boots.

"Let's go," he said.

She held her hand out to him, and he helped her up.

Aaron led her to the parting in the woods behind the barn.

The narrow path was marked by two parallel ruts that led up the mountain.

Iris stepped carefully on the uneven earth as she tried to walk next to Aaron. She fell into step behind him as they entered the forest.

A rustling in the bushes made her jump. She shouted as he

turned.

Cooper stared up at them, panting.

"Jesus fucking Christ," she said, as Aaron laughed at her.

The sun went behind a cloud and the forest grew dark. Cooper sniffed at her heels as they followed the path.

"Stop it," she said.

Cooper waited, then sniffed her again.

Aaron stopped, abruptly.

"Shhhh," he said, pointing at the ground.

Iris saw a collection of tiny bones scattered across the forest floor. Aaron pointed to a tree. Iris looked and saw nothing. He pointed again, bringing her close to him, and had her follow his finger.

She saw the owl, which was sleeping.

Iris stepped anxiously, threading back through the collection of mice and squirrel skeletons. Cooper barked once, and she turned back to the farmhouse.

"What the hell are you doing?" Aaron called to her.

"I don't want to take a walk," she said.

Aaron stood with his hands on his hips, looking at her.

Cooper barked again.

"Shhh," he said, and Cooper sat down.

"I'm going inside," she said.

Aaron took a few steps downhill to her.

"It's okay?" he asked.

"Yes," she said.

"Is everything okay?" he asked.

"Everything is fine," she said, turning and walking downhill.

"I'll be back in about an hour," he called after her.

Paul sat in the last row this year. His desk was one of the new ones, and smelled like mineral oil. Everyone wore new shirts. Two of the girls had begun to develop, and wore sweaters even though it was warm out.

He stared out the tall windows at the treetops.

His teacher, Mr. Bell, stood behind him. He rested a hand on his shoulder.

"Next," he said.

Paul shuffled to the front of the room, and found a piece of chalk. He drew a quick outline of a tree, and then a few circles to represent fruit. Clapping his hands against each other, he tried to clean the chalk from them.

"This summer I went to Florida," he said, as loud as he could. "I lived with my grandfather and we picked oranges."

Paul spoke more quietly now.

"We woke up very early every day and picked the oranges that were very ripe and gave them to a special driver. He drove the oranges to Abraham Lincoln, who also lives in Florida," he said, all at once.

"I never got to meet him," he added, then shuffled back to his desk and slumped into his new yellow chair.

"Paul," Mr. Bell said, and then stopped himself.

The children turned to each other with curious expressions. A few of them began to whisper.

The bus drove them home, emptying slowly until Adam, Paul, and Elisa were the only ones left. They sat in separate seats without talking to each other.

When they arrived at the farm, Adam ran down the driveway as fast as he could, stripping off his shirt, dropping his books on the front steps and looking for Aaron. Elisa walked slowly, stopping when a bee or a yellow jacket buzzed around her, continuing toward the kitchen when they left. Paul walked into one of the front fields and flopped onto his back, looking up at the sky, now full of thin, overlapping clouds that made him think of an ocean topped with silver fish. He counted backward from one hundred by fives and by threes.

Grasshoppers bounded across the tops of the tall grass, sometimes landing on him, then continuing.

II.

Aaron came into the kitchen, just before dinner.

"Effie's giving birth," he said.

"Finally," Iris said.

Elisa sat at her place, fork and spoon in hand, waiting to eat. Adam and Paul jumped up and put on their coats, catching up to Aaron as he returned to the barn.

Effie lay under a bright work light, in a mound of hay. She breathed heavily, her swollen stomach rising and falling in steady rhythm.

They sat on milk crates and waited.

Aaron left without saying anything and returned with three volumes of veterinary books under his arms. He flipped through the chapters, reading a few paragraphs, then searching again.

Iris came with plates of pot roast and beets, and a thermos of black coffee. They sat in silence, stacking the plates on top of each other when they were done eating.

Effie's breathing grew shallow and fast.

Aaron turned to Paul.

"Get me some Vaseline from the downstairs bathroom," he said.

Paul stood up, stretching.

"What time is it?" he asked, faking a yawn.

"Now," Aaron said.

He ran toward the house in the dark night, stumbling but not falling. Cooper ran with him through the mudroom and into the cold bathroom and then back to the barn with the Vaseline.

Aaron was in his T-shirt, his barn coat hanging from a nail.

He removed his watch and his wedding ring and gave them to Paul.

"Put them in your pocket," he said, as Paul ran his index finger along the old face of his grandfather's Rolex, feeling how heavy it was in his hands.

Aaron spread Vaseline generously along his left arm.

Lying down on the floor next to Effie, he spoke softly to her and patted her rump. He slid his arm inside her in one movement.

Adam and Paul stared with their mouths open. Cooper rested his face on his front paws and sighed.

Aaron pulled a gray, bloated piglet from inside her.

It did not move.

Effie's body contorted, and piglets began to slide from inside her.

They wriggled in the warm straw, their eyes closed, their mouths open, showing lines of tiny, sharp teeth.

III.

Paul sat in his room and listened to the static on the radio, switching randomly between stations to create a series of sound effects.

He repeated the sounds to himself while he did his chores outside, feeding the ducks and the chickens and the geese.

Paul went into the henhouse, checking their nests for late

eggs. He found two small brown ones that were still warm. Carrying them carefully, he crawled out and saw a baby duck in the grass. It moved slowly, turning in lazy circles as it tried to stand up. Paul rested the eggs on an open patch of concrete next to the barn and kneeled down to the duckling.

He shoved it gently to its feet, and it fell down.

Paul carried it carefully to the other ducks as they ate the circle of corn he had spread on the ground, hoping to find its mother. He placed the duckling in the middle of their group and waited. They ignored it.

He went to the garage and found an empty shoebox.

Paul secretly kept the duckling in his room, lining the inside of the box with an old shirt. He placed small tins of milk and water sprinkled with corn next to the duckling's bill. Its brown and yellow down had grown damp with sweat.

Paul slept with his reading light on, thinking it would keep the duckling warm during the night.

The next day was Saturday.

Paul woke up to the rooster's crow and saw an early frost on the grass below his bedroom window.

Checking on the duckling wrapped in his T-shirt, he saw that it was dead.

Its tiny brown eyes were open, staring at the books on his shelf.

Paul hid the duckling in his jacket and went outside. The ground was hard and cold already.

He crawled underneath the side porch, where a layer of fine dirt could be broken with his hands. He dug a shallow grave, his fingers getting cuts on small, sharp rocks.

He rolled the duckling into the hollow, suddenly scared to touch it with his bare hand.

Paul thought for a moment.

"See you later, Artie," he said. "I'll see you in heaven, I guess."

He sprinkled a few kernels of corn in the grave.

Paul covered the hollow quickly and placed a pattern of stones around it, in an oval.

He crawled out from under the side porch and stretched. The sun was still low on the horizon, coming through the trees in the apple orchard and warming the frost-laced fields.

Paul threw the T-shirt into some tall grass and started toward the main road without looking back.

The gravel crunched under his sneakers as he kicked dust clouds in front of him.

There were tiny caterpillars, brown at both ends and black in the middle. He leaned down, stroking their odd, furry backs, and then kept going toward the smooth asphalt where he was not allowed to ride his bike, the pair of double lines, the little old graveyard behind some trees to the left, the town eventually to the right. He thought about going all the way to the interstate and never coming back. There would be another family to live with, a color TV, soda, chocolates and a closet packed with every breakfast cereal he could imagine.

PART V.

I.

Iris pulled the Dodge Dart onto the narrow road with the evening sun splashing across her arms. She checked on the cake which sat on the empty passenger seat beside her, as it rattled against the seatbelt.

Rolling the windows down a few inches, she could smell the giant hay rolls that dotted Mr. Lozinsky's fields. The late sky was giving way to blue in her rearview mirror.

She pulled into the driveway and rolled toward the farmhouse in the distance, a lazy plume of smoke twirling from the chimney.

The cake rested on the counter, decorated with pink roses of varying sizes. The children eyed it in silence, chewing their venison stew.

"We made the roses on these giant nails," she said. "You keep the frosting cone in one hand and twirl the nail in the other hand."

Aaron nodded and smiled to himself.

"It's the twirling that makes the flower," she said.

"Are you gonna go every week?" Adam asked her.

"Yes," she said. "A cake a week."

"Okay," Adam said, clearing his plate as quickly as he could.

"So, the people from Pennsylvania are coming on Saturday," Aaron said, after a moment.

"For what?" Paul asked.

"To breed some sows with Boxcar," he said.

"How much?" Iris asked him.

"Two, maybe three hundred," he said.

"Maybe we should feed him some oysters," she said, sliding a bay leaf to the edge of her plate.

"He doesn't need it," Aaron said. "He's pedigree."

Cooper came to Aaron and rested his mouth on his knees.

"It's part of the job," Aaron added, massaging Cooper's forehead.

"What's pedigree?" Adam asked.

"Sort of like royalty," Aaron said.

"Prince Boxcar?" Paul asked.

Aaron laughed and shook his head.

"King Boxcar if he keeps it up," Aaron said, emphatically.

The lights in the kitchen pulsed brightly for a moment and then went out.

The entire house was dark.

"Not again," Iris said under her breath.

"Just stay here," Aaron said.

The family sat around the Coleman lantern in the living room.

Aaron filled the Franklin stove with logs of cherry and maple, leaving one of the doors half-open as it cast a crackly glow.

They had a Chinese checkers competition, with everyone huddled under blankets.

Then, Aaron and Iris took turns reading fairy tales from a giant book in low voices. First was "Rapunzel," because it was Elisa's favorite and they knew she would fall asleep before the boys. Then, "Rumpelstiltskin" and "The Six Swans" for Paul and Adam, who eventually curled themselves into a messy ball with Cooper between them.

Iris made some strong tea with an old kettle on the wood

stove. They sipped in silence, looking out at the bright stars that crawled across the deep blue sky outside the windows.

"Cherrywood smells so wonderful," she said at one point.

Aaron nodded and kissed her slowly, feeling for her beneath the blanket.

Cooper made a strange sound in his sleep and readjusted his position. The boys rolled onto their sides.

Paul began to snore lightly.

The breeders came on Saturday, with a horse trailer full of sows that they parked next to Boxcar's pen. Aaron stood with his hands on his hips, waiting to greet them. Boxcar paced the length of the fence, occasionally sniffing the air near the strangers.

Iris piled the children into the Dodge and waved at the men, seeing them shake hands and gesture toward the hills and the orchard, readjusting their caps and brushing their hands against their wallets.

They drove to the next town.

Here, they searched the Salvation Army for snowsuits and Eskimo jackets that might fit the boys. Elisa held on to the seam of her pants, following her everywhere.

The boys chased each other down the aisles of the giant, dark space.

Eventually, Iris found what they needed and took them across the street for lunch specials at a Chinese take-out counter.

II.

Winter came.

The countryside was dredged in thick, wet snow that curved around the sharp corners of the house.

Icicles grew from the rain gutters.

The snow fell and fell, hiding the Dodge entirely.

Only the Ford pickup could make it down the driveway, after Aaron installed a snowplow to the front bumper.

The children plodded to the main road each morning, sometimes sinking in to their hips. Adam's boots came off sometimes, and he had to walk backward to get his feet back inside them.

They waited for the bus, shivering by the side of the road. It did not always come, and then Aaron would have to drive them.

III.

A half-eaten chocolate cake sat on the kitchen counter. The yellow roses that had decorated it were gone, leaving nothing but tiny depressions where they had been.

Adam and Paul wandered downstairs, their pajamas wrinkled and twisted around them. Adam poured dry cereal into two bowls while Paul got the milk.

Munching in silence, they stared out at the white fields and the pigs in the distance. One of them was sneezing violently.

Adam looked at Paul, and noticed that he was seeing the same thing.

The pig collapsed to the ground.

"Where's Dad?" Adam asked, after a moment.

Paul stood up halfway and looked in the sink. He spied a

white coffee cup and a dirty dish.

"I think he went hunting," he said.

"For what?" Adam asked.

"Deer," Paul said, spooning the last of the cereal into his mouth, tipping the bowl to his lips and sucking out the final drops of milk.

"But it isn't deer season yet," Adam said, confused.

"Never stopped him before," Paul said, standing up and stretching.

He dropped his bowl in the sink and turned to see the cake on the counter.

"Hey," he said. "Somebody ate all of the flowers."

Adam made a funny face, and stood next to him.

He stared down at the cake.

"That's not good," he said, under his breath.

Aaron emerged from the woods in the early afternoon, his shotgun hanging loosely across his back. He stood in the driveway and removed the bullets from the chamber and the cartridge, dropping them into his jacket pocket.

Pulling his boots off in the mudroom, he entered the kitchen.

Iris and the children were finishing lunch.

"Good," she said, quietly.

"What happened?" he asked, pulling the bullets from his pocket and returning them to a small plastic box.

"Two things," she said. "Someone ate all of the roses off of the cake, and one of the pigs is sick."

"What?" Aaron asked.

"See?" she said, nudging the cake. "All of the roses are gone."

"When?" he asked.

"I think it had to be late last night," she said.

"The pig," he said. "The fucking pig."

Iris suddenly grew quiet.

"Me and Paul saw it sneezing and sneezing," Adam said.

"And then, it just fell down and didn't get up," Paul added.

Aaron pulled his boots on and stalked across the field to the pens. One of the year-old sows lay motionless in the mud. The other pigs nosed her, as if their feed was hidden underneath her stomach.

Aaron shouted at them and they scattered.

He went to the barn and turned off the electric fence.

The wheelbarrow was difficult to push through the deep snow which now had a crust of ice on it. He slid it upside down instead, all the way back to the pen. Aaron lifted the sow into the wheelbarrow as well as he could, her body cold and heavy.

He stared at the truck for a moment, so far from them in its spot in front of the house. Paul and Adam stood in the kitchen window, watching him.

"Fuck," he said under his breath, as he kicked the wheelbarrow over on its side.

Hoisting the dead pig across his shoulders, he launched into the field, trying to gain momentum, and almost fell. Aaron steadied himself and slowed down, smelling the pig shit that now coated his back.

When he got to the truck, he dropped the corpse onto the tailgate and caught his breath.

Cooper barked from inside the house and scratched at the front door.

He slid the dead pig into the darkness of the truck bed and closed the hatch.

Aaron lay back into the snow and moved his arms around, making an angel, trying to get some of the pig shit off him.

On the next day, Aaron woke up at dawn.

He fed the animals and ate a plate of bacon and eggs.

Cooper came to him, and slumped to the kitchen floor.

Paul came downstairs and had cereal, sitting next to him.

"I can go with you," he said. "If you need help."

Aaron chewed at his last bite of rye bread and studied the sky.

"Sure," he said.

Paul finished his cereal.

"We leave in ten minutes," Aaron said.

"I'm ready," Paul said.

"Okay," Aaron said, shoving his chair back. "Let's go."

The highway had been plowed, glowing wet and oil-black under the gray sky. The truck tires hummed against the road.

Paul sat with his hands on the dashboard, feeling the tiny vibrations rising up from his feet and through his fingertips.

"What is that noise?" Aaron asked him.

Paul shrugged his shoulders.

Aaron leaned across him and felt the passenger door.

"You didn't close it right," Aaron said.

Paul grew tense.

"I'm gonna hold you by your belt," Aaron said, "and you're gonna open your door just a little bit, and then close it hard."

"Okay," Paul said.

Aaron gripped his pants and his belt in his right hand.

"Now," he said.

Paul opened the door and saw the highway whipping beneath them.

He slammed it closed.

They arrived at the college campus just after noon.

Paul helped Aaron slide the now stiff pig into the

wheelbarrow, then into a laboratory.

Aaron spoke to a professor and his students, who all wore blue lab coats.

Paul stared at the clean metal tables and the charts on the walls.

Aaron shook the professor's hand with both of his and sincerely thanked him.

"Let's go," he said to Paul.

They started toward the truck.

The sky opened up on their way home.

A white sun hung above them, casting bright patterns of highway signs and bare trees across the dirty white pickup.

"Are you hungry?" Aaron asked Paul.

Paul nodded yes, still gripping the giant black dashboard with both hands.

"I'm starving," Aaron said.

Soon, they approached a sign that listed what was available at the next rest stop.

"McDonalds?" Aaron asked.

Paul wrinkled his nose.

"Burger King?" Aaron asked.

"Burger King sucks," Paul said.

"Oh! Oh!" Aaron shouted. "Roy Rodgers!"

"Roy Rodgers?" Paul asked him.

"Roy will never steer you wrong!" Aaron announced, pulling into the right lane and toward the next exit.

IV.

Dinner was over.

Paul and Adam took everyone's plates to the sink.

Iris put some uneaten beans back in the refrigerator.

Elisa stared at the half-eaten cake on the counter.

"No," Iris said. "None of you are having any."

"But why is everybody getting punished?" Adam asked her.

"Because," she said.

Aaron nodded in agreement, and pushed his chair back a little.

Iris made coffee for them, and sliced two pieces of cake.

"It isn't fair," Adam said. "It was Paul. We all know it was Paul."

"No it wasn't," Paul said.

"Until someone admits it," Iris said, "no cake for any of you."

Adam stomped out of the kitchen, through the living room and up the stairs. Elisa went after him. Paul retreated to a corner of the living room and a book about King Arthur.

The phone rang.

Iris answered it.

"It's the college," she said, handing it to Aaron.

"Yes?" he said. "Uh-hunh. That's right."

He leaned against the wall.

"About three weeks ago," he said. "I'll call them."

He listened to them speaking for a while.

"I understand," Aaron said, his voice suddenly quiet. "Just get it over with. All right, thank you—thank you very much."

Aaron held the phone loosely in his hand, almost forgetting to return it to its cradle. His face grew tense, and he set his teeth against each other.

He sighed.

"How about some more of that scandalous cake?" he said, trying to break his mood.

Mr. Lozinsky came early the next morning.

They wandered across the field to the giant pen. Mr. Lozinsky readjusted his John Deere cap.

"Have no see all go sick like this for long time," he said, half to himself.

"It was the breeders," Aaron said. "But there's no way to prove it."

One of the pigs began to sneeze violently. It walked in a strange pattern across the frozen mud.

"We have coffee now," Mr. Lozinsky said, patting Aaron's shoulder.

"They'll just say it was our pigs," Aaron said at one point.

They returned in an hour.

"Which first?" Mr. Lozinsky asked him.

"It doesn't matter," Aaron said.

"No, this your first one?" he asked. "First borned?"

"That one," Aaron said, pointing at Effie.

The maple trees stood in silence.

Paul walked along his secret path, wading through the snow.

A gunshot pinged from down the mountain and made him flinch.

He found the junk pile, where a rusting tractor and curlicued mattress springs poked from beneath the snow.

Paul sat in the seat and pretended to drive, imagining the oranges that hung heavy on branches that brushed against his shoulders.

Another gunshot echoed through the valley.

Twenty-three pigs were slumped in the mud, a red bullet hole in each of their foreheads. The blood trickling from their necks filled the crisscrossing patterns of their tiny footsteps.

Aaron and Mr. Lozinsky hoisted two of them across the wheelbarrow. As they slid their bodies into the truck and started for another, Aaron wiped the blood from his hands against his pants.

He stopped and looked out at the pens as the deep smell surrounded him. Aaron pulled his hat from his head and balled it into his pocket.

"We put Effie last," Mr. Lozinsky said, waiting for him.

Aaron nodded yes.

The bright sun went behind a cloud, and Mr. Lozinsky looked up at the sky.

A red cardinal flew over their heads.

"Maybe snow today," he said.

Paul hid in the woods until the sky began to grow dark. He rolled a series of giant snowballs and began to build an igloo.

A wild rabbit jumped past him at one point, making a zigzagged path through the powdery top snow.

Cooper found Paul, and sat next to him in the half-built house.

He started back down the mountain, resting one of his mittened hands on Cooper's back.

V.

The paintings in the attic were packed in boxes that Aaron found behind the IGA.

Mr. Lozinsky came in his giant, ancient truck and took the chickens and ducks and geese in one trip.

The old rooster that crowed at sunrise had died the night before.

Iris made a strong soup from him, which was dark yellow and had to be cut into squares and diluted after it had been in the refrigerator overnight.

Real estate agents came and went, bringing strangers and odd couples on tours of the old house. Iris tried to bake bread before they came, because she had read this was a good idea in one of her magazines.

Spring came, and the farm was sold to a Buddhist who intended to build a shrine in a clearing halfway up the mountain. Aaron and Iris found a small house at the center of the next town. It had a front porch and a backyard and an upright piano in the living room.

The snow was gone, except for some dirty leftover clumps that hid in the shade of the evergreens. The moving men came and took everything that would fit in the new house.

Aaron piled the boys into the front seat of the pickup, and put Cooper in back.

They drove behind the moving truck, across the stream and through the front fields.

Iris stayed behind to wash the floors and clean the bathrooms.

Elisa stayed with her, sitting at the kitchen table, having a tea party with her favorite Barbie doll.

When she was done playing, she found Iris upstairs, cleaning Adam's bedroom window.

"Mom," she said.

Iris didn't turn to her.

"I was the one who ate the flowers."

PART VI.

I.

Iris thought that the new house smelled like an old age home.

She painted the rooms with the children's help. Aaron built a strong white fence around the backyard to separate them from the neighbors, even though there were lines of bushes, an evergreen, and some lilacs that marked the borders.

They inherited a beagle from Mr. Lozinsky that was too old to help on his farm.

Aaron renamed the dog Pup and built him a tiny house beneath the birdfeeder.

Cooper wandered through the small rooms, searching for unoccupied corners to rest in. He walked through the paint trays sometimes, leaving his paw prints on the kitchen floor. Iris left a few of them in a corner, near the refrigerator.

Summer came early, and Paul caught a cold as soon as school ended.

He slept in his new bed with a fever for a few days. Cooper stayed with him, curled on an oval rug, next to the boxes of books that had yet to be unpacked.

When the fever broke, Paul wandered downstairs to find the kitchen was blue, and the back porch was white, with a brand-new doormat.

"Hello?" he called out, waiting to hear someone.

The house was empty.

He sat on the back steps and scratched Cooper's head,

feeling the warmth of the sun on his face.

Pup came to him, sniffing his bare feet, then taking a nap on the lowest step.

The sounds of the neighborhood sifted toward him.

Someone was mowing their lawn. People from down the block were listening to a baseball game on the radio. Children were shouting.

A football emerged in the air, lobbing back and forth above the bushes of the next backyard.

Cooper searched the ground for a stick that Paul could throw for him, but he had gone inside to watch TV.

After the cartoon shows had ended, Paul played fetch with Cooper. The next-door neighbors were louder, drinking beer and playing music that woke Pup from his nap.

Paul threw Cooper's stick again, and Pup went after it.

Cooper growled at him and bit his neck.

Paul shouted at them, his throat still hoarse from the cold.

He saw Cooper's giant mouth around Pup's neck, flipping the dog's body across the reddening grass.

Pup made deep, gurgling noises as he tried to escape.

The children who played in the next backyard were silent now.

Two gray-haired neighbors rushed down the driveway and to the fence, watching Cooper drag Pup's body into a dark spot under the evergreen tree.

II.

Aaron arranged the boxes of paintings in the attic. Separating the ones with art supplies and unpainted squares of Masonite, he heard someone coming up the stairs.

Adam went quietly to his half of the attic, with the mattress on the floor and the tiny window that looked out on the street.

Cooper came up behind him and rested his face on the boy's chest. Adam stroked his soft, thick ears and whispered a long monologue to him that Aaron could not make out.

He brought a portable easel downstairs to the front room with the piano in it.

Aaron went back to get his paints.

Elisa had a birthday party with all of her new girlfriends.

Paul and Adam hovered in the living room, keeping their distance from the chirping six-year-olds. They eyed the cake and soda and ice cream spread across the table.

Paul and Adam went upstairs and quickly wrapped the lavender Jordache purse and lip gloss they had bought together. "From Paul and Adam," they wrote in a corner of the wrapping paper, and went back downstairs, carefully adding it to the pile at the end of the giant oak table.

The girls were laughing and squealing. Cooper came to them, cautiously nosing the edge of the table. One of the girls grew tense, watching him.

He nosed her hand.

"Get him away," she shouted. "Get him away from me."

Adam took Cooper's new red leash and took him outside for a walk.

The street curved softly along short hills that lead to a park. A summer rain had washed away the final traces of sand and dead leaves from the gutter.

Cooper sniffed at random spots of the sidewalk until he was satisfied, then moved on.

A stray poodle-like mutt scampered past them, barking its high-pitched yelp.

It turned and faced Cooper, snapping at the air between them.

Adam pulled hard against the leash, but could not stop Cooper from attacking the tiny dog.

"Cooper, come!" Adam shouted. "Cooper, come back!"

The dog was already dead.

Aaron ran out of the house with his pants undone.

"Cooper, come!" he shouted, from the top of the hill.

Cooper sniffed the dead body.

Aaron stared at his feet, resigned, as he zipped his pants up and started toward them.

III.

There were wheat fields all around them, dotted with blue wildflowers. Aaron pulled into the slow curve of Dr. Lamson's veterinary clinic.

He turned the pickup truck off.

Iris turned to him, her lips pursed in thought.

"I'll stay here," she said.

Aaron got Cooper from the back.

She stared out the dirty windshield at them as they waited by the front door.

The afternoon sky was cloudless above the field that Aaron carried the giant dog into.

He laid him down gently in the tall grass, smoothing and petting Cooper's body with both hands as he squeezed his eyes closed.

Aaron lay down next to the dog, and held him close for some time until he stopped breathing.

The highway to upstate New York had been empty as Aaron drove the AMC Scout. His newborn daughter sat on Iris's lap. The wind was flying in everyone's hair. Paul and Adam sat in the back seat. Cooper was just a puppy then, a quirky collection of fluffy chocolate fur and expressions.

"So, between a big garden and maybe some chickens it won't be so hard," Aaron said.

"It's so beautiful here," Iris said, breathing in deeply.

"But no bagels," Aaron said. "Hear that, boys? No bagels."

As everyone laughed, Cooper jumped out the window.

"Cooper, come back," Paul said.

"What?" Aaron asked, jerking his head around. "Where's Cooper?"

Paul pointed at the meridian passing outside his window, which separated the two halves of the highway.

Aaron looked into the rearview mirror and braked hard.

He ran out of the car.

Reaching a rise and taking a few steps, he saw Cooper in a heap of scraped fur at the bottom of the hill.

"Cooper, come," he said, frightened.

Cooper got up and ambled toward him, swerving and drooling.

"Christ," Aaron said under his breath. "Stupid dog."

Aaron brought him back to the car, with a giant smirk across his face.

"Windows up until we get to the farm," he announced, getting back in the driver's seat.

no deposit, no return

I.

My father pulled us onto the main road as the wheels of the white Ford spun hard on the asphalt.

The wipers swung out of time with each other.

I leaned forward in the big black seat and looked at him for a short time. He had lost a lot of weight after the divorce, but wore the same clothes. They hung from his shoulders, making him seem even thinner. Giant shirt cuffs hid half of his hands.

My father fixed his hunting hat and eyed me.

"I think there's a music store in Garrisonville," he said.

"Good," I said quickly, and nodded.

"But you'll pick it up," he continued. "I don't understand these things."

I pursed my lips into a smile, waiting for him to see it.

"What's to understand?" I said, not really asking a question.

"You're the only one of us that isn't tone-deaf," he said.

I sipped from a foam cup of coffee, leaned back into the seat, and watched the road disappearing behind us in the rearview mirror.

The music store was open, and my father pulled into a space in front of a fire hydrant.

"I'll stay here," he said, reminding me.

I went in quickly, spying the glass case where the harmonicas were displayed, sitting on top of their boxes. A teenage salesman was on the phone behind the counter. He noticed me, and made a face that asked if I needed any help and told me to wait at the same time.

There was not much of a selection. Just Marine Band harps with nickel plating, some chromatics, and a few wooden ones from China that were really just kids' toys.

I bought a Marine Band blues harp in C and asked him to press it against the hand bellows by the register to make sure all of the notes worked.

"You gotta break it in before it sounds good," he said as I paid.

Back in the truck my father nodded once and turned on the ignition.

"Do you want to see it?" I asked.

He shook his head no and turned the radio on.

A few hours later we pulled up to the mammoth house and parked in a gravel lot. The rain was coming down in big fat drops.

My father turned the truck off.

My stomach growled, long empty from the jam and toast we had eaten in silence at the kitchen table while it was still dark outside.

I looked out at the entrance and thought one of the curtains shifted behind a window, as if someone had been watching us.

My father sighed.

"He's waiting," I said, after a little bit.

My father raised his head up, his palms catching the shadows of the raindrops.

"But he's okay. He's going to be okay," he said, as his head sank to his chest. "There's something I want to tell you," he continued between slow, measured breaths. "I let things roll off my back, but Adam—he just takes everything inside him."

A small tree branch fell on the hood and slid onto the

ground.

"I think he is some kind of sponge," he added.

My stomach gurgled again and I felt embarrassed.

"That's what must have happened," he said. "He just took too much inside him."

I tried to ignore the strange feeling that I was wet.

"I don't understand why people say he is nuts. I mean, just because you do something crazy, you're automatically nuts?" I asked, jumping forward in my seat, convinced I was sitting in a puddle of cold water that had started seeping into my jeans.

"Why is he in there and I'm not?" I asked. "I think he is way less crazy than I am."

My father looked at me, anxiously.

"I just want to know that he's okay to leave," I said. "Maybe he likes it here. Maybe he doesn't want to come home."

"He's waiting for us," he said.

"Alright," I mumbled, seeing the seat was bone dry.

The rain came down even harder, making giant pancakes on the windshield. We watched them, and prepared to get out.

"Ah, fuck it!" my father said and bolted for the house. I pulled my coat tight to my chest and followed him, slipping sideways in the mud a few times and almost falling down.

The earth smelled of rotting leaves and dog shit. I tried to scrape it from my boots on the front porch. I decided to pull them off instead and walked around in my socks.

A man in a white coat greeted us and brought us to my brother who was peeling potatoes in a very big kitchen.

"Paul!" he said, looking up suddenly and dropping the peeler on the table. He was pretending to be surprised.

My father hugged him first, robot-like. Finishing his embrace like a pair of vise-grips springing apart, I leaned in next.

"Hey little bro," I whispered, squeezing him carefully. He felt frail, as if the bones in his chest had become soft.

He took us on a tour of the place, but I could not listen to the sweet talk he made about group therapy, the individual sessions, and the long salt baths, instead studying my brother's hands and how he ran them against each other. The missing digit was still red, and had black string poking from it. His hands wove in a sort of pattern that seemed like they were finding the phantom limb that was gone now.

We sat down for some lunch, and the man in the white coat disappeared. My brother was across from us. He closed his eyes for a few moments and let air come out of his lips with a hissing sound.

"Sue?" my father asked.

A young woman placed bowls of soup in front of us.

"Her name is Amanda," my brother said, smiling openly.

"Then who is Sue?" my father asked.

"That's what I say when I pray before eating," my brother said, motioning to Amanda that we needed spoons.

"Hunh," my father said, staring into his soup.

"Try it," my brother said.

"Sue," we said slowly, together.

"Spooooons," I said, trying for a laugh as Amanda brought them.

My father craned his head around.

"This needs salt," he said.

My brother looked around the table.

"I can get you some," he said.

"Nah," he said. "It's fine."

My father stared at a plate of bread for a moment.

"You know, you can ask me anything." My brother said. "It's okay."

My father stepped hard on my foot under the table. I wished I hadn't left my boots on the front porch.

"Okay," my father said.

"Well, I do have a few things to say," my brother said, growing serious.

I rested my spoon on the edge of my bowl.

"I do absolutely believe that there was a man that was Jesus Christ. I don't know if he died for our sins or all of that magic stuff like coming back from the dead—but I do definitely believe that there was a real guy and most of what he did, it's true," he said.

My father sighed and stared into his soup bowl.

"Okay," he said, quietly.

I looked at my brother's bright, blue eyes.

We nodded at each other.

"This soup is awesome, isn't it?" my brother announced so the people around us could hear him.

We drove home in the same rain, singing along to Glen Campbell songs on the AM station. My brother sat in between us, looking far off at the road and the sky.

I started to feel jealous of him.

II.

The wet landscape grew lush and green. The sun was coming out, dotting bright spots on the low stone walls and farm ponds we were passing. I rolled down the window, the wind whipping my hair around, breathing deeply.

It was dark by the time we pulled into the parking lot at Price Chopper.

I found a cart that had four good wheels. My brother jumped on the front and I pushed him into the store. We had agreed on vegetarian lasagna, and made our way through the aisles.

Halfway between the crushed tomatoes and the grated cheese canisters, my father stopped us. He did not say anything as he tiptoed to the end of the aisle and back to us.

"Your mother is here," he said under his breath, then broke into nervous laughter.

My brother was still hanging from the front of the cart. I rolled us back to the vegetable aisle. I looked at the grapes for a while, then plucked one and ate it.

"They're good," I announced. "Let's get some?"

My father shook his head no.

He went toward the registers and spied around the corner. My brother looked at me and made a funny face like a question mark. I shook my head.

"That's fucked," he said.

"I know," I said, stealing another grape.

"The whole world is fucked," I added.

He rested his hand on the grapes, suddenly looking very tired.

My father came running back to us.

"I think she saw me," he said in a loud whisper.

"Let's go to the milk case," I said. "She only drinks soy now."

My father was dancing as we rolled ahead, shaking his head to himself and laughing nervously.

III.

The dog came running out from behind the tiny house to greet us, jumping around the tires as we pulled up. My brother had fallen asleep, and we decided to leave him until he woke up.

I stretched my legs and started for the grocery bags, then found myself staring out at the lake below us. I had been here for two days, and had not even looked at it until now. The water was clear and dark blue. Swarms of bugs danced on the surface as birds swooped through them.

I cooked in silence with my father. He chopped vegetables and boiled water. I made a loose sauce, and combined everything quickly, not tasting to see if it needed seasoning.

The screen door opened and my brother shuffled inside, then sat at the big kitchen table, as if he would just wait there for dinner to be ready.

The lasagna really did need salt but nobody mentioned it. My father put on a film he had rented about a little boy who saves a whale. We all sat awkwardly in the living room. It seemed like the room was never used, as if that morning there had been sheets draped over the couch and the chairs and they were rolled in a ball on the porch now.

My father announced he was going to bed during the final credits, and the dog trotted after him. We listened to him pulling back the covers and arranging the pillows.

He blew his nose a few times, then clicked off the light.

A low roll of thunder punctuated the silence.

My brother motioned toward the side porch with his head, and we made our way through the dark house to sit outside. I stayed in the kitchen, trying to remember if there was any beer in the fridge. Opening it, I saw there was none. Looking under the sink, I found a dusty bottle of Chartreuse.

"What the hell is that?" my brother whispered.

"The fuck if I know," I answered.

I poured some into a jelly glass with some ice cubes and a splash of water from the sink.

Outside, the air was warm and soft in the half-light of the porch.

We sat for some time, looking out at the lake, listening to the thunder in the distance.

"Think it's coming this way?" I asked at one point.

My brother nodded yes.

He cleared his throat.

"Remember much from when we were little?" he asked me. "I mean, in Brooklyn."

"Of course," I said. "We had that hot babysitter with the long dark hair, and she helped us make a fort in the living room when we watched *Yellow Submarine*."

"And do you remember when they put both of my legs in a cast so I looked like a frog, and I just crawled around on the floor for like, six months?" he said.

I nodded yes, sipping the syrupy, foul-tasting liquor.

"And every time some kid tried to mess with me, you protected me," he said.

"Yeah," I said, half laughing.

"That was a very cool thing to do," my brother said, as if he had rehearsed the conversation many times.

"So, how do you feel now?" I asked. "Being outside."

My brother shrugged his shoulders, and pursed his lips together.

"Sometimes people just go out of your life," I said. "You can't control it."

His shoulders turned in, and he did a somersault into the wet grass, then got up on his knees.

"Look," he said. "Mushrooms."

He brushed his fingertips across the tiny caps pressing between the crabgrass.

Thunder broke, close to us now.

"Man—Dad has really changed," he announced, as if he had also practiced saying this. "He finally got another dog."

"I didn't talk to him for a while," I said.

"Yeah, I know," my brother said.

He stood up, brushing dead leaves from his muddy knees.

"Remember when we were kids and we were so fucking scared of him?" he asked. "Like the sun came up behind his head?"

I nodded and tried to smile, sipping from the glass.

"Remember when we put a bottle of Tabasco in the grape juice so Elisa would drink it, only Dad did instead?" I said, stifling a laugh.

"And he chased us around the house like a *Road Runner* cartoon?" my brother added, snorting and slapping his hands against his legs.

I yawned, suddenly feeling tired.

"And now, he's like some confused little kid," he said, sitting back down in the lawn chair.

"You know, he's trying so hard not to upset us," I said, "and is sort of doing the opposite."

"It's about all he can do," my brother answered, quickly.

I slapped at a mosquito buzzing around my ear.

"I'm not staying very long," he said. "I'll be gone in a day or two."

I nodded, approving of his plan.

"Think we'll end up like him?" I asked.

My brother shrugged his shoulders and pretended he was going to roll into the grass again.

"Him and Mom are from a different time. They had no idea what they were doing. Everyone from that time is a shit parent, but they all think they did a great job," he said.

"I guess I'd like to have a kid," I said.

"I could be the uncle that teaches them to swear really good," my brother added.

I finished my drink and smacked my lips.

"Let's go down to the water," he said, abruptly.

The path was steep, and we held on to the trees to keep from slipping on their muddy roots. I smelled moss, and pine. The lasagna came back up into my mouth, sour and bland.

The water was not cold.

My brother went in first, and I followed, trying not to imagine what was swimming around below us in the dark.

He went under the water for a long time, enough for me to get scared.

Thunder cracked close to us, and I bloomed with regret, wishing we had all gone to sleep when Dad clicked off his light.

My brother surfaced, flying above the bugs, spouting a giant stream of water from his mouth.

"I'm a whale!" he shouted, laughing and splashing around.

Some people on the neighbor's dock told us to quiet down.

We treaded water, close to each other. My brother was laboring, his breath heavy.

"You okay?" I asked.

"I'm awesome," he said. "I've got a new harmonica and I think I'm gonna go to Alaska. They have these giant cabbages there."

moon like a dandelion

I began to walk the two-mile stretch of highway with my eyes closed in the middle of the night. With my palms extended and my thumb barely touching my first finger I wandered forward. My feet traveled beneath me. The smell of cow shit and rotting hay was to my left, wildflowers and a breeze to my right. Cars could be heard from a distance, and I would crouch down in the ditch waiting for them to pass. My boots sucking in the mud, I found the high slope of the median and continued.

Eventually the curve of the approaching village arrives.
I open my eyes.
Here is the general store with hard peaches that they wrap two at a time in cellophane on Styrofoam trays.
A tiny Madonna leans sideways on the front lawn, staring past me into the darkness of the no-mooned night.

I bring down the gallon jug of Carlo Rossi and a small glass.
Sitting on the front porch and sipping the sour Paisano, the crickets chirp so loud their violin song seems almost visible, hanging in the air like waves that roll in slow-motion down the empty curve of the road.

There is only sulfur water here. The showers and sinks smell of rotting eggs. I never feel clean. I pour salt and chili in my pasta water, trying to offset the foul taste.

There is no TV.

There is no radio.

My cassette tapes are arranged across green milk crates that were my father's. They are a long way from Brooklyn, in an attic room in this small town. I listen to Patti Smith, The Sex Pistols, Syd Barret.

Late one night, rolling off the mattress on the floor, I stood up, suddenly wide awake. I lathered my head with soap and shaved my long hair off with a disposable razor, running my fingers along to make sure I didn't miss anything. The tiny sink filled with wet curls.

The blood on my fingers turned them pink.

The field climbs gently toward a rise that I cannot see past. There are tiny wildflowers, white and lavender and deep purple. They bend in the light wind and I part them carefully, wading through the tall grass. I do not trample a single one of them.

Now far from the road, I breathe in the smell of wet earth. There is a small army of insects swirling above me. Magnificent stacks of clouds do not move.

I think I can see the moon hanging in the afternoon sky behind one of them.

I close my eyes.

There are blackbirds flying around me. Their patterns intersect with the telephone wires sagging from old poles. I imagine their flight paths, seeing their trails as long lines that hang in the blue air.

There are patterns to be read. I can make sense of them. There are secrets in their movements.

I take a small book and a pencil stub from my pocket. Holding the paper open, I do not look down. I watch the birds, letting the pencil follow their movements.

I will look later.

The pencil scratches.

I must keep my eyes on them as they disappear past the rise in the earth I cannot approach.

I am not ready to go there.

Maybe at the end of the summer. Maybe before I go.

Walking to work through a light rain I taste the drops sliding down the stubble on my head and into the corners of my mouth. The water has a faint sweetness.

A handful of puddles reflect the flat gray sky in my field.

Kneeling by the shoulder of the road as pickup trucks swish past me, I rest my hand on some wildflowers. Closing my eyes, I pull on their long stalks. I whisper to the field and ask permission to take them. I promise to water them, to keep them on a windowsill.

"My name is Paul," I whisper, and pull them in one swift motion, their roots clumped with dirt. "I will be very good to them."

It is the midsummer night. The moon looks like it is three or four feet away. I can see every leaf. Every road sign in the distance.

There is no sound.

No cars.

Just my boots scraping on the highway.

To fill the silence, I begin humming. My field is approaching on the right. On my left, a muddy cow pen, a sagging barbed wire fence.

The fence posts are staring at me. I do not like the left side. I am sure the sulfur water comes from there.

I imagine my field wants to tell me my secret name. It wants to give me something, to share a collection of letters that describe who I truly am. A black bird flits over my head. I see it draws the letters for me. I hum them. This is my new name and I will tell it to no one. No person will know it. I will never write it down. Someday I will die and maybe I will whisper it. Yes, it will be on my gravestone. Maybe I should be buried in this field, just after the puddles, just before the rise.

The blackbirds are circling the mud field on the left now. They are talking to each other in blurts of sound. Squawks, chirps, long, low whistles are rolling toward me. The moon is really over there, just behind a giant maple tree.

I feel sorry for that field. I have rejected it and understand the birds are telling me I must also have a name from there, one from each side.

"I don't hate you," I tell the field to the left, standing in the middle of the highway.

I sing both names to myself, my hands reaching out as far as they can.

I close my eyes.

Moving toward the town I drag my heels, hoping to keep the road beneath me.

The ground is dry now.

August has brought a low sun and honeybees. I run outside with some blankets rolled tightly under my arm.

I buy some white bread and peanut butter from the store downstairs just as they are going to close. The old woman plunks her keys down on the register with a massive slap. She turns it off as soon as I pay. The lights click and everything goes dark before I reach the screen door.

In the field I spread the blanket out as well as I can.

My pocketknife is yellow. It was my grandfather's, and then my father's, who used it to castrate baby pigs when I was a boy.

I make peanut butter sandwiches with that same knife and eat them slowly, watching the sky turn purple and blue, then orange. I lay back on the uneven earth. I will sleep here tonight.

Maybe I will dream what is beyond the rise.

I am not scared any more.

I smell cow shit and salty grass from across the road.

Sitting in the kitchen, I drink black coffee and eat buckwheat pancakes. The wildflowers are drooping from an old cup. I will put them in a cigar box tomorrow.

I need to find one somehow.

I feel terrible that I took them. I should not have. It was the left field that made me do it. I know that side is just evil. It tricked me. It wants me to think there is both bad and good in all of us.

Everyone has two names.

The phone rings.

I listen through the receiver and say nothing. There is labored breathing on the other end. I am sure it is my mother. I hear a tiny sound through the wire, a mouse whisper. There is a rush of air.

A dog barks and I cannot tell if it is from outside the windows or over the phone.

The other end hangs up.

I go to the tiny sink in the bathroom, catching my face in the mirror. It is suddenly unfamiliar.

I vomit everything inside me in long yellow strings of mucus.

Washing my face with the lukewarm sulfur water, the foul smell of split pea soup and rotten eggs swirl around my eyes in the reflection beneath the single light bulb.

Down the stairs, I wander the countryside shirtless. I follow the highway that brings me past abandoned houses, trucks left to rot on cinder blocks, carcasses that disintegrate into the grass. I search for a cigar box, but do not find one.

I carry an old blue bottle in my hands.

This, I will take with me when I go.

Leaning against the window of my father's pickup truck, I look out at the green landscape whipping past us. The milk crates are in the back with my blanket and books.

Everything I own.

We will pass the field in a moment.

I think to stop him, to run and throw some pennies there. To stand in the tall grass once more.

To take a picture.

The mud field passes on my side. I see an old brown cow there, staring into the horizon.

This is what I will remember.

no tattoos

I.

I don't know anyone here.

Breakfast is easy as long as the bacon and sausage are on the flattop by five. There is nothing like the sound of cracking an egg and then scrambling it. That slap of the fork, the smell of hot coffee. A man does not need much more than that.

There are days when we are in the chop, and we are only supposed to make toast. The fryer is off then, empty. We put some fruit out. Canned peaches go fast.

"Pauly Boy—how come you got no tattoos?" Howard asked me today.

I looked at him for a while.

"Alright, no tattoos you showing," he added.

"Never wanted one," I said, breading more chicken, trying to keep one hand for the wet bath and one for the flour.

"You double dunking, right?" he asked me.

I showed him a piece. He smiled, flashing that gap between his front teeth.

"You a Jewboy?" he asked me. "Jew got no tattoo."

My face may have gone red for a second, but the galley was dead hot so maybe he didn't notice.

"Nah, not a Jew," I told him, the toes curling up in one of my boots.

He shook his head, laughing his little laugh like a puppy scratching on a door.

"How come you got no tattoos?" I asked after dunking a few more pieces of chicken.

"What the hell a black man want, getting a tattoo? Black and blue on brown, that ain't pretty. Looks like shit," he said. "Besides, I don't like needles."

Someone poked their head in the door.

"Fried chicken," they called out, into the hallway.

II.

I walked around on the top deck after lunch service.

It started to snow.

The flakes were tiny and there was not enough wind to keep them afloat, so they melted as soon as they touched the ship.

I ate some grapes I snuck into my pocket, spitting the seeds over the railing, one at a time.

Little ideas I could tell her turned over in my head. I imagined her making excuses, plenty of tears and mascara on her cheeks, and I was like a cowboy, eyes squinted looking off into the distance. I knew right from wrong. I would make her suffer. The door would close. I would still put everything in storage, still walk away with that pair of twenties in my pocket.

I swore a school of fish passed the boat then, shiny and silver just under the surface.

III.

One of my teeth hurts like hell.

There is even a dentist on the ship. A barber, a part-time priest.

Mostly I want some needle and thread because half of my buttons are about to fall off. But that is something I think about when I eat, hunched down in the back by the ovens. There is no time here, just work.

I drink milk.

I make bread.

I chop onions, peel carrots and potatoes because there is no fight down here. There are just light bulbs, the flour on my arms, sweaty faces, empty dishes, full dishes, dirty dishes. If you ask people what day it is they might have no idea. Tacos are on Tuesdays, pizza on Fridays, the rest is unknown. Canned corn, mashed potatoes, no wondering what will happen tomorrow.

IV.

Howard gets letters from his wife.

He has three kids.

If the mail comes while we are in the middle of service he just looks at me and I take over for five minutes. His fingers go pale, holding that letter so tight.

I ladle soup, beans, looking at the faces with no need to ask, they just nod at what they want.

Howard comes back, maybe clearing this throat. I step away, go back to making tossed salads. The letter pokes from his back pocket. There must be pictures in there, smiling faces on the front lawn before the first day of school, or maybe someone winning an award. I bet they throw him a birthday party even if he is thousands of miles away, pulling more Salisbury steaks from the freezer.

V.

It is late.

I haven't been topside for days. These light bulbs are the sky. There is no war down here, no roar of jets, no angry slap of helicopters. There are just boxes of frozen manicotti. There are knives that we sharpen once a week.

Yesterday never happened. Last year never happened. It all goes down the drain with soap bubbles and bits of food.

They like what we cook, no complaints.

I don't worry about what will happen tomorrow.

VI.

There was some accident today. I saw him, blood covering his head and arms. His hands were shaking, leaving red prints on the blank walls. He did not cry. Someone walked on each side of him.

He said he could make it to the infirmary.

"A Navy man is one tough motherfucker," Howard said to me, not looking away from the chickens we were trussing.

He shook his head to himself a few times.

"Think he'll be okay?" I asked.

He made a face at me like I was a fly in his kitchen.

"Maybe when he gets better we can make him a cake," I said.

"A get-well-soon cake?" Howard asked. "Or a go-home-soon cake?"

I stared at the pink chickens for some time.

"I was mostly just thinking a chocolate cake," I said.

Howard laughed like crazy, slapping the chickens like they were bongo drums.

"Pauly is making a chocolate cake," he said in a big voice. "Sunday night."

VII.

I had a dream.

There was a big long wood table and a bowl full of boiled human hands. I sat down, and I did not want to eat them, but I was starving. Closing my eyes, I bit into them, wobbly and soft, the skin like jellyfish must taste when you cook it. Chewing through the rubbery meat, I got to the cartilage, which made these ugly popping sounds as I got through them.

I felt cold, terribly cold, but still hungry.

VIII.

I keep the coffee coming in the middle of the night.

Some guys want scrambled eggs. Some want pie. Their faces are empty, gray. The crack of thunder feels more like a dull thud down here, but it is not thunder. No one speaks, just a gesture toward what they want.

I see it all on them.

None of this matters, and none of this is real.

For a second, I smell a woman's perfume.

I think of that bar, the old guy and the pretty girl with the big eyes, those freckles, soft lips that she bit when she was listening. I watched them for hours, how he drank her in, how she sucked up the attention, their little whispered jokes to each other, her hand on his arm, his faded black T-shirt, the gut pressing against his belt buckle. And then I watched them stumble out to the sidewalk still wet with rain, ducking into his old green muscle car, the engine gunning before they pulled away. Me making notes on a scrap of paper, not expecting to find the bones of a story that night, just cold beer and distraction.

"Snapshots of Heaven" took me months to write and it came out like shit, like a lopsided cake, half burnt, half raw. I erased it all, threw the pages out. I don't even like to say the title any more. It sounds like a commercial for Polaroids.

IX.

Meat and bones and skin, from the freezer to the ovens or maybe the fryer. Salt, pepper, butter, oil. Sizzle, boil, baste, scrape, flip, melt some cheese on top. Nothing fancy, no parsley on the corner of plates here. Just meat and bones and skin going inside or making bones and skin and meat into tiny bites, washed down with iced tea or just water. Eat, shit, fight, wash, sleep.

I need to buy a new razor.

X.

We docked today. I am not supposed to tell anyone where we are. It is cold here, no palm trees or beaches. I can say that.

Howard left early.

I handled breakfast myself.

He came back before lunch, his eyes glazed over. I wondered if he got stoned or not, because he sure looked like it. A few mumbled words, some head nods, a promise to be back in a few hours.

It was strange to wear a scarf and pull a hat down over my ears, feeling the weight of a warm coat on my shoulders. If I had anyone back home I would get some souvenirs, but it has been years since I talked to any of them except my little brother, and I don't think he wants any refrigerator magnets.

I changed fifty dollars at an exchange and wandered around looking up at the buildings that curved on long streets, the warm orange windows that people lived behind. People worked and came home and maybe played with babies. People who had dogs to walk grabbed hot shits in plastic bags before anyone stepped on them.

It started to snow.

I thought about staying here, getting a job washing dishes in the first place that would take me, living in a room I rented by the week from an old woman who asked too many questions, which luckily I didn't understand. I could sneak past Howard and go get my notebook, maybe make a new story because it had been years since I tried to write. Maybe here it could all turn around, a little angel would appear late at night and whisper in my ear and that bestseller would happen.

Cars are rolling slowly down the narrow streets like the snow was unexpected and they have the wrong tires on.

It sounded like someone was singing opera when I turned into an alley. I stood for some time trying to figure out where the sound was coming from, eventually accepting that it was just in my head.

There was a bar, and an old man was wandering toward it. I thought to follow him, to order a beer and a whiskey and stare at the faces inside, or maybe the news in some crazy language on the TV.

I bought a street sausage first, mustard sliding around the

insides of my mouth, shoving it into my face, gulping down giant bites. I threw some bits of bread crust to some pigeons who looked like they were sharing it peacefully.

This is such a weird a place, I said to myself.

Even the birds get along.

The bar was hot and I took my coat off. There was no TV, just some jazz playing from an invisible jukebox. Pointing at the tap the bartender nodded as he poured a beer for me, tiny bubbles dancing around the foam. It was the most delicious thing I ever tasted.

For some reason I stared at my hands for a very long time. They did not look like they were mine.

I ordered another beer and a shot of some kind of whiskey.

Making my way to a chair in the corner, I felt my legs going like they were crumbling out from under me. I rested my head against the wall, seeing the clock, knowing I was already late for dinner service. Howard would be swearing and smacking his palm against something, saying my name. Or maybe not, thinking I was doing the right thing, that I was brave to walk away from the boat and the kitchen and the war. I could just sit here, while back home everyone was still sleeping, some half-awake pulling at the corners of pillows, whispering in each other's ears, wondering what time it was.

Yes, the sky would be getting brighter at the edges. The moon was left over somewhere by a water tower.

A little draft moves the curtains. A dog nudges its master's hand asking to go take a pee. A garbage truck groans from the street.

In the wee small hours of the morning, people are finishing their dreams.

I am waking up next to her, trading little kisses and loose hugs. We are waking up in each other's arms on the couch and the TV is still on. We are making love in the soft warmth of the covers. We are turning off the alarm clock.

yellow pencils

The yellow pencils were going to poke me in the eyes.

It was in gym class, as the dodge balls were whipping past me, that I realized I was in constant danger from the pencils.

I froze up, not scared of Fat Irwin or Scotty Jordan. I was too small and too fast for them. A few slipped past me, like a tooth plucked from my gums after biting into a hard, sour apple. I felt maybe my eyelashes would work perfectly now, protecting my eyes.

I curled up on the floor as the balls pelted against me.

A note was pinned to my parka, and I figured it out on the way home. I told my parents about the danger of the yellow pencils and we went to the doctor the next day.

I know that things were discussed that night, after I had gone to sleep, after the bath in the kitchen sink in my underwear even if I was too big for that now.

In the hospital, my parents signed me in. My little brother and baby sister sat on the edge of my bed, wondering if I would live.

The nurses and the anesthesiologist were trying to tell me jokes. I could hardly hear them, thinking there were so many sharp things in the operating room. They placed the mask across my nose and mouth and made their faces look as kind as possible.

Someone asked me to spell my name.

"P-A-U-L," I mumbled.

They asked me to count backward from one hundred.

I spent a few days in that room—or so I imagined—eating ice cream, taking long naps and feeling like my eyes were safe, now that nothing could poke into them.

the year of the horse

PART I.

I.

The window shades moved slowly in the breeze. Slivers of afternoon light grew and disappeared at their edges as the sound of children playing filtered up to Paul. He lay on his back, running a finger along his teeth.

He smelled black tar, and thought he could hear the machine that rolled it out smooth as beads of water formed on the surface of the giant drum.

Paul splashed cold water on his face, sucking the moisture from his lips, salty then sweet.

He merged with the crowd, dragging his feet behind a family with two young boys. Collections of people were gathering in lazy groups, making their way to the river. The low sun slammed back from the windows of the tall buildings across the street. A stray dog nosed in an overturned garbage can, finding half of a sandwich it chewed in large bites, smacking its lips against the roof of its mouth.

Paul reached out to pet the dog and it barked, baring its teeth and finishing the sandwich. Paul suddenly felt dizzy. He started down Clinton toward Delancey smelling stale beer. The Williamsburg Bridge seemed to hang in the sky, a gray erector set left out to rust in the July sun.

The crumbling promenade was full.

Paul pressed his way past Mexicans and teenagers in ripped jeans, past Polish women and random faces. He kept going all the way to the Brooklyn Bridge until there were fewer people. The rotten smell of the fish market came up to him and he stopped, leaning against the rail, looking down at the dark water. The sky had gone from pink to violet in a short time. Thin clouds hovered over the East River. Brooklyn was already dark. Lights were coming on in windows. People emerged on rooftops in the distance.

A giant woman stood next to him. She produced a bottle of wine from her purse and uncorked it, splashing some into a plastic cup. A tiny man next to her took it. She poured another in silence and they toasted. Paul stared at the great fat rolls on her neck, her breathing labored, the sound of the wine smacking against her lips. The tiny man held her hand in his, twisting her fingers, playing with the cup until it grew empty and she refilled it.

Paul thought of how he had come down to the river with her that summer, how she always smelled of oranges, clutching his arm, pressing against him as he brought her through the crowd to an empty spot along the fence. He thought of her long blonde hair and how she would brush a piece away from her face when she talked.

The fireworks began.

People shouted randomly. Someone turned their radio all the way up. "The Star-Spangled Banner" played, crackling and drifting around the dial. Paul tried to guess what shapes and colors were coming as giant pompoms scattered across the sky then reflected on the river.

Paul's hand jumped awkwardly as the smell of smoke blew across his face. His arms grew cold, covered in goose bumps. Trying to breathe, he opened his eyes, seeing the dim sky above them revealed by the next splash of color and brief light. His hand went to his chest, feeling for something he had hidden in one of the kitchen cabinets for some time now.

Paul studied the little man's eyes, how he raised his hands high in the air, shouting *hurrah, hurrah, hurrah!* He managed a sort of smile. The tiny man produced a third cup from the giant purse. Splashing from the bottle into it, the woman shoved it all at once into Paul's hands. She wrapped his fingers around the cup and said something in French he could not hear, or understand.

Paul did not drink.

The smell of gunpowder grew thick around them. His eyes began to itch.

The tiny man threw himself into a crude salute waiting for Paul to notice him. Letting out a long breath, Paul drew himself into a proper salute, setting his feet apart, straightening his hips, his shoulders, his chin. Fingers positioned to the right of his eyebrow, Paul waited for the little man to correct himself, but he was already refilling his cup and drinking again.

He let his hand drop, shoving his fingers inside his jeans.

Paul sipped on the wine.

All at once the fireworks stopped.

The last explosion echoed through the city.

A deep cheer rippled down the promenade.

Across the river in Brooklyn, people were setting off bottle rockets that shrieked into the sky in angry red arcs.

Sunburned and tired, the crowd shuffled back toward the heart of the city. Paul looked out at the black water for some time, then poured the rest of the wine onto the ground.

He bought two hotdogs to go from Katz's and a six-pack at the corner bodega.

Upstairs, he sat in the kitchen with the lights off, resting the food on its brown paper bags, sipping slowly on the cold beer.

Paul went back to bed.

II.

Paul got off the bus at 86th Street, crossed Madison and bought a liter of Coke at a hotdog cart. He made his way into the park as the sky went black. Swarms of bugs twirled around the lights that dotted his path. The zoo had been closed for hours already, the trash cans emptied, the flat stones swept of ice cream wrappers and scraped of bubble gum. The air was sweet and warm on his arms. He wiped a tiny insect from his cheek and went into the office.

His uniform was worn at the edges, fraying at the cuffs because they slipped under his heels, his shoes chewing a half-circle from them.

He punched in, and made his walk.

The sea lions were swimming effortlessly, surfing below the water's surface with just noses and whiskers above, and then disappearing into the cool water. Their bodies full, they did not bark or splash. They did laps, always counterclockwise it seemed. He watched them for some time, seeing their pale underbellies, anticipating their breathing as the water swelled.

The small birds were already sleeping, their heads turned under wings, huddled in groups. Paul looked at the floors of their cages, splattered with white patterns of shit. He drank from the cold bottle of soda, wiping the condensation against his forehead, closing his eyes and trying to hear nothing but the sounds of their sleep.

He saw the new guard through a window. Paul raised a hand in greeting and closed it quickly. He pointed toward the polar bears, motioning for him to go there. The new guard made his face into a question mark. He turned on his walkie-talkie, his voice crackling across the speaker, his accent thick and musical. Paul did not reply, pretending his did not work. He made a bear drawing on the window.

"Da sea lions?" the young guard asked him.

Paul shook his head no.

He swigged from the soda bottle.

"Ah," he said. "Da bears."

Paul nodded, giving him a thumbs-up.

Outside the bird house he sucked on the night air. Paul closed his eyes, hearing the low pulse of traffic from the East Side. His hand went to his back pocket, feeling for the tiny book of crosswords and replacing it, then to his shirt pocket making sure the pen was still there.

He checked his watch.

Almost ten.

Paul sat on a bench, trying not to guess what time it was. He finished the soda in short sips, tossing the bottle toward a garbage can, then watched it bounce off the rim and roll across the ground. He thought about leaving it, then found himself throwing it away.

The penguin room was thunderous, the throngs of tiny birds running to the edge of the murky green water, splashing, twirling, careening off the thick glass and heaving onto the flat concrete. The room reeked of piss and fish. Paul gazed at the long window from the back wall, imagining it was a CinemaScope film. He counted them, made up names for them. Paul checked his watch. It was after eleven thirty. He lay on his side, propping the watch upright on the floor next to him.

The penguins shrieked and jumped, over and over. He let his eyes go blurry, the cascade of black and white and green playing over him.

He reached for the walkie-talkie.

"Hector," Paul said quietly.

"Over," he heard.

"I'm in the penguin house now," he said.

"Copy that," he heard.

There was a brief silence.

"Everything okay?" Paul asked.

"Affirmative," he heard.

"Bears sleeping?" Paul asked.

"Almost," Hector said.

"Okay, thanks," Paul said, resting his head on the cool floor.

The walkie-talkie sputtered for a moment, a series of clicks.

"Over," Paul said, and closed his eyes.

A heavy thump on the glass woke him. He let his eyes adjust to the light of the room. The penguins were still at it. A handful of them slept against the back wall of their enclosure.

Paul tried to breathe through his mouth as the stale air swirled around him.

He saw something in the tank, and rose to his feet. A new baby penguin was there, skipping around the water's edge. He pressed his face to the glass, mouthing out a hello in some kind of code. Tap tap. Tap, tap, tap.

The tiny bird jumped into the water, bobbing like a dry cork, then back onto the concrete and to its mother.

Paul wiped the sleep from his eyes and found his watch on the floor. It was almost two. He pressed the door open, feeling a sudden draft as he went outside.

III.

Paul sat in the kitchen, the table littered with bills. He ripped the envelopes open, throwing their carcasses to the floor. He scribbled amounts on checks, yanking them jagged from the book, forcing them into the new envelopes and setting them in piles next to him.

He searched in a drawer for postage stamps and found them. He went through the piles, licking them all closed.

A low moan came from the bathroom.

He stopped, craning his neck.

All at once, a massive thud echoed through the narrow apartment.

Half of the bathroom ceiling lay on the floor in a pile of wet, mildewy plaster. He stared up at the naked beams and the underside of the bathtub from the apartment above his. A slow trickle of water ran down the walls.

Without thinking, he opened the medicine chest and saw it was soaking wet. Paul grabbed a pot from the kitchen and put everything in it. Razors, Band-Aids, half-empty sticks of deodorant.

He opened the lower chest as rolls of toilet paper swollen with gray water fell out with a dull thump. There at the bottom was a plastic tube. He knew it was hers. Paul grabbed at it and tried to flush it down the toilet then watched it float back up.

He thought of her running out into the middle of the street as cars screamed down Second Avenue.

He remembered stumbling off the curb past the taxis barreling down on him to grab her arms, her fighting him across two lanes, the cars swerving and then honking wildly. He tried to shout but no sound came from his throat suddenly the size of a pinhole. He forced her to the sidewalk. An old woman was staring at them and screaming, saying she was going to call the police. The old woman said, "Suicide" over and over. He did not let go of her. He could not hold back the broken thundering in his ears. His fingers pressed into her arm, pushing right through her.

She refused to go back to the hot, cramped apartment to lie in bed and watch TV. She would stomp across the sidewalk swearing in Russian, talking to herself under her breath. He trotted after her, resting his hand on her shoulder. She shrugged it off. They walked more than twenty blocks this way until she ducked into a pizza place, the pies going stiff under the heat lamps. She plopped into a booth after seeing a man and a woman go into the bathroom. They sat there for more than thirty minutes as people came and knocked on the bathroom door.

Paul sent them off.

"Yes, somebody's in there," he said, nodding toward each of them.

The young men behind the counter did nothing, huddling for a moment and whispering together.

"You should eat something," he said to her at one point.

She shook her head, her sigh curling into a snarl.

He stood up and ordered a plain slice and a Coke. He paid, eating methodically, the cold cheese and grease painting his lips. His stomach no longer empty, he asked her if they could go home. He promised to find a new place she would like, even outside the city. She stared up at him, her eyes bloodshot and wild.

He turned his finger across his heart.

Paul nodded slowly.

"*Ladno,*" she said, under her breath.

"Okay?" he asked.

She nodded once.

As he threw the pizza plate in the garbage, a solid thump came from the bathroom door as it jumped on its hinges.

"Lets get out of here," he said quietly.

She stood up, shaking. He wrapped one arm around her, pressing the side of his body against hers. She was cold, as cold as ice, he thought.

Late that night, she slept.

Paul watched reruns on the TV, imagining what it would be like to leave the city, to put everything in boxes from the liquor store down the block.

He poured himself a glass of scotch and drank it in tiny sips, gazing out the kitchen window at the empty skyline where the towers had stood two years ago. They were gone now, the way baby teeth could be pulled out with a piece of string.

He stood over her, watching the sleep move across her face. He saw the twisted corners of her mouth, her throat clenching then relaxing. Paul threw the rest of his scotch back and got under the covers, forcing his arm under her head so her cheek rested on his shoulder.

Tomorrow was Saturday and he would not have to work.

IV.

There was a light knock on the door. Paul rolled across the sweaty sheets, glancing at his watch. Ten thirty.

"Yes," he called out, his voice strange in his throat.

Paul stared at a patch of sunlight on the living room wall for a moment, blood rushing through his fingertips.

He looked through the peephole at a tall thin man, his nose a broken shape like the beak of an exotic bird.

"Is Misha. I meet you two time, three time. Long time before," he said. "Brother of super."

"Ah," Paul replied, flipping the deadbolt.

"I fix floor," he said.

Paul stopped opening the door, confused. He pointed up.

"Ah, no," Misha said. "Up floor."

"Ceiling," Paul said.

"Yah, yah," Misha said, sliding into the apartment, then into the bathroom. He stood with his hands on his hips for a bit.

"Fucking mess," he said, half to himself.

Paul nodded, thinking to make some coffee, but only for himself.

Misha turned to him, looking down his crooked nose, beads of sweat forming a ring around his bald head.

"You take fish, make him to survive," he said, suddenly coughing. "But he say what the fuck is water?"

Paul shrugged his shoulders, offering a weak smile. He started to make coffee in the tiny aluminum pot.

Misha left, returning with a tackle box full of tools and string.

"You got paper?" he asked.

Paul craned his head from the kitchen.

"Not yet," Paul said.

"Not news," Misha said. "Piece."

"Ah," Paul replied, grabbing one of the empty envelopes from the floor. Misha looked at it, his lower lip jutting out in some sort of approval.

He went to the bathroom, making measurements he repeated to himself, scribbling away. After a while he emerged, standing with his hands on his hips.

Paul looked up at him.

"I go now," Misha said. "Later, I back."

"I might have to go to work when you get back," Paul said.

Misha twisted his mouth around.

"Maybe you wife home then?" he asked.

Paul looked at his hands for a moment.

"No," he said.

"She not you wife?" Misha asked.

"No," Paul said.

He opened his mouth, but said nothing.

Misha wiped the sweat from his forehead. He craned his neck, peering into the apartment.

"I no see you. No ever see you," Misha said. "Sleep day, work night."

Paul stared at him.

"I no see you long time," Misha said, waving his hands around the tiny kitchen. "She go?"

Paul nodded, digging something out of his teeth.

"Five years ago," Paul said. "Just about."

Misha shook his head to himself.

"Fucking hell," Misha said. "Czech girl better than Russian girl."

"What?" Paul asked.

"She Russian, right?" Misha asked.

"Moldovan," Paul replied.

"Same fucking thing," Misha said, spit flying from his lips.

Paul wiped some from his arm.

"Czech girl no leave you," Misha said. "No never go. Never."

Paul stared into Misha's face.

A garbage truck rumbled from the street.

Children were shouting in the loose spray of a fire hydrant. A sweet smell came in the window, green and luscious.

Misha rested a hand on Paul's shoulder and patted him once.

"We fix," he said, then let himself out.

PART II.

I.

The boy moved in his sleep, and flipped his legs on top of her, pushing off the covers. Anya drew the blanket back across them, cradling him against the inside of her elbow. Pasha grabbed at her, his lips pursed.

She brought one of his fingers to his mouth.

He pulled at her shirt.

"No," she whispered to him. "Not until morning."

Struggling with the shirt she had pulled down, Pasha began to cry.

Anya sighed, now wide awake.

She let him nurse.

The sky was black outside the windows.

Her breath hung in the cold air, making wet clouds above them.

Pasha gurgled and smacked his lips, eventually going back to sleep.

Anya looked inside the wood stove, at the logs that had turned to ash during the night. She smoothed Pasha's long hair from his face, resting her hand on his shoulder.

The sun pushed its way into the tiny room. Pasha rose in silence, careful not to disturb her.

He crawled from under the covers, and picked through a lopsided box of toys. He found two giraffes, and positioned them next to each other on the table in the corner of the room. Next, two lions. There was only one in the box, and he searched for the second one.

A man's silhouette stood motionless outside the window.

Pasha played Noah's Ark with a series of tiny objects lined up in twos. A pair of used matches were snakes, a pair of peach pits were walruses. He searched the lopsided drawers by the sink, finding two copper kopeks. He turned them in his fingers, feeling their weight. He returned to the boat, a blanket twisted and knotted into some kind of shape.

He smelled a cigarette then looked up at the window.

Pasha stood perfectly still.

The man disappeared.

She lit the flame with a match, then rested it on the edge of the counter.

Pasha's mouth twisted around as he thought.

"Grechka?" he asked

Anya splashed some oil across the bottom of an old pot and dumped in the last grains from the bag.

"Can you get water?" she asked him.

"But it's too heavy," he said.

"Just a little," she said. "Enough for this, and tea."

Pasha primed the pump in the garden, listening to the odd sound of the water rising. He caught the first drip in a bowl, then pumped a few more times until it was full. The sun was already high above the apple trees. He tested the sand that filled an overturned tractor tire. It was cool and wet. His toys seemed stuck in time, as if they could lurch into motion as soon as they were warm enough.

As he gave her the bowl, Pasha looked out the window.

"Papa was here today," he said.

The bowl crashed to the floor.

Water was everywhere and Pasha laughed without thinking.

"The flood!" he shouted, running to the makeshift boat and nudging the train of animals inside it.

Anya leaned against the counter.

"What did you see?" she asked, almost whispering.

Pasha made a series of animal noises.

"What did you see?" she shouted at him.

Pasha pointed a finger at the dirty window, caked with a milky dust.

"You were sleeping," he said. "He was there."

Anya went outside. There was a group of footprints in the mud. She kneeled down, measuring them with her hands. She saw a cigarette butt in the grass.

Anya began to breathe.

"Mama!" Pasha called from the window. "Something is burning!"

She ran inside, sliding in the mud and almost falling. She caught herself at the corner of the tiny house.

Anya pulled the old pot from the flame, seeing the grains were black. She went to the window, pulled it open and threw them out.

II.

Pasha kicked a half-deflated ball across the backyard.

Anya sat in one of the folding chairs reading a mystery novel. She smelled something. A foul, chemical smoke moved past her. Craning her neck, she saw a smoldering garbage pile behind the next house. She could make out a tall man standing over it, poking and adjusting pieces of clothing, furniture, and books.

Pasha ran to her.

"What is he doing?" he asked.

"I don't know," she said.

Pasha stood next to her, his hand resting on her elbow.

"That's him," he said after a while.

"Who?" she asked.

"My Papa," he replied.

Anya sighed.

"Is that the man who was outside the window?" she asked him.

Pasha looked up at her and nodded.

She shook her head.

"That's just some neighbor," she said.

Pasha pressed his lips together.

"So Papa is still on the moon?" he asked.

She looked at him standing next to her, the ball caught under his arm.

Anya brushed his hair from his eyes and held his chin.

"Yes," she said. "Your Papa is still on a very long trip, but he is almost to the moon."

"And is he gonna bring me back a moon rock?" Pasha asked.

Anya stared at him.

She shoved the center of his back.

"Go play," she said.

He threw the ball as far as he could and shouted as he chased after it.

The man standing over the fire looked at her in the distance. One of his hands flinched at his side as if to wave at her, but then he did not.

She stared at him for a while, through the bare trees and the smoke.

Anya found her place in the book and went back to reading.

III.

A car approached, laboring along the muddy, narrow road, then stopped. Anya waited to hear the sound of the doors opening, then closing. She thought to close her eyes and pretend she was sleeping.

Pasha looked up from the sandbox.

"Mama," he said.

She kept her eyes closed.

"Mama!" he said as loud as he could. "Grandma is here!"

Tossing her book to the ground, she stood up. A heavy man wearing a fisherman's cap made his way through the weeds and tall grass. Her mother was behind him, a white purse caught in the lock of her elbow. Her bright red lipstick was fresh and clean, standing out against the trees and the pale blue sky. She noticed the burnt *grechka* on the ground, frowning, shaking her head and letting out a long sigh.

The fat man stood with a cluster of plastic bags in each hand, waiting for her to tell him what to do with them. She waved a hand toward the massive refrigerator behind the screen windows. It stood open, rusting in the darkness. He placed everything carefully on the ground, the bag of eggs last. He rubbed his hands together, making little sounds to himself.

Her mother started into the house, returning with a heavy ceramic bottle and two small glasses. She poured, filling them both to the edge.

"*Samogon?*" he said, half to himself, and clapped his hands together.

They toasted in silence, quietly looking at each other. The old woman nodded once and drank the glass empty. She placed hers on the wood table and reached inside her purse. He let out a sort of laugh and a cry. She nodded, putting her purse down and poured him another.

"For the boy," he said, raising the stubby glass and slurping it down.

"Pasha!" the old woman said. "Get him an apple."

Anya sat in her chair watching.

The boy ran to the trees and shook them until one fell.

The old woman pulled out 300 rubles and handed them to him. He jumped back a little, gesturing and shaking his head. He pressed her money back toward her.

Pasha returned, polishing a green apple against his shirt.

"So tiny," the man said, patting the boy's head and taking it from him.

He bit into it and made a face.

"Sour?" the boy asked.

The man nodded yes.

"Very sour?" the boy asked.

The man shook his head no.

He ate the seeds, the core and even the stem. Checking his watch, he smiled at the boy and made his way back to the car.

The old woman primed the pump and cleaned the two glasses, filling one and drinking the water slowly.

Anya stared at her, hands folded in her lap.

The old woman ran her hand through the boy's hair. She felt his shoulders.

"You definitely grew," she said to him.

"Really?" the boy asked.

"Show me something," she said, squeezing his hand.

He brought her inside, explaining what animals were in his boat now.

Anya's stomach made noises, empty except for the black tea she had made earlier.

IV.

Pasha slept in the front room on the old sofa. A book about a dancing doughnut hung loose in his hands. The old woman closed it carefully and drew a blanket across him.

She went to the kitchen and found places for the groceries in the lopsided cabinets. She searched the drawers, quietly yanking them open until she found a can opener. She filled a pot with water, slicing onion and carrot in her hands, the tiny knife moving toward her as the pieces fell. She opened a tin of beef and let it slide into the water, a ring of white fat making it bob on the surface.

Wiping her hands on a towel, she went outside.

Anya looked up from her book.

"Who was the man at the window?" the old woman asked her.

"I have no idea," Anya said. "I thought he was making it up, but there are footprints there."

The old woman stared off at the horizon for a while.

"I didn't give you this place to have affairs," she said.

Anya opened her mouth.

The old woman put her hand out in the air.

"Fucking strangers is what got you here," she said, baring her teeth.

Anya stopped.

"This place is for the boy," she said. "He needs to have a simple life."

Anya nodded once.

"He is a beautiful child," the old woman said. "And I want him to stay that way."

A sparrow flew into the yard, searching in the tall grass for something. Another followed it. They hopped around, chirping and flapping their tiny wings.

"How often does he nurse?" the old woman asked.

Anya frowned a little, lowering her gaze.

"How much?" she asked.

"In the morning" Anya said, under her breath. "And so he will fall asleep."

"Good," the old woman said. "It's the best thing for him. It keeps him close to you. It keeps him healthy."

Anya stared at the old woman's purse.

"Just one?" she asked.

The old woman nodded.

Anya pulled a cigarette from a long white box inside the bag. The lighter was next to them.

She lit it quickly, inhaling as deep as she could. Her eyes grew wide as if she was just waking up. Anya held the smoke inside her for what felt like a minute, then let it out in a noisy gray whoosh. She tapped a finger on her lips then inhaled again.

The old woman zipped her purse closed. She brushed some crumbs from the tiny table then repositioned it so it did not wobble on the uneven grass.

"The soup will be ready in about an hour," she said and started toward the road.

The two sparrows flew straight up into the sky.

"Don't forget to turn off the stove," the old woman called as she disappeared around the corner of the house.

"Goodbye," Anya said to herself.

V.

She dreamt she was fighting in a war.

The moments passed like a film, full of smoke and bright flashes in the sky. The bullets did not seem real as their screams whipped past her in perfect stereo.

Anya was stuck in enemy territory. She kept a gold pistol inside her shirt, tucked beneath one of her breasts, against her

skin. It felt cold and warm at the same time.
Her flag had a series of white stars on it. This, she knew.
The stars changed from white to red.
She fired three shots, her hands shaking, then steady.

PART III.

I.

Paul rested his coffee cup on the edge of the old blue sofa. The newspaper felt damp in his hands, as if it had just been printed.

A rolling thump came from the bathroom, punctuated by Misha's cursing. Paul's hand jumped to the coffee cup, thinking it was about to fall. He gulped from it until it was empty, then went back to reading.

Misha dragged debris to the hallway, leaving the door open as he waited for the tiny elevator to arrive. There would be a few minutes of silence, a breeze from the stairway making its way into the apartment. Paul stared at his watch. It was hours before he should go to work. He yawned, noticing the dirty soles of his feet on the old wood floor.

Misha stood in the doorway, pausing dramatically.

"I killing *tarakhan*," he said. "White *tarakhan*."

Paul craned his neck, wondering if Misha was talking to him or himself.

"*Tarakhan!*" Misha said, pounding his fist into his palm.

Paul shuffled over to him.

"What's that?" he asked.

Misha opened his hand, showing him the broken body of a pale, white cockroach.

"What the hell is that?" Paul said under his breath.

"They make new skin," Misha said. "Like snake."

Paul paused in thought.

"Like shark tooth," Misha said.

Paul shook his head to himself.

They stood motionless for a short time.

Paul's stomach growled.

"Is like white rabbit," Misha said. "Pink eyes."

Paul took a step back.

"You have pink eye?" he said.

"I have brown eye," Misha said. "Animal, no color making pink eye."

Paul cleared his throat once, then again.

"I have to go to work," Paul announced.

Misha shrugged his shoulders.

"Give me fifteen minutes, okay?" Paul said, motioning toward the bathroom.

Misha stared at him.

"Can you come back in fifteen minutes?" Paul asked him, in a loud voice.

Misha did not blink.

He turned and sat on the stairs, pulling a soft pack of cigarettes from his shirt pocket.

Paul closed the door.

II.

Walking across 91st Street, Paul saw a couple running, hands clasped, her dress flapping around her legs, his tie dancing around behind him. The park was only two blocks away and he guessed they were going to a wedding in the Conservatory Garden.

They stopped at a giant, dark church. Crossing themselves three times on the front steps they bowed their heads in a strange rhythm.

He recognized it now. The backward sign of the cross, hands first to the forehead then down below the chest then left across the heart, then to the right, hands curled against themselves. He watched them go inside, still out of breath.

Paul stood at the steps. The heavy doors closed very slowly, giving a short view inside the dark building. He looked up at the stained-glass windows hidden under thick plastic.

A mailman rolled his cart along the sidewalk, whistling to himself. Paul took a small step toward the church to let him pass.

The doors opened.

A young woman with a screaming baby came outside. A kerchief hung lopsided from her head, about to fall. She rocked the baby as it grasped the air with tiny hands. She shushed and cooed.

Paul did not move.

The woman looked at him from the corner of her eye.

He checked his watch calmly, occupying himself.

Paul squinted his eyes, looking toward the park pretending he was waiting for someone.

The baby was still crying, but less.

The woman was singing, pressing the baby to her shoulder. It knocked her kerchief to the steps. Paul took a small step toward her. She kneeled down and grabbed it quickly, forcing it into a ball then shoving it into her purse in one motion.

Paul looked at his watch again and scratched his chin.

He headed back down the sidewalk.

III.

Paul sat on a stoop across the street from the church. A takeout cup of coffee and a brown paper bag lay next to his hand. A crowd of people spread across the steps now. Men wore wrinkled beige suits with pointy white shoes that had gone yellow over time. There were women in tight skirts twisted sideways, with shiny kerchiefs wrapped around their hair. Children ran up and down the sidewalk, hiding between parked cars.

A white limousine pulled up, with a giant plastic ring attached to the sunroof.

A man came through the main doors, bald, a bit heavy. A great smile pasted across his face, he was sweaty and was yelling something about getting drunk. Shoving both of his hands in the air, a cheer came up.

"*Gorka! Gorka!*" they shouted, randomly.

A young woman came out—tall, thin, wobbling on her heels. The white dress fit strangely. She broke into nervous laughter, her horselike face and bare shoulders poking into the sunlight, the long train wrapped around one hand.

Some champagne popped open.

"*Gorka! Gorka!*" they shouted, now together. The children stopped playing and watched as they kissed on the steps, his arm reaching around to the small of her back. Her stiff, awkward, embarrassed.

The crowd cheered.

A man ripped open a column of plastic cups, tossing the wrapper to the pavement. Champagne flowed, messy and fast. The children went back to their game.

The couple made their way into the limo and poked their heads from the sunroof once they were inside. The car throttled and drove off in a noisy burst, the gold ring on the roof jiggling back and forth while they waved.

The woman from earlier with the baby stood in the gutter, one hand in the air, watching the empty street after they had disappeared around the corner.

Paul reached for the bialy, chewing long and slow on the stale bread slathered in butter.

She looked at him.

He lowered his eyes.

A man sat down next to Paul.

Paul fidgeted.

"Please, don't get up," the man said with a light accent,

one hand extended in the space between them.

Paul looked at the dusty edges of the man's black pants and his cracked shoes, his long black robe and the wooden cross hanging from his neck.

"Every wedding is beautiful," the man said, breaking the silence.

Yes," Paul said quickly, catching a glimpse of the young priest's wild hair, his giant beard, and eyes that seemed too pale blue for his face. They did not blink.

"Gorka?" Paul asked. "What does it mean?"

"Aha," the priest said through a little laugh. "Literally, bitter. But we say this after the wedding, so that when they kiss, they kill all bitterness."

Paul nodded.

"To make life sweet," the priest added.

Paul nodded vigorously.

They sat, watching the children playing hide-and-seek, as the champagne bottles emptied and new ones popped open. A breeze pushed the tops of the trees around. A fire siren gurgled in the distance.

"Do you have other questions?" the priest said.

"No," Paul said. "Ah, no Father."

"Father Alexander," the priest said.

"Paul." He extended his hand.

In a sloppy, awkward motion Paul tried to complete the handshake, but Father Alexander put Paul's fingers together, then rested one of his on top of them. He pushed down once and then pulled his hand away.

"Bless you," Father Alexander said.

Paul smiled at him, without realizing it.

Father Alexander closed his eyes dramatically.

"Come—visit me," he said, opening them.

Paul made a face as he looked at his watch.

"I have to go to work," Paul said.

Father Alexander pressed a business card into his hand.

"It is a lovely church," Paul said, not knowing what else to say.

"Cathedral," Father Alexander said. "It's a cathedral."

Paul nodded, making a face as he grabbed the empty coffee cup, smashing the brown paper bag inside it.

"Goodbye," the priest said.

"Dasvedanya," Paul said as the word came to him, turning and heading toward the park.

IV.

Paul changed into his uniform in the windowless room. The door opened and Hector came in. Paul nodded once, tying one of his shoes.

Hector's head hung forward, his chin on his chest. Paul tied his second shoe and heard Hector's breathing, a wet, slack sound in the quiet room.

"I'm gonna get a Coke," Paul announced. "You want one?"

Hector sighed, a small whine coming out of his mouth.

Paul stood up, tucking his shirt into his pants. Hector wiped his nose against the back of his hand.

"You got a tissue?" Hector mumbled.

Paul searched his pockets.

"Nope," Paul said. "Sorry."

"It's okay," Hector said, as tears dripped from his face onto a folding chair and made little bell sounds.

Paul picked an imaginary hair from his sleeve.

"What happened?" he asked.

Hector shook his head.

Paul stood with his hands on his hips, his chin jutting into the space between them. Hector hung his head between his legs and cried out, gasping for air.

Paul left, closing the door as quietly as he could.

Outside, he turned toward the edge of the park. Making his way through a late crowd of people, he found a hotdog cart and asked for two bottles of Coke.

"From the bottom," he told the scrawny man. "Cold ones."

The man nodded, silently taking his five and giving him back a dollar in quarters.

Paul headed back to the zoo where a handful of police officers were guiding people away.

"Nothing to see here," one said.

"Keep it moving," another said.

Paul watched the people mumbling among themselves, shaking their heads as they passed.

He approached one of the officers, a tall young man with shiny black hair.

"What happened? he asked, gesturing toward the badge embroidered to his shirt.

The officer made a face, then pointed toward the arch, and the mechanical clock with bronze animals that danced every thirty minutes.

"Guy was standing there, taking a picture of his wife and their kid," he said, unflinching.

Paul looked at an area that had been taped off, at the plastic barriers that stood in the middle of the sidewalk.

"Not a kid, a baby," the officer said. "Six months old or something."

A couple pushed past Paul, entering the park.

"The park is closed here," the officer said to them. "Enter at 72nd Street or 96th Street."

They went uptown.

"So the guy was gonna take a picture of them—his wife and his kid. Tree branch falls, kills the baby right there," he said, moving a hand across his face. "Mother's in the hospital.

Concussion.”

Paul nodded once.

“And if anybody asks?” Paul said.

“Technically it’s not the city. The tree is under the Wild—”
He broke off.

Paul watched a child kicking a ball and then his mother
screaming at him, chasing him out of the park.

“Reed!” the officer shouted.

A woman turned, a walkie-talkie loose in her hand.

“The Wild—” the officer said.

“The Wildlife Conservation Society,” the woman added,
then went back to listening.

“Shit,” Paul said. “That’s us.”

The officer cleared his throat.

“What’s done is done,” he said.

Paul nodded once, and went back to work.

PART IV.

I.

Anya took an enamel bowl from the cabinet and went outside. Past the sandpit and the water pump, she searched the ground for apples. They made bell-like thumps as she tossed them into the bowl. Brushing a dead wasp from one of them, she smoothed her hair back, ran a finger along her teeth, and pinched her cheeks as hard as she could.

She crossed the low stone wall and entered his backyard, her feet squashing weeds and dandelions.

He looked up at her, letting the stick and the hunting knife in his hands hang loose. He rested them on the ground and began to get up as she arrived.

"Sit. Sit," she said, standing over him, her hands on her hips.

He squinted up at her, the bright blue sky turning her long hair into a messy halo. She extended the bowl of apples.

"They are a bit sour," she said. "But juicy."

He nodded a thanks to her.

Anya polished one against her long blue dress and took a giant bite. She showed him its inside, juice dripping from her fingers.

He nodded, smiling anxiously.

"Do you have a cigarette?" she asked, suddenly.

He reached into his shirt pocket and tapped the pack until one poked out. She leaned into him, plucking it out with her wet fingers. He lit it for her, shaking the match and tossing it onto the pile of ashes next to them.

"Thanks," she said, sucking hard, her cheeks going hollow.

He fished one of the apples out of the bowl.

"So, you got cold?" she said, pointing her chin toward the burnt pile of garbage.

"Something like that," he said.

"Do you—" she began and stopped as he turned quickly, looking toward her little house.

Pasha stood on the grass in his underwear, a stuffed rabbit hanging from one hand. He rubbed his eyes.

"Mama," he cried softly, then louder. "Mamaaaaaah."

She took a heavy drag, then let it out slowly, handing the cigarette back to him.

"I'm here," she said.

Pasha made his way to them, wiping the sleep from his eyes and crawling across the low stone wall with awkward movements. The man stood up. He was tall and thin, his pants a little big. His belt was cinched tight to keep them up.

Pasha went straight to the burnt garbage, and the remains of a small radio.

"Hello," the man said.

Pasha looked up at him, making a face.

"Those are my apples," the boy said.

"Pasha," Anya said. "They are a gift for our new neighbor."

The man cleared his throat.

"Igor Kirilovich Ibramov," he said, holding his hand out once again.

The boy held it hard and did not let go.

"Pavel," the boy said.

"Just Pavel?" Igor asked.

The boy nodded.

"What is your father's name?" Igor asked.

The boy shrugged his shoulders and pulled his hand away.

"He's a cosmonaut," Pavel said, his voice sad and angry.

"You must be hungry," Anya said, pushing the boy back toward their house. Pasha dropped the stuffed animal and she snatched it from the ground, grabbing both of them up in her arms.

II.

It rained all day, the sun hovering at the edge of a shelf of low clouds, then giving way to an early moon. Anya lined up the dirty cups and dishes on the little table in the backyard thinking they would get clean all by themselves. She watched them fill, then overflow, the soft drops making giant bubbles on the water's surface. She remembered being a child, and how someone told her this kind of rain brought mushrooms.

Pasha was angry, stomping around in his underwear, banging on the windows and singing a made-up song as loud as he could, over and over.

After it grew dark, Anya retreated to the front room with the kerosene lamp and a mystery book. Curling her feet under herself, she fell asleep this way, half-dressed.

III.

The earth was soft and turned easily under the spade. Anya made crude rows, sketching out a messy rectangle. The mud smeared under her fingernails and in her hair. She worked barefoot as the sun walked tall above the trees.

Bees were buzzing.

A train whistle blew in the distance.

The smell of dead grass and wet earth filled her lungs. She pumped water and drank from the spout, letting it splash across her face and neck.

Pasha lined up tiny plastic soldiers in his sandpit, an elaborate war taking shape.

Anya went inside.

Searching the back of a closet, she found the cool clay jug. Pulling it out, she rested for a moment. Uncorking it, she slugged once, the harsh honey-perfumed liquor burning her throat. She sat back, wiping the sweat from her forehead, smelling the horselike stink of her armpits.

She slugged again and put the bottle back.

The box of seed packets was there.

Outside, she scattered the seeds then pressed them down with her toes. Anya planted cucumbers and cabbage, carrots and turnips.

"Pasha," she said.

He stayed on his stomach, whispering to a toy soldier.

"Pasha, my feet are dirty. Can you get the old potatoes?" she said. "The ones that are growing arms and legs."

He shook his head no.

Her empty stomach turned on the samogon. She grew hot and a little dizzy. Anya sat on the ground, wiping her dirty hands across the tall grass.

Pasha looked at her for a moment, his eyes big.

"The old potatoes in the kitchen," she said. "Please bring them."

"Landmines," he whispered to a different toy soldier. "Must be careful of landmines."

All at once, Anya lurched to her feet and tossed the water from the bowls and cups on her legs then crossed the grass and into the kitchen.

The drawer stuck.

She rattled it from side to side until it opened. It was empty, just a few of Pasha's peach pits rattling around the bottom.

"Pasha!" she yelled, her hands shaking as she went back to him.

"Where are the old potatoes?" she asked.

He sang his made-up song, quietly.

"What did you do with them!" she shouted.

His shoulders shrank together. The small of his back

pressed his stomach against the sandpit.

She kicked him once with her bare foot.

He shrunk away from her.

"Where?" she shouted.

He curled into a ball, hugging his knees to his chest.

She clapped her hands together, next to his ear. He dug his chin into his shirt.

Anya smacked the back of his head.

She yanked on his long, messy hair.

A few strands came off in her hand as he slumped to the ground.

"Where?" she said, her teeth set against each other.

Pasha shook his head no.

She yanked his arm and dragged him into the house.

IV.

Pasha waited until she fell asleep, then went quietly. A full moon sat fat above the chimney of Igor's house. He dug his hands into the sandpit. Shoveling as hard as he could, eventually he found six of the old potatoes, soft and shriveled, the white sprouts rubbery between his fingertips.

He found the spade where she had left it and dug six holes.

Pasha pressed them deep, covering them with handfuls of the dark earth.

He went to the dishes on the table and stacked them inside each other, shivering once in the cool air.

Crossing into Igor's backyard, he retrieved the burnt radio from the pile.

One of the knobs still worked.

He pressed it hard to his ear, then whispered inside it.

"Space control," he said, waiting on a reply. "This is space control."

Lightning broke, silent and bright. Pasha's eyes grew large. Thunder coughed softly, then louder.

The wind seemed to blow backward. He pressed the radio hard against his cheek.

It started to rain again.

PART V.

I.

A broad-shouldered priest sang with a deep voice as an incense burner swung from one of his hands, thickening the air with a smell like burning wildflowers. The great space was empty of chairs and benches, just the plain wood floor and a dark red carpet dividing the place. A cluster of people turned toward him, taking miniature steps as he circled them, always keeping their faces toward the incense and his voice, crossing and re-crossing themselves.

Paul stood among them, turning with their shuffling steps, his hands limp at his sides, his face lowered as he watched from the corners of his eyes. The priest sang long and loud, with giant lips poking from his massive face, the ancient Russian tumbling into the silence with no organ or choir to support him. The singing became a sort of crying, Paul guessed as the words turned desperate. A question without an answer, he thought.

A round little man with wild curly hair bumped up against him.

"Sorry," he said.

Paul nodded once, his eyes on the floor.

A shiver moved through him and Paul sneezed violently.

"Budzdarov," people said in random whispers.

The little man motioned to Paul to cross himself, showing him slowly so he could copy him.

"Just observing," Paul said under his breath.

The little man screwed his face around.

"Father Alexander invited me," Paul said. "Just to watch."

"Aha," the little man whispered, one of his hands jumping into the air and moving back slowly. "First time?"

"Yes," Paul said, staring at the priest with the incense as he made his way back to a wall that showed saints and angels, old men, and young mothers holding babies in their arms. A room could be seen beyond an archway, past painted doors. A soft, warm light grew there as Father Alexander emerged, now in a white robe with gold trim.

Paul stood as everyone did, his legs growing tired. Shifting his weight from one foot to the other, his hands in front and then behind, he listened. The words were impossible to recognize, even simple particles that he knew. He began to imagine what was being said, maybe some request or wish. Forgetting the stiffness in his legs, his thoughts wandered along the walls, following angels and clouds until his head tilted all the way back. The bright circle of the dome in the ceiling calmed him.

The speaking ended.

A hand rested against his shoulder.

"Hungry?" the little man asked him.

Paul shrugged his shoulders and nodded yes.

"Eli," the little man said, holding his hand out.

"Paul," he replied, shaking it once.

People were shoving past them.

"This way," Eli said, pointing toward a door to one side of the great room.

Leading him down a dark stairway and through a windowless corridor, Eli paused for a moment.

"Smell that," he said, breathing in through his nose and letting the air out with a flourish.

Paul saw a long window looking onto a large kitchen. Old women stirred and chopped as young ones carried giant pots in a choreographed silence. A man with a mustache and a white suit stood in front of them. He spoke to the women in aggressive bursts, waving his hands with a mixture of direction and disappointment.

"That's Volodia," Eli whispered to Paul. "He runs the kitchen."

"But he doesn't cook?" Paul asked.

Eli shook his head no.

"What is he saying?" Paul asked.

"My Russian is not so good. But I think it's something about the soup. I think they made too much," Eli said. "Or, too little."

A young woman produced a container of orange juice and began pouring it into plastic cups that Volodia lined up across the counter.

Eli made a face and shrugged his shoulders, laughing a little. The line of people moved forward. Eli poked his head into the kitchen, peering at different aluminum trays.

"Is there a menu or something?" Paul asked.

Eli laughed again.

"Two soups, two cutlets and, what is that, *kartofel* puree?" Eli said in a loud voice to an old woman.

She nodded and filled their plates.

"Ah, *svekolnik,*" Eli said, his nose drifting across the steaming bowl of soup.

 she said.

"Even better!" Eli announced as they balanced their trays and entered a room jammed with low tables. They sat in a corner. Paul paused, waiting for Eli to eat first.

"Don't wait," Eli said to him. "The priests will say something later, and we pay when we leave."

Paul's spoon swooped into the bowl.

"What do you think?" Eli asked.

"Pretty good," Paul said.

"I mean about this place," Eli continued.

"Seems nice," Paul replied.

"It's very humble," Eli said after slurping a few spoonfuls. "I mean, all Russian churches are humble. You know, no one is better than anybody. We all stink. The priests are just regular guys."

Paul nodded his head as he listened.

"Okay, they have a special table, but we all eat the same food," Eli said, waving his hand toward the priests as they entered.

Father Alexander and the others made their way through the room as people stood up. Clasping their hands together, the priests touched them once and then moved on. Young women brought plates to a long table in front of some stained-glass windows. Everyone sat back down.

Eli pulled his wallet out and began searching through it. Paul wiped his lips, licking the salty, fatty broth from the corner of his mouth, buzzing from the taste of hot pepper. Eli flapped a photograph of two girls around.

"My daughters," he said.

Paul looked at their round faces, searching for a hint of Eli in them.

"They don't live here," Eli said.

"They have your eyes," Paul said, taking a piece of black bread from a bowl on the table.

"Divorced," Eli said. "They live in Arizona but I go to see them when I can."

"That's something," Paul said.

"It's pretty nuts," Eli replied, his voice straining above the noise in the room. "I was born a Jew, met a Russian girl and converted."

Eli grabbed at a piece of the bread, sniffing it once before shoving some into his mouth.

"Then she left me," he continued, sliding the photograph back into his wallet and putting it away.

"It happens," Paul said, after a moment.

"You too?" Eli asked him.

"Long time ago," Paul replied. "We got married, but not in a church, just at city hall. She wasn't religious or anything."

"Every Russian believes in something. Maybe religion, maybe money, maybe revenge," Eli said. "But, they're believers."

"Maybe," Paul said.

"Kids?" Eli asked him.

"No," Paul said, shaking his head.

"Big difference," Eli replied.

They ate in silence after this. Paul studied the room, looking at faces, at who sat with whom. He did not see the mother with the baby.

Father Alexander returned to the long table and said a brief prayer. Everyone lurched to their feet, crossing and re-crossing themselves. He finished, and made his way to them. Paul began to stand, after having just sat down again.

"It's okay," Father Alexander said in a low, soft voice.

Paul nodded, resting the plastic spoon on a tiny napkin.

"Please come to visit me," Father Alexander said, turning and acknowledging Eli. "I want to hear your what you think of our home."

"I will," Paul said.

"This is the real church," Eli said, pointing at the empty soup bowl after he left. "This is where it all happens."

II.

Paul lathered his face and shaved, craning his neck to see himself in the steamy reflection. A deep blue sky dangled outside the tiny window that was half open. The sound of tiny balls thwacking against concrete from the handball court downstairs rose above the steady hum of traffic.

Brushing his teeth, he spit red into the sink. The mirror, now patched with sweat, showed his gums ragged and bloody.

The walls and ceiling smelled of fresh paint.

The bus was half empty, running along First Avenue. Paul got off at 86th Street, the black asphalt cooking in the midday sun. The new button-down shirt felt stiff at the cuffs and around his neck.

Taking the stairs that lead below the sidewalk, Paul pressed the bell for one long ring.

A moment later the door buzzed and he entered the hallway, dark and cool.

Father Alexander stood in front of his office door and took one of Paul's hands in both of his.

"Welcome," he said in a quiet voice, then opened the door.

Paul sat.

"Did you read the books?" Father Alexander asked him, as he arranged some papers.

"Yes," Paul said.

"And do you have any questions?" he asked him.

"No," Paul said, after a measured pause.

"Alright," Father Alexander said, looking directly at him. "We need to select a name."

Paul opened his mouth, then closed it.

"Normally, something like Pavel, or Petr would be correct," Father Alexander said. "But in your case, I think it is more wise to choose a name, a name that means something to you, with nothing to do with the name your parents gave you."

Paul nodded slowly.

Father Alexander cleared his throat.

"It must be a saint's name, right?" Paul asked.

"Yes," he said.

"Maybe a modern saint. One that is not so old?" Paul asked.

Father Alexander pressed his fingertips together and closed his eyes for some time.

"Silouan," he said. "A humble man. He could hardly read."

Paul shifted in the chair, thinking to cross his legs. There was nothing in the room. No sound. No movement, just the two of them breathing.

"Tikhon," Father Alexander said, opening his eyes. "A man who lived in difficult times, not so long ago. His name comes from *tikhe*—to be quiet."

Paul felt the corners of his mouth turning. He held his lips over his teeth, hiding them.

"Good," Father Alexander said, clapping his hands together. "Now, who will be your witnesses?"

Paul sighed.

"No one from your family?" he asked. "Maybe an aunt or an uncle?"

Paul shook his head no.

"I have not talked to any of them for a very long time," he said.

Father Alexander scratched his chin.

"Almost twenty years," Paul added.

"We will solve it," the Father said. "You will need to bring two white shirts. One you should already be wearing."

"Okay," Paul said.

There was a knock on the door.

"Come in," Father Alexander said.

A woman entered, her eyes lowered, the scarf around her head hiding her face. She moved to the priest's side and whispered in his ear. Paul looked away, then recognized the woman with the baby.

"Paul," Father Alexander said, standing up. "I have some urgent business. I will see you on Tuesday, at three o'clock."

"Thank you, Father," Paul said, dropping his head, then trying not to look back at her, wondering if she remembered him.

III.

Paul stood on the sidewalk downstairs from his apartment, blinking in the fierce afternoon sunlight. His stomach growled. Feeling for the bag on his shoulder, he imagined the new shirt inside it, still wrapped in cellophane from the store.

A very tall man ran down the middle of the street toward the cars that honked at him. A brown paper bag was clutched in his arms, his long hair flying violently around him.

"No!" he shouted at them. "I can't stop!"

Paul craned his neck and saw the man stop at the corner. He pulled kitchen tools from the bag. A spatula. A broken whisk. A knife.

He dropped them one at a time into the sewer.

Satisfied, the man stood and clapped his hands together, then put them on his hips.

"Okay!" he announced to an imaginary audience. "Show's over!"

"Joseph!" a woman called from the other end of the block. She ran, laboring her way down the sidewalk.

A taxicab roared around the corner and lurched to a stop in front of Paul's building.

"Hey!" Eli said, leaning over from the driver's seat.

Paul jumped a little.

A middle-aged woman sat on the passenger side. She smiled at him, and fanned herself with a piece of paper.

"This is Natasha," Eli announced, waving Paul to get in. "She is your mother today."

"Hi," Paul said, getting in.

"Beautiful day," Natasha said through her thick accent, grabbing his hand and patting it once.

IV.

"All of your sins are now erased," Father Alexander said to him, leaning forward.

Paul nodded once.

"You are only a child," he continued. "Innocent."

Water was dribbled across his forehead from a silver bowl.

The great room stood dark, the walls disappearing into black corners. Eli and Natasha behind him and to the side, with half-smiles on their faces as they nodded and bowed and crossed themselves.

Father Alexander had Paul roll each leg of his pants up to the knee. Kneeling, he painted myrrh on them, reciting a prayer.

"This will protect you," he whispered as he stood up, painting on the insides of Paul's wrists and his forehead.

The brush tickled, but Paul stood still. He wondered what the second shirt was for and if it was even for him.

Father Alexander opened a very old book, pressing his palms against the pages as he recited from memory in a low voice. Paul watched his closed eyes, the long curls of his beard, the deep lines of his forehead as he spoke.

"You can change the shirt now," he said, opening his eyes. "You must never wear the old one again. You may keep it, but never wear it."

"I'll throw it away," Paul whispered.

Father Alexander nodded once, a tiny smile on his lips. He moved to the corner of the room where the candles and icons were sold. Paul turned to look at Eli and Natasha. The little man gave a quick thumbs-up.

Paul found himself smiling.

The new shirt felt good on his arms, as he pressed the tails into his jeans.

Father Alexander returned with a folded piece of paper.

"This is a record of today," he said.

Paul nodded.

"Your name, your witnesses, and my name," he added, his finger running across each word. The Cyrillic was beautiful and odd, blue ballpoint swirls he half recognized.

"Which is Tikhon?" Paul asked.

Father Alexander's finger ran back to a short word with a backwards N and an X in it. He pressed a small wooden icon into his hands and a tiny silver cross that dangled from a red string.

Paul pulled it over his head and tucked it inside his shirt.

"*Pozdravlayu,*" Natasha said, jumping forward and grabbing his hands in hers.

"Congratulations," Eli announced softly. "She says big, big congratulations."

They stood together in a messy circle for a little while, saying nothing with happy crooked smiles on their faces.

"Bless you," Father Alexander said. "Every one of you."

He turned and left, disappearing behind the side door that led down to the basement.

Outside, the street was bright and warm on their faces. Paul walked slowly, closing his eyes and feeling the sun on his skin.

"Feel different?" Eli asked.

"Maybe," Paul said under his breath.

A red bird fluttered down from the trees to sit on the gate. Natasha's hand jumped to her mouth.

"What?" Eli asked.

Natasha shushed him.

Paul opened his eyes and looked at it.

The red bird turned in circles, then flew away.

"I never —" she said.

"What?" Eli asked her.

"It is very good," she said. "Very good."

Paul rested a hand on each of their shoulders.

PART VI.

I.

There was a light knock on the back door. Pasha looked up from the floor. Anya repositioned a fork on the table, her mouth twisting. She raised an eyebrow and tossed her head to the side. He saw three dishes set out.

The boy went to the back door and opened it.

"Good evening," Igor said, stepping inside.

Pasha shook Igor's large, flat palm.

"Quite the little man," Igor said, looking at Anya from the dark porch.

She raised her eyes slowly, leaning across the table, holding his gaze and saying nothing.

Anya did not blink.

Igor rubbed his feet on the mat and struggled into the room, ducking his head as it almost touched the ceiling. He placed a bag of candies and some black bread on the table.

"Everything is ready," Anya announced. "Pasha, wash your hands."

The boy ran to the backyard.

"Thank you for inviting me," Igor said after searching for the words. "I am a terrible cook."

"Don't assume I am much better," Anya said, bringing a bowl of boiled potatoes to the table. She rolled up her sleeves and peeled an onion, slicing off the brown parts then placing the rings on a plate.

Pasha came back inside and squeezed his nose between two fingers.

"Fooo," he said.

"Sit," she said.

Pasha pulled his chair out and rested his chin on the table. He began to whistle.

"Not in the house!" she snapped.

The boy jumped.

"You only whistle for a bad woman," Igor said, the words tumbling out.

Anya cleared her throat.

"Apologies," Igor whispered. "That is what my mother told us."

"What is a bad woman?" Pasha asked.

Anya ripped open the plastic container of pickled herring and placed pieces over the onion slices. Wiping her fingers on her apron, she smoothed the hair from her face with the back of her hand.

"Let's eat," she said quietly.

"But what is a bad woman?" Pasha asked. "A witch with spells?"

Igor sat up straight and looked at her.

"May I?" he asked.

She nodded.

"A bad woman is a woman that cannot love," he explained. "A woman that doesn't even know what love is."

Pasha rolled his eyes for a moment, then nodded once. He stabbed his fork into a potato and dragged it onto his plate.

"Well done," Anya whispered in a low voice as she leaned into his ear. "My mother would just tell him a man should only whistle if he wants to find a whore."

Igor flashed a satisfied grin.

"But she thinks all women are whores," she added.

Igor stuck his fork into the bowl and pulled a potato onto his plate.

"Do you have children?" she asked.

Igor shook his head no.

"My ex-wife," he began. "She couldn't."

"It happens," Anya said after a moment.

Igor held the plate of fish for her and she took a piece, dragging the raw onion through the oil after it.

"And what is your work?" she asked.

Igor paused after filling his plate. He pressed his hands to the table.

"It is not a job to talk about around children," he began.

Anya made a face, half-surprised.

"Mama," Pasha said.

She cut her fish carefully, packing the fork with all three items before she ate.

"Mama," Pasha whispered, leaning across the table.

She stared at him, chewing slowly.

Pasha threw up onto his plate, the insides of his stomach splattering across the fish and the potatoes. Anya's arm burst out, grabbing the bread. Pasha began to cry as long strings of mucus hung from his mouth. Igor stood up from the table, his hands held in the air.

"Get some water," she told him.

Igor loped into the darkness.

He saw the boy's silhouette clinging to her as she wiped his face with her apron. Igor came back inside, resting the bowl on the table.

"I should go," he said.

"No," Anya interrupted, smoothing the boy's hair and caressing his back.

Pasha let out a low moan.

"Can you boil some water?" she asked. "There are some eggs on the porch."

Igor shrugged his shoulders and went for them.

Thunder rolled in the distance far beyond the apple trees. Igor stood in the dark as the hairs on his arms danced in expectation.

He waited to see lightning flash, to see it paint the trees for a moment.

II.

Rain pattered against the windows. Anya pulled herself from the bed, twisting the boy's arm back on him.

She stood naked in the morning air, seeing his flushed cheeks and the bowl on the floor half-full of vomit.

She took it to the back porch and threw it into the grass, then left the bowl on the ground. The moist air felt cool and warm at the same time on her skin. Glancing through the windows, she stepped outside, raising her hands high in the air, washing her armpits with her fingers. Anya looked down at her pale skin, the hair on her legs, the scar across the red bulge of her stomach.

Back inside she sat at the kitchen table and peeled a cold egg in messy chunks. Anya salted it and ate it in two bites. Pasha made a sound, and she went to him, wiping her hands on her thighs. His arms reached out and she placed them on her chest, sitting on the edge of the bed as she guided him to find her. Once he'd had a few mouthfuls, she leaned back against the headboard and closed her eyes. His mouth pulled the milk softly from her, with no sound.

Pasha's face was hot against her.

She began to fall back to sleep.

A shadow passed the front window.

Anya opened her eyes just enough to make out the tall form, the size of the man's hunched shoulders. His fingers rested on the windowsill.

The rain stopped abruptly, and great blue splotches of sunlight filled the room. She knew he could see her naked, the brown birthmark on her hip, the fat pink nipples crusted with milk.

Igor's silhouette remained.

She watched through the slits of her eyes to see if he was still there.

Anya began to make small whining noises, her lips sagging

forward. She let a cry out as if she was dreaming. A line of drool oozed from her mouth, plopping on the boy's long hair.

She began to whimper, like a small dog locked inside a car.

All at once, her eyes opened wide and she stared into the bright light. The man's fingers did not leave the windowsill. Not blinking, she held him there, flipping her hair from her shoulders and sitting back. Lowering her eyes, she poked her chin into the air and ran a hand across her chest then let it rest on the bed.

Anya spoke to him but he could not hear her through the glass.

He raised one hand, palm upward as if to ask her what she was saying.

Anya motioned toward the kitchen jabbing her thumb in the air.

Igor repeated the gesture.

She drew the blanket off her feet and stood up, guiding Pasha to the middle of the bed.

Anya started toward the kitchen, wondering if he would already be standing in the doorway.

By the time she reached the table he was there. It was littered with eggshells and corners of black bread.

Anya pulled a chair in front of herself, hiding the long scar across her stomach.

Igor rested his hand on the edge of the door and leaned inside.

"Take your shoes off," she announced.

He kicked one off then struggled to untie the second one.

Anya turned at the corner of the table so her back faced him. She piled the dishes in the center of the plastic cloth. Spreading her feet apart, she took a step back and rested her hands on the edge.

"Don't look at me," she said.

"What?" he asked from the dark room, staring at two giant red pimples on her ass then giving his shoelace a final yank that broke it in his long fingers.

"Eyes down," Anya said through her teeth.

"Agreed," Igor answered as he tiptoed into the kitchen.

"Come on," she said, taking another step back and waving one of her hands around between her legs. She pressed her red pimples into the air between them.

"Agreed, again," Igor said, unbuckling his pants and spitting on his hands.

Anya stared at a trail of vomit on the floor in the bedroom that had missed the bowl. She spit on one hand and fingered herself quickly.

He lurched into her. She felt his knees against the backs of her legs.

Igor cleared his throat quietly.

"Do I look old?" she asked after a moment.

"No, no," he blurted.

"Don't lie to me," she snapped, wiggling around once.

"Not—not at all," Igor said, stuttering and groaning.

There was no sound except for the creaking table.

"Would you like to breathe with me?" Igor whispered.

"What?" she asked.

"I read about it," he said. "Now, in—"

Anya breathed in.

Igor grabbed at her hipbones.

"Now, out," he said, pulling her away.

Anya rested on her elbows.

"Don't get creative," she mumbled. "You can't learn to fuck from a magazine."

Igor stood motionless for a few breaths then pressed back into her.

Anya cleared her throat once.

Igor reached for one of her breasts and she swatted his hand away.

"What kind of work do you do?" she whispered, craning her neck around.

"Ah," Igor replied. "I did not want to say around the boy."

"So?" she asked as she looked back at the floor and twitched twice.

"The earlier you get in," he said. "The earlier you get out."

She turned the expression over in her thoughts, trying to remember where she had heard it.

"Show me your tattoos," she said after a few thumps.

"I have none," he said. "I was not a prisoner."

"Aha," she whispered.

"I was a guard," he explained.

She glanced back at him, seeing there were no marks on his slack white chest.

"Do you like it like this?" he asked her.

"There are no former policemen," she said with a small, cruel laugh.

Igor went faster, his fingers digging into her hips. He made small, sad noises and stared at the two red pimples.

"Don't finish inside me," she warned.

"Okay," he grunted.

Pasha stood in the doorway, watching them.

The boy pressed his lips together and began to whistle.

They did not notice him.

Pasha watched Igor's red face, eyes rolling wildly at the ceiling. He saw the stack of dishes wiggling in tiny jumps. Anya looked angry.

Pasha whistled louder.

Anya howled at the boy, her breasts swinging, her mouth a red blur.

Igor grabbed his pants and ran outside.

Anya screamed and screamed, her eyes closed now, her hands thrashing the air.

PART VII.

I.

Paul shoved his hand deep in the kitchen cabinet, his fingers feeling for a new bag of coffee. He pulled it out, holding nothing. Cracking open the bottom door, he looked quickly past a pile of old envelopes and the rumpled phone book. Wiping the sand from his eyes, he took the loose papers from the kitchen table and went to stand in front of the bedroom window.

Looking out for a moment at the morning sky, the black glistening fire escape, and the old bricks, he read from one of the dog-eared pages.

"Oh Christ our God," he whispered while crossing himself. "Who at this hour didst stretch out thy loving arms upon the Cross that all men might be gathered unto thee, help us and save us who cry out unto thee, Glory to thee, O Lord."

A maple seed spun and glanced off the fire escape then rested on the windowsill.

"Through the prayers of our holy Fathers, Lord Jesus Christ our God, have mercy upon us and save us," Paul read, now a little louder. "Amen."

He crossed himself and folded the papers closed.

Yawning and stretching, Paul thought to go back to bed, but went to the bathroom instead.

A yellow Post-it reading "wet" was stuck to the door where Misha had left it. Paul stood in the tiny space, smelling the fresh paint, the smooth walls, the new ceiling shining above him.

He showered, the steam reflecting his face soft in the tiny mirror.

"Fuck," he announced.

Going back to the pile of papers on the bedroom windowsill

he saw that the midday papers were on top. He thumbed to the morning prayers and scanned them.

"Fuck," he said under his breath.

Paul went back to the shower.

"Coffee, Chief?" the man behind the counter asked as Paul hovered in the doorway.

Paul nodded yes.

"And two scrambled with bacon on a roll," he added.

"Okay, Chief," the man said, repeating the order to the young Mexican at the grill.

"Salt, pepper, ketchup?" the boy asked.

"Salt, pepper," Paul said, loud enough for him to hear it.

Paul listened to the eggs cracking. The man behind the counter snapped a lid onto a blue paper cup and slid it toward him.

Paul sat on the front steps taking a giant bite of the sandwich, getting some of the paper with it. A skinny woman in ripped jeans stopped and sat on the sidewalk near him. Paul nudged his breakfast closer to him. She coughed once, leaned sideways and sent two fingers in the air, then tapped them against her mouth. She looked at him.

"Don't smoke," Paul said.

She nodded.

Her eyes were red, and a line of white puss oozed from one of them.

The woman rocked from one foot to the other, clenching her teeth.

"That was some fucking party," she said in a loud voice. "We had a good time, hunh?"

Paul put the sandwich on his knees and shrugged his shoulders.

"I am the fucking Queen of New York," she continued, her hands striking crude ballet poses in the air. "Am I right?"

Paul nodded, feeling a stray bit of bacon sliding around his mouth. The woman coughed again, her body thrashing around, her shoulders curving in.

The woman walked away, and stood at the corner watching the traffic light. She turned and stalked back to him.

"You know—" she began, then stopped.

Paul sipped from his coffee.

"What?" he asked.

"I had an idea a long time ago. A place for families. A place for kids. You know—rides and shit," she told him.

"Like Coney Island?" he asked.

She shook her head no.

"No, big. Real fucking big. With a castle. With princes and princesses. Kings. Queens. Horses," she said, standing up.

Paul pulled his feet up to himself.

"They stole fucking Disneyland from me!" she yelled at a taxi as it passed. "It was all my fucking idea!"

Paul scratched his head and looked at his shoes.

The woman stood on the edge of the sidewalk, her shadow drawing across the concrete.

"It was my only good dream," she said under her breath.

"It was a great idea," Paul answered.

Her teeth bared.

Her shoulders slumped. She picked at something inside her nose for a moment.

"I'm sorry they took it from you," Paul said, looking up at her silhouette.

"People need to know," she mumbled, and walked off.

Paul looked at the perfect shape of the single bite in the sandwich and wrapped it back up.

The subway smelled of detergent and the cool pocket of air that came before the train. Paul got out at 103rd Street and walked west past Park Avenue to the Conservatory Gardens. A string of limousines and horse carriages lined the gutter. He stood outside the main entrance, watching the spray of the main fountain turning into a wet cloud. People were coming and going, dressed in suits and shiny dresses, all smiles and big hellos.

He walked through the park, smelling the fresh-cut grass, watching squirrels chase each other across tree limbs.

II.

The service had almost started. He let his eyes adjust to the dark room, staying close to the giant doors. A line of people formed on the left edge of the space and he could see Father Alexander standing at the front with a sort of easel and an icon that rested on it.

He stepped into the line and the man in front of him turned for a moment, nodding his head.

Paul nodded quickly.

The man turned his head again.

"Ah, hello," he whispered.

Paul tried to smile a little.

"You prepared?" the man asked.

Paul wrinkled his forehead.

"You did not eat today, right?" the man whispered.

Paul nodded once, wondering if he would smell the egg sandwich on his breath if he said anything.

"Good," he whispered and turned forward, tucking his fingers together behind his back.

The priest with the black beard sang now, his thick red lips quivering in the dark air. Paul stared at him as people draped their heads forward, rocking back and forth on the balls of their feet, crossing and re-crossing themselves in random waves.

The line inched forward.

Father Alexander wore a gold robe, his hair rough around him, his glasses a bit crooked.

Paul imagined his shoes under the shiny fabric, cracked and old. He craned his neck around, looking at who was behind him in line, searching for the woman and the baby.

Folding his hands, he lowered his gaze and tried to ignore the gurgling sounds his stomach was making. The man in front of him approached Father Alexander, kissing his hands then kissing the icon after they spoke in low voices for some time. Father Alexander slid his glasses up the bridge of his nose, resting a hand on the man's elbow, guiding him to kiss the icon once more, then sent him to enter the throng of people.

Paul approached.

Father Alexander looked at him suddenly.

"You prepared?" he asked.

Paul nodded.

"And you did not eat today?" he asked.

"No, Father," Paul said.

"What will you confess today?" he asked after a moment.

Paul cleared his throat.

"I raised my voice to my wife in anger. We fought. We argued all of the time, terrible awful fights," Paul said, the words tumbling out of him.

Father Alexander rested a hand on one of his.

"Sometimes we threw things. I threw a glass, a plate," he mumbled. "She threw a knife at me once."

"I would tell you something," he said. "An expression from my childhood."

Paul looked into his bright, blue eyes, waiting.

"You are not the sugar," he said, measuring the words out.

Paul was confused.

"You are just a man," Father Alexander whispered to him, leaning right against his ear. "I am just a man. We are all sinners. You do not need to be so perfect, so sweet."

Paul chewed the insides of his cheeks for a moment. He thought of the bite from the sandwich and wished he had not.

"It is understood," he added, "that we are not angels."

"But what I did was wrong," Paul whispered back.

"This fighting was some time ago, yes?" Father Alexander asked.

"Many years ago," Paul said.

"And did you love her?" he asked.

"Yes," Paul said.

Father Alexander stood still for some time.

The room grew quiet.

Paul's thoughts skipped from argument to argument as he shifted his weight from one foot to the other.

"We thought we knew everything," Paul blurted out. "Actually, we were a couple of idiots."

"You do not catch Russian expressions so well, so I will quote from one of the books I gave you," Father Alexander said, half to himself. "Do you know it, the Song of Solomon?"

Paul shook his head.

Father Alexander stared at him.

The room grew dark around them.

"Nothing lasts in this world," he recited slowly. "Not even sorrow."

Paul let out a deep breath he did not realize he had been holding.

Father Alexander grabbed both of his hands, his eyes wide.

His breath smelled like mud.

"This is how the world was built," he said in a low voice. "From suffering."

Paul waited for him to say more, then leaned forward and crossed himself, finding the icon that he pressed his lips against. He made his way to the center of the room, rubbing against shoulders without looking back, and then stared up at the bright circle in the ceiling. Priests he did not know brought a small table and a giant bowl to the front of the room. The man who had stood in front of him in line guided him. His hand in the center of Paul's back, he brought him to hold a heavy metal cup that was offered.

People with children rushed forward, jostling to run the cup against their lips. Paul waited, awkward. The man rolled his eyes a little.

"Children are always first," he whispered. "They do not have to give confession."

The last child cried out, wine dribbling past his cheek and onto the floor as his arms waved in the air. It was the woman, with the same scarf around her hair. Paul stared at the baby, trying to find some resemblance.

"Your name," the man whispered in his ear. "You must tell them your name."

"Paul," he said quietly, as they offered the cup to him again.

One of the priests made a face.

"Your baptism name," the man said to him.

"Tikhon," Paul mumbled.

"Tikhon," the man said to the priests in a full voice.

They recited a short sentence that included the word *Tikhon*.

"Drink," one of them said.

Paul tossed the sweet wine to the back of his mouth as it turned on his tongue and danced down his throat. There were tiny rounds of bread to eat next. He took one, working on the dry pieces until he could swallow them. The man patted his shoulder, smiling at him.

"How do you feel?" he asked in a low voice.

"Dizzy," Paul said.

"The first time is always like this," he answered. "See you downstairs?"

Paul pressed through the crowd to lean against the cool

walls.

He stepped outside into the shadows of the leaves and headed for the park. A car honked at him as he crossed the street against a red light then slowed to let him pass.

He turned left once, passing the stone wall and made his way to the children's zoo.

He showed his badge at the ticket booth and let himself in, suddenly surrounded by children and mothers and fathers and grandparents. They were watching the tortoise turning in small circles and the ponies that craned their necks across the fence, looking for something to eat or just to have tiny hands feel the soft hair of their noses. The goats were noisy, jumping from rock to tree stump, kicking their front legs in the air.

A boy began to cry when he got close to him.

III.

The penguins shrieked and splashed in an endless series of dives. Paul wrapped his jacket into a ball and rested it on the floor. He closed his eyes, smelling the hot, foul fish they were fed, lost bits of chewing gum on the ground, and the church incense from that afternoon.

He imagined the perforated box that the priest swung, spreading smoke around the crowd as he circled them. Paul rolled onto his side, folding his hands under his cheeks as he found sleep.

A door cracked open and the hum of morning traffic filtered in. Paul rolled onto his back, seeing the ceiling, understanding where he was. The penguins had calmed down.

He rose quickly, tucking his jacket under his arm, and snuck out the back door.

A light rain pattered on the trees. He made his way to the office and saw his time card had been punched out already.

Changing back into his Sunday clothes, he thought to borrow a slicker from the closet and then decided not to.

Walking out into the wet street, his shirt sticking to his arms, he shoved his hands into his pockets.

Inside the bus, he took a window seat and looked down at the puddles and the umbrellas and the people going to work. Paul closed his eyes, feeling the cold air conditioning running along the back of his neck.

He shivered once, then sneezed.

"God bless you," an old voice said, after a moment.

He nodded without opening his eyes.

IV.

Paul left the lights off in the apartment, going to the refrigerator to check the near-empty shelves. There was a half-empty bottle of vodka in the door. He turned on the oven, kneeling on the floor with a lit match until the pilot light came on. He pulled a rumpled box of fish sticks from the freezer and arranged them on a scrap of aluminum foil that sat in the middle of the oven.

He pulled from the vodka, smacking his lips and rubbing his palms together.

A fire engine blasted once from the street below, and roared away.

A collection of empty boxes lay in a pile next to the

blue couch. Paul dragged them all together to the bedroom and began to fill them with the contents of the drawers and the clothing on the floor. He emptied the closet next, leaving nothing but a yellow sundress in the back under a clear plastic cover, and a navy uniform.

He turned the stove off and pulled the foil out quickly, dumping everything onto the kitchen table.

Paul ate standing up, munching on the fish sticks and washing every other bite down with a slug of the vodka. When it was all gone, he dragged the boxes into the elevator and took them out to the street.

The moment he left them, the woman with the infected eyes appeared. She grabbed them, ripping the tops off. Paul stood behind the front door, watching her examine his shirts and old jeans. She took a number of them, looking up and down the street as if she were being followed.

V.

Paul wandered the empty rooms then sat in silence at the kitchen table. His face turned up, forcing a smile.

He pulled the papers from the cabinet.

Reading softy to himself, his lips moved in a slow and steady rhythm.

Paul flipped to another page, and cleared his throat.

He began again in a deep, loud voice, stopping and looking up from the paper out the kitchen window.

"O Lord, deprive me not of thy heavenly good things. O Lord, deliver me from eternal torments. O Lord, if I have sinned in mind or thought, in word or deed, forgive me. O Lord, deliver me from all ignorance, forgetfulness, faint-heartedness, and stony insensibility. O Lord, deliver me from every temptation," he said.

Pigeons clumped on the rooftop of the next building and looked like they were fighting.

"O Lord, enlighten my heart which evil desire hath darkened. O Lord, as a man I have sinned, but do thou, as the compassionate God, have mercy on me, seeing the infirmity of my soul. O Lord, send thy grace to my aid, that I may glorify thy holy name. O Lord Jesus Christ, inscribe me thy servant in the Book of Life, and grant me a good end," he continued.

Paul stared at the floor for some time. He ran his finger along the page, looking for where he had left off.

"O Lord my God, even though I have done nothing good in thy sight, yet grant me by thy grace to make a good beginning. O Lord, sprinkle into my heart the dew of thy grace. O Lord of heaven and earth, remember me thy sinful servant, shameful and unclean, in thy kingdom," he said, then whispered, "Amen."

PART VIII.

I.

Pasha turned in bed, feeling for the radio on the tiny table next to him. His fingers found the knob and turned it, waiting for its soft click.

"Papa," he whispered. "I still don't feel good."

He imagined the broken plastic box was making sounds now, clicks and hums and fragments of voice.

"Papa, I can't hear you," he whispered. "I will try later, after the moon comes."

He rolled back onto his stomach, leaving his hand close to the radio.

"I don't like this neighbor," he added. "Igor Kirilovich."

Pasha coughed into the pillow, trying to be quiet.

"He smells like fish and he worked in a jail. Only bad people are there," Pasha said. "I know it from his face."

Anya came into the room, the angry slap of her bare feet. She pressed the back of her hand on his forehead and then his cheek.

"Just rest," she said to him.

He turned his back to her.

II.

Pasha held the sheets over his head with both hands, standing on the bed, making a bright white sky around him.

He slumped down on his back, letting the sheets drift down to cover him, imagining he was in a tiny spaceship on a solo mission passing through a nebula. Pasha could not decide the details of his trip, just that it was going to save the planet. He created an imaginary schedule for his father— brushing his teeth, doing zero gravity exercises and recording a daily report.

He would record messages for his son, explaining why he had to leave when he was just a baby and how the space mission was more than half-over, and that maybe in three years he would return to earth's orbit and splash down somewhere in the Pacific Ocean, or maybe the Atlantic. There was time to decide. A room full of men at mission control with computers and slide-rule calculators and notebooks full of equations would bring him home safely.

After the splashdown he would need to be decontaminated, as surely he would have been exposed to radioactivity and delta rays, gamma rays, and maybe even beta rays on his mission.

Pasha imagined his father had dark hair but blue eyes just like his. He imagined he had a long chin and a beauty mark on one cheek.

He ran his hands along the inside of the sheets, bringing them right up to his face. They were big now, because things grew faster on spaceships than on earth. They had almost doubled in size and could smash watermelons with the slightest squeeze.

The air in the room grew still. Pasha felt a quick shiver grow down his body as goose bumps ran along his arms. The curtains flipped into the room, then were sucked backward outside the little house.

Rain began to fall in fat drops against the dirty glass.

Pasha drew the sheet around his shoulders and wobbled into the kitchen. His mother stood at the back door, silhouetted against the apple orchard.

Thunder smacked once and a collection of crows flew from the trees. Pasha jumped, steadying himself against the edge of the table.

Anya did not flinch.

Pasha spied a pencil stub on a chair and grabbed it.

Thunder broke again and the sky grew darker. He pulled himself back to the bedroom, climbing onto the pillow and standing on it. He clicked the radio on and adjusted it to the right imaginary frequency. Pasha rested his cheek against the cool wall. Running his hands out, he saw how far they could reach.

"Course correction in progress," he whispered.

Pasha drew a circle on the wall with the tiny pencil and then a larger one next to it.

"Sun, Earth, Moon," he began.

Pasha made some little dots around them and stopped in concentration.

"Mars, Pluto," he added.

He drew two more circles and bit his lip.

Thunder broke again, this time softer in the distance.

Pasha drew a tiny spaceship close to the first circle and then a dotted line describing its path. He continued past the edge of the bed into an empty space.

"Three more years," he whispered, then curled back up under the sheet and closed his eyes tight.

III.

Her face hovered over his in the dim light. She stared at the pimples on his forehead, the slack edges of his mouth, the air chugging into him. Anya smoothed her dress and ran a finger across her teeth.

The bottle of samogon was pulled from the closet. It was light now, less than half left.

Anya opened the back door with slow, quiet movements and stepped into the grass. She moved quickly, straddling the stone wall and then, next to Igor's wooden chair, the latest burnt objects, black and blistered in the center of the firepit.

She knocked on his back door once, then again.

A train whistle blew in the distance.

Anya knocked once more.

There were movements inside.

Igor opened the door, his pale, thin frame glowing in the dark.

She raised the bottle up, waving it in the space between them.

He frowned for a moment, scratching the stubble on his chin.

She pouted and rolled her eyes.

He rested his hands on his hips.

Anya pushed past him and sat at the tiny table in the kitchen.

The countertops were littered with empty sardine cans and half-empty cups of tea with oily splotches on their surfaces.

Igor grabbed at a pack of cigarettes and lit one, moving to sit next to her.

She slid one from the pack, pulled his from his lips and used it to light hers. She coughed once, wiping some imaginary dot from the tip of her tongue. Anya rested the clay jug on the table with a thud.

She ran her hands across her face.

"So?" she said, abruptly.

Igor fished two shot glasses from the sink and wiped them clean with a rag. Just as he rested them on the table, she was already pouring into them.

Raising her glass, Anya's hand shook as some dribbled down her arm.

"To Pasha," Igor said after a moment.

Anya's face turned in on itself.

"No," she said. "To freedom."

The glasses touched and they stared at each other, tossing the alcohol back in one smooth movement, eyes closing at the same time.

Anya sucked on the cigarette and waved her hand in the air.

"Hurrah," she whispered.

Igor refilled them.

"I am——" he began.

Anya rested a finger on his mouth.

She shook her head.

Sucking on the cigarette, she closed her eyes and held the smoke inside her for as long as she could. Letting it out in a noisy rush, her eyes grew wide. She slapped her hands together.

The glasses were raised, elbows on the table now.

"Your turn," he said, forcing the edge of a smile onto his face.

She stared at the glasses, eyebrows twisted, her pulse racing along her neck.

"To my mother, the land," she mumbled.

"What?" he asked.

"To the motherland," Anya murmured.

"The motherland is calling!" he said, making a clownish salute and splashing samogon onto a saucer. They drank and Anya lowered her face to the tiny plate and licked it clean.

"Waste nothing," he whispered, still trying to be funny.

"No," she said, shoving a hand into his underwear. "Waste everything."

Igor jumped halfway to standing then slumped back in his chair. She worked quickly, pulling at him. With her free hand she poured one just for herself and drank it in two small gulps.

"Good morning," she said to him when he looked at her. Igor stretched a hand inside the neck of her dress.

She shook her head, then pressed it away.

"Close your eyes," she announced.

Igor stared at her.

She stopped and began to take her hand away. He grabbed her wrist, holding it there.

"Don't fucking look at me," she said.

Igor closed his eyes and let his arm hang against the back of her chair.

IV.

Pasha woke in silence and went to the kitchen. The table and counter were empty. Pulling the bread drawer open, he found nothing.

A bag of macaroni sat on a shelf and he pulled a chair to it, climbing up and grabbing a handful. Crunching on each one, he let them soften in his mouth until he could swallow them.

Pulling on his shoes, he leaned against the back door until it swung open.

A bowl of water sat next to the pump and he drank from it, picking dry bits of macaroni from his teeth and then swallowing them.

A motorcycle gurgled in the distance and then pulled onto some road close to him.

He imitated the rumbling sound, holding his arms out and

running in circles around the tiny backyard.

Pasha jumped from the tractor tire and disappeared into the trees.

V.

The apples on the ground were soft and brown under their skins. Pasha poked one with his toe, feeling them wobbling on the forest floor. He spit on them.

Crows gathered in a tree, squawking and flapping their wings in bursts. He tried to count them.

The sound of an old car approaching sent them back into the sky.

The car stopped.

Pasha shook one of the trees until a few apples fell with dull thumps. He grabbed one in each hand and then tucked more in the hook of his elbow.

"Grandma!" he shouted. "I'm coming! I'm coming!"

As he ran, one fell but he left it there.

Skipping into the backyard he smelled smoke. Igor stood over his firepit poking at some books and an old chair as the flames grew higher. He had no shirt on, just pants hanging from his hips.

Pasha stopped shouting as he stepped on one of Anya's arms.

She lay on the ground, her dress loose around her. A long line of snot and drool snaked across her cheek. Her eyes were closed, her skin cold and wet.

Her arm flinched under his shoe and curled under her back.

Pasha ran to the road, but no car was there.

"Grandma!" he called once, dragging the word out.

Pasha ran around the entire house once in a long circle, ending up in the backyard.

Igor watched over the low stone wall. A line of blood ran down the side of his face, starting from somewhere under his hair.

Pasha stepped back.

"I'll have one," Igor called out to him.

Pasha took another step back.

"Just one," Igor said, raising a hand out then wiping the blood caked on his face.

"These are family apples," Pasha said, his voice growing with the words as they tumbled out of him. "And you are not my father."

He stood, feet apart now.

"I eat dry food like a real astronaut, like my father," he said. "You were not a guard. I know you are lying. You were a prisoner."

Igor laughed once and looked at the blood on his hand, distracting himself.

"The little hero," he said, half under his breath.

Anya threw up into the grass.

She cried out as she twisted into a ball and emptied herself, then raised herself to sit up.

"Your father—" she began, and then threw up again.

"Your father lives in New York and he does not want you," Anya said.

Igor grabbed at Pasha's shoulders holding him in place.

Anya stood now, wobbling on the balls of her feet as she stumbled to them, her legs stiff, not bending at the knees.

"He did not want me," she said, her teeth clenched. "And he did not want you."

Anya fell, and her arms did not reach out to catch her. Her face slapped hard against dirt and stones that filled the ground by the well.

Pasha did not move, as Igor's hands rested on his shoulders. He could smell the vomit and bile on her as she began to stand up.

Anya stumbled forward, lunging at him, slapping at his face and arms. Pasha felt Igor pulling her off of him, her screaming and her body shaking in waves. He heard his own voice, as if it was someone else's, saying something about Venus and Mars, about recordings.

Igor's face hung down over his, drifting closer until their noses touched.

"Run," he said.

PART IX.

I.

Paul leaned against the rail, looking down at black water and the reflection of the bridge. He thought he saw his face. His head spinning, he threw up the fish sticks onto his shoes and the crumbling sidewalk. His stomach twisting, he threw up until nothing but air and sour burps came from inside him.

A sunburned man emerged from the shadows, carrying some fishing poles. He passed him, saying nothing, navigating around the mess on the ground between them.

Paul stepped out of his shoes and wiped them on the wet grass. He pulled his socks off and used them to wipe his face, then threw them as hard as he could into the water. Poking a finger in each shoe, he carried them barefoot and began to make his way uptown.

The streets were empty as the occasional taxi roared through the silence, scraping around corners, suspension squealing. He could smell fresh bread on Mott Street, sweet and warm, but it made him feel sick. He turned East to Bowery.

The sun was edging the water towers.

His feet felt the sharp prickle of the sidewalk.

Paul stood in front of a hardware store, resting his hands on the gate. A sign in the door said they opened at eight.

He saw a man in a janitor's uniform walking towards him.

"Excuse me," Paul said in a quiet voice once he grew close.

The man stopped.

"What time is it?" Paul asked.

"About five," the man said, not looking at his watch.

Paul leaned against a fire hydrant and pulled his shoes on.

"There's a 24-hour place on 23rd," the man said. "Vercesi's."

Paul looked up at him as a shoelace broke off in his hand.

"23rd and Lex." The man said over his shoulder as he walked away.

II.

Paul paced up and down the narrow aisles, talking quietly to himself. He counted on his fingers, squinting his eyes in thought, examining wood screws and sandpaper.

A man approached with a shopping basket.

"Do you need one of these?" he asked.

"Yes!" Paul announced, grabbing it.

The man stared at him, hiked up his jeans, then cleared his throat.

"Do you need something specific?" he asked, his words measured.

Paul smiled at him, standing perfectly still.

"Magnets," he said. "Let's start with magnets."

"For what?" the man said, looking once at the front counter.

"Cabinets," Paul said. "You know, so they stay closed."

The man turned, gesturing to the end of the next aisle.

"All along the second shelf," he said.

Paul studied the tiny plastic packages and put a collection of them in the basket.

"And a paint scraper," he said.

The man pointed toward the next room.

III.

Paul rested the bags on the kitchen table. First, he plugged the charger in for the cordless drill. Next, he pulled all of the windows shut and began scraping the old paint from them. It danced in giant flakes across his arms and onto the windowsills.

Stretches of bare wood were exposed, pale and pockmarked. The apartment began to smell like old books. Paul worked without pausing, switching the scraper into his left hand when he got cramps.

The sun reached its fingers into the rooms, catching the dust in the air as it danced in slow-motion. Paul swept everything into the plastic bags the tools and hardware came in, tying them into parcels and lining them up next to the front door.

Staring at the can of primer, he bit his lip.

"Fuck," he said to himself, then rifled into the kitchen drawers until he found an old butter knife that he pried the can open with.

Paul shook the brush over the kitchen table, whacking it against his palms as loose hairs fell out. The primer smelled like gasoline.

He painted the bare wood quickly, wiping his overruns on the glass away with his fingers. Sweat was pouring down his cheeks, dust caked in the corners of his mouth. Finishing the first coat, he washed the brush in the bathroom sink and left it there.

Showered, his stomach empty, Paul walked north on Second Avenue. He closed his eyes at the corner, waiting for the light to change, and imagined the soft click of the cabinets with the fresh magnets in them. His found his hands leaping to his face, wiping a quiet satisfaction from his cheeks.

Turning onto Tenth Street, Paul thought of the first letter he had sent to her. He marveled at the odd fortune of their meeting and the color of her eyes. He sat at work staring at the penguins, wondering if she would find a description of them interesting, then wrote about the sea lions instead.

The post office was open now, and an instinct brought him to the door, to go inside and see if somehow there was a new letter for him, held at the registered mail desk. His hand rested on the handle, and a postwoman made a face at him from behind the glass, asking if he was coming in or not. He shook his head no and she pushed her way past him.

"Gonna be a long day," she mumbled to herself, stepping into the bright sun.

He thought of the letters she wrote to him, each more brief than the last. At first, she admitted her loneliness, then the suffocating shadow of her mother, then stories of being stalked by a strange man and how she ran toward her apartment, keys in hand every time she came home. Paul never knew how to reply beyond bland words of support. Her letters grew further apart. She accused him of being a dream, a fabrication of her imagination to fight her fears, to fulfill her needs.

He called her sometimes, in the middle of the night from one of the phones at work. Their voices rang hollow, shy. He listened to her breathing when they could not think of what to say. He told her not to worry.

"My prince," she always said when their conversations had come to a close. "My prince on a white horse."

A dog barked, lunging against its leash, and Paul stepped from the post office door.

"Sorry!" a young woman said, yanking the leash and pulling the dog to her side.

Paul blushed, shoving his hands in his pockets.

The dog lunged again, teeth bared.

"Buddy!" the girl shouted, yanking hard as the dog spun in circles and made choking noises on the bright sidewalk.

Paul walked on the east edge of Union Square Park. The green market was working today. There were tables full of foxgloves and tiger lilies, of irises and late cherry blossoms.

He bought a small bouquet of white flowers, not sure what they were called, their stems wet and cool in his hands.

IV.

A police car sat half on the curb next to the side entrance of the cathedral. Paul stood just inside, listening to voices coming down the hallway, smelling ammonia and incense mixing with the light, fresh smell of the flowers in his hand. He rested against the wall, cool against his sweaty back.

Volodia turned the corner, a cardboard box in his hands.

"Ah," he said, stopping in the doorway. "You can help, yes?"

Paul stood for a moment, then reached his hands out to take the box.

"No, back there," Volodia said, tossing his head to the side.

Paul passed him, making his way to Father Alexander's office and the kitchen.

The door stood half-open and he could see a policewoman taking notes in a small book. The door swung open and Eli stepped on Paul's foot, another cardboard box in his hands.

"Oh, hello," he said as he handed the box to him.

Paul rested the flowers on a chair.

Back in the hallway, he squeezed past Volodia.

"Back seat," he said. "Put in back seat."

Paul rested the box on the hood of the police car and opened the back door. It smelled of hot vinyl and coffee.

"Where is Father Alexander?" Paul asked Eli when he took the next one from him.

"Not now," Eli whispered under his breath. He stared at Paul, not giving him the box until he felt his hands had taken the full weight of it. "Later."

The work went quickly. Paul enjoyed the moment when he returned to the cool darkness from outside and the breeze that ran through the hallways.

They stood in Father Alexander's office after the last box had gone to the car.

"I think I go," Volodia said to them as he waved a hand toward the street. "Go with them."

Eli twisted his mouth around.

"No," he said. "I can do that."

Volodia stared at him, then smacked his hands together trying to wipe the dust from them. Paul folded his arms across his chest, standing by the chair he had sat in so many times, looking at the old clock on the wall and the giant desk that somehow looked smaller now.

"Elena is sick," Eli said. "How are you going to feed everyone today?"

"I am not cook," Volodia said.

Eli nodded, letting out a slow breath.

"I can cook," Paul said in a small voice.

They looked at him.

"I cooked in the navy," he said a little louder.

"What can you cook?" Volodia asked.

"You know, meat, soup, rice," Paul said. "Macaroni."

The policewoman hovered in the doorway.

"Two minutes," Volodia said, looking at her quickly.

She nodded once as she snapped her pen closed and went toward the street.

He held his hand out in the air.

"Come," Volodia said and motioned for both of them to follow him.

The kitchen was bright, the giant pots hanging on hooks above the six-burner stove. A pair of brushed steel tables sat in the center of the room.

Volodia swung the double doors of the refrigerator open.

"Look," he said, pulling Paul to them.

He studied the collection of shopping bags, the green tips of vegetables poking from some of them.

"Look!" Volodia said again, yanking one of them open.

Eli took a giant soup pot down from a shelf and rested it on the stove. He toyed with the knobs until he found one that lit, and moved the pot to a different burner.

"Should I put some water?" Eli asked.

Paul chewed the inside of his cheeks, resting his hands on the empty tables, then spying a box of onions under them.

"No," Paul said. "Peel onions."

Eli turned the burner off and pulled the box of onions to the table.

"Wash your hands first," Paul said. "We all have to wash our hands."

Volodia stared at him, then smiled.

"Eli, you go," he said. "I stay."

Paul stood next to Eli at the giant metal sink and washed his hands.

"I'll explain when I get back," Eli said in a low voice, then left the room waving his hands around to dry them.

Volodia held a bag up in the air.

"Chicken," he announced, then banged it against the table showing it was frozen.

"Soup, or with rice?" Paul asked.

"You chef today," Volodia said.

Paul fingered through the bags and packages on the shelves. In the bottom of one he found a five-pound bag of rice.

"For how many people?" he asked.

Volodia scratched his nose.

"Maybe thirty today," he said. "Not like Sunday."

Paul poured half of the bag into the big pot on the stove.

"And hot summer now," Volodia added. "People not so hungry."

"Better too much than too little," Paul said as he pulled a knife from the drying rack next to the sink.

People filtered into the kitchen. Two young women arrived with bags of tomatoes and cucumbers that they washed and sliced over large metal bowls with tiny knives. Paul kept an eye on the flame under the big pot, making sure the bottom did not burn.

Cups were pulled from the closets.

A row of eight plates were lined up at one edge of the table. Volodia stood over them, mumbling to himself. He removed one of the plates.

Paul looked at him at the same time.

"For the priest table," Volodia explained. "Today, seven."

A bell rang upstairs.

Knives were placed carefully on the cutting boards.

Everyone in the kitchen stopped and turned to a corner of the room, looking up at an icon on a triangular shelf. Crossing themselves, moving their hands in loose rhythm, they repeated the words under their breath.

Paul followed along, thinking about the rice and wondering if it was done yet.

An old woman came into the room, heading straight to the back as she pulled a vase from a shelf. She filled it with water and arranged the flowers that Paul had left on the chair in the hallway. He thought about saying something, but watched her instead, wondering if she would take credit for buying them, but she said nothing.

She wiped her hands on a towel, said something under her breath, and then brought them to the dining room.

The chicken and rice was spooned into plastic bowls. Faces loomed in the window that opened onto the hallway. Volodia pulled Paul's shoulder and led him to the back of the kitchen.

"Let woman work," he said. "You do good job."

Paul's hand leapt to his chin as he smiled shyly.

"Very great chef!" Volodia said in a big voice.

Paul cleared his throat.

"Where is Father Alexander?" Paul asked.

Volodia held a hand out to him.

"And why the police?" Paul continued. "Was something stolen?"

Volodia flicked his head to the right and went to a back room. He motioned for Paul to follow him.

A heavy door squeaked on its hinges and opened onto a tiny dark alley, walled in by three other buildings. Paul looked up and saw a piece of sky above the cathedral.

An empty can of peas sat on a ledge, half-full of ashes and crumpled cigarettes. The sound of traffic ricocheted around them in the narrow space. Paul had to stand sideways to make his way.

Volodia lit a cigarette and held the smoke inside. He gestured to Paul, offering him one. Paul shook his head no and Volodia breathed out.

"Thanks you again, Paul," Volodia said at one point, dabbing at the tip of his tongue for some spot. "Good man."

Paul scratched the back of his head, suddenly unsure what to do with his hands.

"Father—" he began.

"Father Alexander piece of shit," Volodia said suddenly, swerving and looking up at the back of the stained-glass windows of the cathedral. *"Gospodi."*

He crossed himself, bent his head to his chest and recited a short prayer.

Paul looked directly into his eyes as he finished.

"He steals money, they think," Volodia said. "And he make girl with baby. This is true, truth."

Paul shivered once.

"And he also have wife in Kaluga," Volodia continued. "Nice young girl."

"So, this woman with the baby and no husband," Paul said. "The baby was Father Alexander's?"

Volodia rested a hand on Paul's elbow and nodded once.

"The pretty woman with the blue scarf," Paul added.

"Lubov," Volodia answered.

"That was her name?" Paul asked.

Volodia let out a giant laugh, then dragged hard on the cigarette.

"Lubov," he said, "is her name. Is also love."

Paul watched him tapping ash into the tin can on the ledge. A pigeon swooped down into the alleyway then arced back up toward the sky.

"All for love!" Volodia said in his loud voice, tilting back and talking to the sky.

The door cracked open. A woman gestured for them to come back inside.

The priest who had sung stood in the middle of the kitchen. He spoke quietly in Russian to the women around the table.

Volodia pressed the center of Paul's back until he stood in front of him.

"Father Kirill," Volodia whispered in Paul's ear.

They bowed their heads as Father Kirill blessed each of them, holding their hands in his, one at a time.

"*Spasiba,*" he said to Paul after he lifted his eyes. "Thank you."

A woman leaned against Volodia and whispered something

to him. He shrugged his shoulders.

"Paul," he said. "Yesterday?"

Paul stared at him, confused.

"Ah!" Volodia said. "Tomorrow?"

He pointed to the stove and the tables, making a chopping motion.

"What time?" Paul asked without hesitating.

Volodia slapped his shoulders and grabbed two bowls from the shelf.

"Come, we eat," he said, leaving the room. "Real plates."

V.

Paul stood at the corner of 91st Street and Fifth Avenue. He thought to walk to the gardens and watch the people getting married, the fountain with the girls dancing while sagging roses perfumed the afternoon air. He turned south, passing museums and tourists, hotdog carts, horse-drawn carriages, police cars, the zoo where he would not work today, old women in giant sunglasses, little boys in new suits. A light rain began to spit across the sidewalk. He thought to walk fast, maybe duck into FAO Schwartz on 58th Street until it passed, but he did not.

Paul stared up at Tiffany's, wondering if he would ever go inside, if he would ever take a woman to the fourth floor or the second floor or wherever the engagement rings hid under bright cases.

He shivered once.

The rain smacked against him, his shirt and pants growing heavy.

Paul wove through the crowds, never bumping a shoulder, never nudging a baby carriage as he made his way downtown. He looked quickly at the stone lions in front of the library. He had heard their names once, but today he could not remember them.

Now on 34th Street, he didn't look up at the Empire State Building, because it scared him to lean his head back that far, even if the top was hidden in fog and mist.

He thought of the apartment, smelling of fresh paint, the closets empty, the dust in corners where he had not swept. She had made him paint when she arrived.

"White," she said, the moment she entered. "It must be white or it is bad luck."

He had been scared to send her pictures, the old windows and the wobbly fire escape would make her change her mind.

She sent him to the hardware store.

When he returned she was stripped down to her bra and panties, one of his old T-shirts wrapped around her head like a turban. They painted long into the night, then he threw everything out in one single plastic bag, the cans, the wet brushes, the rollers, the T-shirt, leaving it by the curb.

She stood naked in the darkness when he was back.

"Wash your hands," she said, in a low voice.

He did, leaving his dirty clothes on the tiny bathroom floor.

"Tomorrow, you buy a new mattress," she said. "I don't want to know how many girls you fucked here."

His hands jumped. Goose bumps ran up one of his arms.

She went to the bed and drew herself across it. Her arms spread, her breasts sliding flat, her cheek turned to one side.

"Come on," she said in the same low voice. "Like you did when we met. Like you did in the hotel, the last time you were in Moscow."

He kneeled, his head on her stomach, his hands pressed against her hips. Paul pulled himself straight, spooning next to her. He kissed her neck, twisting her hair in his fingers. She turned away, arching her back once then flopping back to the messy sheets.

Birds were flapping around the windows.

A police siren grew close, then stopped abruptly.

Paul let out a breath and climbed on top of her. She lay motionless, her legs stiff.

"It took so long for you to come here," he whispered to her.

She turned her face to give him her cheek.

"So, so long," he continued.

Anya moved once against him, and then he was pressing inside her in a steady rhythm. A light filled the sky for a moment but neither of them noticed it.

He finished quickly, holding on to her breasts like they were life preservers.

She began to cry in the darkness.

He pulled away.

"That hotel," she mumbled. "It's gone now. They tore it down."

Paul thought of the worn red carpets of the hallways, the dark fake-wood panels on the walls, the bright lights in the elevator.

"And now, you fuck me like I am some whore," she said, and stood up from the bed.

The streetlight changed and Paul did not cross, staring at the pavement while the Empire State Building loomed above him, the top in that same wet cloud it had been in for the past few hours. He shivered again, and stifled a sneeze. The light changed again and he ran across the street as a truck barreled through the potholes and the black puddles in between them.

VI.

A woman wrapped in a blanket stood at the corner of Second Avenue and First Street. She shouted at the traffic weaving toward Houston and the Williamsburg Bridge. Her hair was wild, like steel wool that had gone bad. She rolled her eyes at him.

"No motherfucking Reese's Peanut Butter Cups for you, shithead," she said through clenched teeth. "Not even the mini ones."

Paul nodded once, and held out a hand asking if she would like some help crossing the street.

"I'm not going over there," she grumbled. "Fucking one-foot mafia junkie house."

He nodded once, taking a step back.

"Never cross Second Avenue," she said. "If you know what's good for you."

Paul watched the light change to green and crossed the street.

"Asshole," she shouted at him, waving a dirty finger in the air.

He hovered in the door of the Mars Bar. A few stools had people on them, nursing bottles of beer. A young man with hair slicked back sat with a guitar case next to him.

"Hey, one more whiskey please," the man said through a thick Southern drawl.

A Shangri-Las song came on the jukebox.

The skinny blonde behind the bar in a torn shirt with tattoos running up one of her arms leaned toward him and splashed bourbon into the glass until it reached the brim.

"Thankee," he said after slapping his hand on the bar.

Paul went inside and sat a few stools away from him.

The pay phone began to ring.

Paul looked at the lost expressions on faces that stared into the bottoms of their beer bottles. No one moved.

"Should I get it?" the man with the guitar case asked.

The bartender shook her head no as she washed glasses.

The phone kept ringing.

She slid a cold beer in front of Paul.

"Shot?" she asked, placing two glasses next to each other. She filled them halfway and toasted to him all in one motion.

"I even gave you a clean one," she added, slapping the empty down. "Welcome to New York."

Paul sipped once from his, then pulled on the beer.

"I live here," he said quietly.

The man with the guitar case broke into a strange laugh.

"Welcome to New York!" he repeated, sliding his glass down to touch Paul's. "Where you from?"

"Down the block," Paul said, trying to keep from smiling by staring at the names carved into the wood in front of him.

The man with the guitar case pretended to sip some of his drink as he snorted. The bartender topped his off as the pay phone began to ring again.

"Answer it," she said. "And tell them Sid isn't here."

Paul leaned back in his seat and grabbed the receiver. A woman was speaking quickly on the other end.

"Sid's not here," he said, interrupting her, and then she hung up.

The room percolated with small chuckles as he sat back down.

"I'm ordering Mexican," the bartender announced, leaning toward him. "You want something?"

Paul thought for a moment.

"If you are gonna sit here and drink you should put something in your stomach," she added.

"Just no chicken," Paul said after a moment. "Too much chicken today."

The man with the guitar case began making clucking sounds.

"Hitch!" the bartender said, leaning forward as her T-shirt hung loose from her shoulders. "Lay off him—he's from out of town."

Rain smacked against the old windows as red brake lights and neon glowed outside them. The bar was hot and damp, with people crammed around the jukebox and the pinball machine. Paul stood next to Hitch now, his guitar case knocking against their feet. A man with a twisted spine sat in the corner, his body a sort of curlicue, one shoulder hunched tall over a mug full of ice that he filled bit by bit from a bottle of beer. He stared at him, and the man barked back impossible words, hands jerking in circles, his mouth half-full of tiny yellow teeth.

"Lulu!" Hitch called out to the bartender. "Translation?"

She looked up, as she opened a beer with each hand.

"Charlie has two basic conversations," she shouted back above the roar of the jukebox. "He likes you, or he doesn't like you."

Paul looked at Charlie, trying not to stare. He raised his bottle to him and nodded once. Charlie's hands fell, suddenly going quiet.

A woman with red hair and a leopard-spot jumpsuit stood in the doorway, her hands on her hips.

"Sid!" she shouted.

No one noticed her, and the next song came on.

Lulu reached beneath the bar and the music got quieter. Someone shouted to turn it back up.

"Mil," she said, leaning across the bar.

Paul turned, trying to get the red-haired woman's attention.

"Hey," he said, pointing at Lulu.

"He's in the corner," Lulu said.

The red-haired woman craned her neck and saw a man with his head against a narrow shelf, sleeping by the front window.

"How the hell can a guy sleep here?" Hitch asked Paul, nudging his elbow.

"Sometimes you just have to," Paul said, shrugging his shoulders.

Lulu came back down the bar to them.

"The real question is what he did to get that tired," she said in a loud whisper.

The red-haired woman stood over him.

"Sid!" she said, dragging his name out.

"That ain't Sid," Hitch called to her. "That's Amazing Sid."

She frowned, waving a middle finger at him.

Charlie's hands were in the air again as he barked his impossible words. Paul thought of the sea lions and how they must be swimming with just their noses above the water. They always did this when it rained.

"He don't like Sid," Hitch said, banging hard on Paul's elbow.

"Nobody does," Lulu said, from the other end of the bar.

She turned the music back up.

"If it's "Delia's Gone," I'm turning that shit off," she shouted. "I've fucking had it with that song."

Someone yelled at her.

"Yeah, and no Chemical Brothers too," she added.

The red-haired woman stomped outside, her heels making snapping noises on the old floor.

At the far end of the bar, in the darkness close to the pair of bathrooms, the crowd turned in a slow circle. A Sinatra song came on the jukebox. All at once, Paul saw a man strip naked, his old lumpy body climbing onto a stool and then the bar as random hands steadied him, balancing his soft white skin. He sang along with the music, his head brushing against the bulbs that hung from the lopsided ceiling fans. He held his hands out for balance, not unlike a ballet dancer. Lulu made change and slapped fresh beers onto the counter. Someone howled. Charlie put a hand over his face. Paul watched the old naked man navigating around the empties on the bar, nudging them with his feet. A fire truck barreled down Second Avenue and the room bloomed with red light.

"Alright, get the fuck down," Lulu said, finally looking up at him. "It's too early for this stupidity."

The man wiggled his ass in her direction, handfuls of pale skin dancing. A camera flash went off, then another.

"How about you, baby?" the old man cooed to Lulu.

She shook her head no and gestured for him to get down. Paul smelled smoke.

The red-haired woman stood in the doorway.

"Sid, you motherfucker," she shouted and went into the street.

Rain thwacked in giant pancakes against the sidewalk.

In the corner, Sid moved slowly, then began dancing around.

His shirt was on fire.

People pulled back, cramming into the small space between the pinball machine and the front window. Charlie snapped. Lulu looked up from the far end of the bar.

Hitch stepped into the empty space and grabbed Sid's collar, the flames jumping around the arms of his jacket.

"Come on," he said, pulling him outside.

"Holy shit," Paul said, mostly to himself.

Hitch rolled Sid across the puddles on the sidewalk a few times.

"He's fine," Hitch announced, poking his head back in the door. Sid stood behind him now, wobbling from one foot to the other. Hitch pulled him back inside, giving him his seat.

"Give this man a drink," he said. "On me."

Sid burst into tears and rested his face on the bar. His hair and shirt reeked of burned plastic and smoke.

"Thank you," he mumbled through a thick Manchester accent.

"Who is that woman?" Hitch asked, after a moment.

"That would be my wife," Sid said.

VII.

"Say, friend," Hitch said, leaning close to Paul's ear. "I'm doing a late-night show in a bit."

Paul said nothing.

"It's free," Hitch added.

Paul shrugged his shoulders, pretending to yawn.

"Lulu, you coming?" Hitch asked her. "You get off at ten, right?"

She rolled her eyes.

"Are you any good?" she asked.

"I'll sing you some Elvis," Hitch answered, dragging the words out with his accent.

Paul finished his beer.

"Outstanding!" Hitch said, slapping his hand on the bar, right next to Sid's ear.

The hotel smelled of vomit and sweat. Hitch lead Paul and Lulu up narrow stairs, into a dark hallway.

"Ten bucks a night," he said at one point.

"You get what you pay for," Lulu replied.

A short, fat man and a tall, thin one were running up and down the hallway.

"Gentlemen!" Hitch said in a big voice.

"Cowboy Joe!" they said, all together.

Lulu stood with her hands on her hips.

"Oh, Jesus Christ," she said.

"Miss Lulu!" the short one said through an excited lisp. He bowed once. The tall one just stared at her.

"Eugene," she said, in a low voice. "Clem."

Clem stared at her T-shirt.

"I hope you finish your homework, before you go out to play," she added.

Clem looked at his feet. Eugene opened his mouth, speechless, then his lips slowly turned into a tiny O, then a smile.

Hitch opened a door and rested his guitar case on the floor.

"Sit, sit," he told them, waving toward the bed.

Lulu shook her head no and leaned against the wall with her arms folded across her chest. Paul found a place next to her.

Hitch tuned the guitar for some time. The little man and the tall one galloped the halls in random spurts.

"One song and I'm out of here," Lulu whispered to Paul.

Paul nodded slowly and pressed a finger to his chest.

"Me too," he added.

"Okey-dokey," Hitch said with a flourish and a sour open chord. "This one's for Amazing Sid and . . ."

"Millie," Lulu interrupted.

"And Ginger Millie," Hitch mumbled. "I think we all got a Ginger Millie in our life, right?"

He closed his eyes in quiet concentration, then launched into a series of messy chords. Lulu tapped against Paul's leg once and raised an eyebrow.

Well, a hard-headed woman
a soft-hearted man
been the cause of trouble
ever since the world began.

Oh yeah, ever since the world began.
A hard-headed woman been
a thorn in the side of man.

As Hitch muddled his way through the words, Paul began to feel dizzy. He leaned hard against the wall, steadying himself, and one hand reached out into the air as he slid down to the floor.

Adam told to Eve,
Listen here to me.
Don't you let me catch you
messin' round that apple tree.

VIII.

There was a pale light outside the window. He saw the narrow bed, the empty beer cans on the floor, the guitar resting on top of the case. Hitch snored lightly, one hand tucked inside his jeans, another over his face. Paul breathed in quietly, smelling perfume, wondering if it was Lulu's. He pulled himself to his knees, finding his balance, and then stood up.

Pigeons were making noises on the windowsill. A garbage truck groaned from the sidewalk.

He unlocked the door and closed it carefully, turning the handle in tiny motions until it made a soft click.

There were long puddles in the street. He wandered around them, starting back uptown. The sun reached past the water towers and slanted down into the valley of the Bowery as Paul stood in the early light, finding it warm on the back of his neck.

His stomach turned, sour and empty as he waited for the light to change.

Paul's feet knew the way and his mind wandered as the streets and tiny parks flitted past him, as he imagined the warm kitchen, the giant pots, and the soup he would soon be cooking.

IX.

Paul steadied himself against the steel tables. Someone placed a paper cup of water next to him and he sipped from it randomly. The faces were asking him things and he could not tell if they spoke Russian or English. He forced half-smiles, shrugged his shoulders, waiting for them to be satisfied with the vague answers he offered.

Volodia stomped into the room in a wrinkled white suit.

"Smell good chef!" he announced. "So, so good."

Volodia left the big room and came back with Eli. His hand gripping Eli's arm, he guided him to the stove. Volodia whispered in his ear.

Eli leaned to Paul.

"You taking short break," he explained.

"But, the soup," Paul said.

"It can wait five minutes," Eli explained. "You come with me."

Paul lowered the flame.

Volodia stood in his place, his eyes fierce, his hands on his hips.

"I watch," he called to them. "Nobody change soup. No *kapusta*."

Eli brought him to a different hallway and a tiny door. All at once it opened onto the main room. The choir was singing at full volume. People were clumped in the center, necks craning.

"Excuse me," Eli said, pressing past the first ones.

He clutched Paul's arm the same way Volodia held his.

"Come on," he said. "This is important."

Paul wobbled on his heels feeling the soft incensed air around him.

"*Astaroshna*, excuse us," he repeated in a quiet voice. People eyed them and saw Paul's white apron. They began to help Eli, pulling at each other's shoulders, making a loose path for them.

In the very center of the crowd there was a small pedestal. An icon was perched on it, under glass. It looked old to Paul, older than anything else on the walls or the ceiling.

"You can ask her for anything," Eli explained. "She will give it to you."

Paul shook his head without realizing it.

His stomach growled and he thought he might want to throw up. He burped the Mexican food Lulu had ordered last night.

Eli pressed the middle of his back.

"Okay, you are next," he whispered.

Paul approached the icon and went to his knees. His chin to his chest, he imagined the apologies he had written to her but never sent. He thought of her sad, angry eyes and how she never said that she loved him. Paul thought of her running into traffic that night, replaying the car horns and her low scream and how he did not hesitate, following her.

The icon was flaked with gold, the woman's giant almond-shaped eyes staring back at him, kind, unflinching. Paul kissed his hand and rested it on the glass, then leaned forward and kissed her eyes with his lips as gently as he could. Someone raised their hand in the air as if they objected to what he was doing.

Eli took his shoulder and helped him to his feet. Paul stumbled toward the front doors, the ground giving way underneath him.

Outside on the front steps, birds were chirping.

Eli fished a Kleenex from one of his pockets.

"Here," he said, pressing it into Paul's hand.

"My friend, you are so moved!" Eli said. "First a chef, now this. You are full of surprises."

Paul wiped his eyes and understood he had been crying.

"The soup," he said, as he went down the stairs toward the door that led to the kitchen.

Father Kirill entered, blessing the women who lined up the plastic bowls and the ones who sliced cucumbers and tomatoes.

Paul held his hands out as he approached.

"Bless you," Father Kirill said in his low growl.

Paul nodded once, adding, "Thank you, Father."

"Do you have a passport?" Father Kirill asked him abruptly.

"Ah yes, I do," Paul said quickly.

"Come with me," Father Kirill said, leading him into the hallway and then to Father Alexander's office.

"Wait here," he said, his voice growing thick and slow. "If you are tired, please rest."

He motioned toward a folding cot that leaned against the wall as he closed the door behind him. Paul thought to sit in the big chair behind the desk just for a minute, then went to the cot.

Paul folded his hands across his chest and listened to the quite thrum of the clock.

There was a small tap against the sole of his shoe, then another. Voices improvised in the dark room. They discussed something, asking the same question in hushed bursts. Paul recognized Eli, then Volodia.

"Well, he definitely needs to eat something first," Eli said at one point.

Paul stopped pretending to be asleep and opened his eyes.

Father Kirill and Volodia looked down at him. Eli leaned into his ear.

"Just say yes, okay?" he whispered.

"Tikhon," Father Kirill began. "Are you ready to do God's work?"

Paul pulled himself up, and stared at his hands for a moment.

"Yes, Father," he replied.

"Bless you, Tikhon," Father Kirill said, pulling him to his feet. He turned abruptly and spoke in Russian to Volodia who nodded vigorously as he listened, smacking his hands together once, then again.

"You passport here?" Volodia asked him, pointing down.

"No, it's at home," Paul replied.

Volodia turned to Eli, shoving his shoulder.

The taxi creaked as it bounced across the potholes on the FDR. Paul closed his eyes with the window open, feeling the cold air whipping against his cheeks.

"You are doing a very good thing," Eli told him. "This will come back to you. I just know it."

The streets clicked by. Eli took the corners hard after turning onto Houston. Whenever a light was going to turn red he beat it. They never came to a full stop until he pulled over on First Street.

"Be right back," Paul said.

A bulb flickered in the hallway. He could smell pot smoke and maybe black beans as he climbed the stairs.

Paul tried not to look at the empty rooms, or the bed, just the kitchen drawer where the box with the ring and passport were. The apartment smelled of paint and somehow cigarettes. Paul pocketed his documents, suddenly turning and standing in the arch that led to the tiny living room. He leaned against the wall, counting out the arguments, the nights he slept on the couch, the morning he woke up and understood she had really gone, that quicksand undertow of the empty rooms, the abrupt silence.

Paul called the zoo and explained he had a family emergency and would be out for a week.

There was a light knock on the door.

Paul turned, seeing he had forgotten to close it.

Misha forced his head in, flashing a quick smile and held out a hand.

"Hello," he said.

Paul nodded once.

"All is okay?" Misha asked, craning his neck to see inside the apartment. "I smell paint."

"Ah, no. The bathroom is fine," Paul told him. "I was just fixing up the windows."

Misha nodded, approving.

"Okay," Misha said. "I no see you for five years, now so many times."

Paul motioned that he was leaving. Misha backed into the hallway. He shook Misha's hand vigorously, then went down the stairs two at a time as his steps echoed around him.

"So, you didn't eat today?" Eli asked as they pulled away.

Paul shook his head.

Eli looked back quickly and pulled the taxi all the way around to the left, hard onto Houston, and then gunned the engine to make the light as they went up First Avenue.

He pulled over at Tenth Street in front of the Five Roses pizzeria.

"You want a meatball parm?" he asked. "What am I saying, everybody wants a meatball parm."

He slammed the door, waving his hands around.

"Back in ten," he said. "Rita, I'm baaaack!"

Paul slumped back in the seat, listening to the bicycles

whizz by, bits of people talking.

The sandwiches were huge, wrapped in tinfoil. They balanced their paper napkins on the dashboard and tore into them. Paul sucked on the sauce, smacking his lips, pulling the cheese in long strands and chewing on everything.

"The call those telephones in Italy," Eli said in between bites. "These are fucking good, right?"

"Amazing," Paul said and took the next chew, the bread soft and wet and then crusty on the outside.

"Give," Volodia said, holding his hand out.

Paul gave him the passport.

The door to the consulate opened. There was a dull thud and the smell of old roses. Volodia stalked the halls. Paul followed him, seeing big rooms with their lights off, lace curtains behind glass.

A door opened.

Volodia motioned for Paul to sit outside in the hallway.

He rested, tasting garlic and oregano rising from his stomach as he stared at the old carpet.

Volodia came from the room with papers for him to sign.

In the cathedral, Father Kirill placed the icon in a padded aluminum case. He spoke words over it, folding an old cloth, praying and resting his hands on it. He motioned for Paul to approach.

"She is in your care now," he explained. "In Moscow, Father Dmitry will take her from you, only him."

"How will I know if he is Father Dmitry?" Paul asked.

"He has a birthmark on one cheek," Father Kirill said, pointing at his own face. "And he looks like me."

"Ah," Paul said, taking the case slowly.

"He is my brother," Father Kirill said. "My real brother."

Volodia rested a hand on Paul's elbow.

"No first class," he said, handing him an envelope. "Maybe you sit nice girl next to coach."

Volodia laughed nervously.

"You carry our mother now," Father Kirill said, cracking a smile behind his beard. "Anything is possible."

There were kisses on Paul's cheeks in the giant dark room, faces that were familiar but with names he did not know. Faces rough with beards and stubble, soft and young, old and wrinkled. The case already felt heavy in his hands. He stood up straight, carrying it in front of his chest then leaning his head back to remind himself of the paintings on the ceiling and the bright circle where the sun came in.

Eli drove in silence. The sky turned pink and lavender, stretching beyond the bridges.

All at once, night fell.

"You cold?" Eli asked him.

When he pulled up to the departure gate, Eli jumped from the wheel and went to the trunk.

He handed Paul a windbreaker.

"Someone left it," he said. "I knew it would find a good home someday."

Paul pulled it on, seeing how it was short in the sleeves.

"Thank you," he said.

Eli wrapped his arms around him in a bear hug.

"Bless you," he said. "Bless you, Tikhon."

X.

The flight was delayed for more than an hour. Paul sat on an edge of a window that looked onto the planes that silently taxied to their gates and the ones darting into the sky in the distance. His skin was hot and he touched his forehead more than a few times, trying to understand if he was running a fever.

Then, he grabbed the case tighter, feeling the cold aluminum against his fingers, imagining this would cool his entire body and bring him back to normal.

When the gate did open, there was a mad rush of passengers, some with giant bags, some with crying children, one with a cat or a small dog in a special case.

Inside the plane, an old woman sat in the seat next to his. Bags wrapped in plastic were crammed around her legs, stuffed into the empty spaces. He sat down, resting the case on his lap. There were heavy thumps under them. The plane rocked slowly back and forth, in tiny movements.

Paul closed his eyes for some time, trying to understand if he was really sick or not. He imagined the icon inside the case, and how nothing bad could happen as long as he carried it.

He opened his eyes.

"I go home," the old woman said, looking at him quickly and waving a finger in the air.

He smiled and nodded.

The loudspeaker came on and a man spoke in Russian.

The old woman laughed once, and clapped her hands together.

"Year of horse," she said to herself.

"Excuse me?" Paul asked her.

The loudspeaker started again, now with the same man speaking in labored English. "Ladies and gentlemen, our apologies for the brief delay. It was unavoidable, but not due to any technical issue. We have some important passengers with us today. As you may have noticed, we have some heavy cargo being loaded. These are ten Lipizzaner show horses that are returning to their stables in Moscow. Please know that they are being handled very carefully to make sure they are comfortable. Again, we are sorry for any inconvenience. We should be leaving the gate in the next ten minutes."

Paul looked at the old woman, trying to find what he could say.

A smile stretched across his face. His hand jumped to his cheek. She closed her eyes once and nodded, then she pulled a pillow to the side of her head and wedged it against the window and closed her eyes.

He felt the gentle rocking under his feet stop. Paul imagined the great white horses in the darkness, tired and nervous. He wondered if they understood they were traveling across an ocean tonight. They must be scared, he thought. But at least they are together, going home.

Acknowledgments

I was lucky enough to work with some fabulous editors while writing this book. Kristin Kimball, Peter Bricklebank, and Jenny DePierre navigated these stories through the roughest seas, and somehow into your hands. To be an editor is a bit like being a parent. The job changes by the moment—from psychologist to grammarist, from Sherpa to reader. If writers are anything like tightrope walkers, then editors are both the balancing pole and the safety net—without them, we writers are doomed.

A college professor named Howard Enders gave me all of the tough love and salty encouragement that a young writer could ask for. I remember reading that first draft of Cooper's Farm in his class so many years ago, and how he championed it. It meant the world to me, and I am sorry he is not alive to see the fruit that eventually grew from that tree. Another teacher from SUNY Purchase, Richard Stack, taught me how to write a sentence, as nutty as that sounds. We wrote nothing but sentences for an entire semester, and I am all the better for it. Rome was not built in a day.

I met Jack Micheline in the Mars Bar one night, and we became fast friends. He treated me like a son, and we wandered the streets together. His finger pointing furiously in the air, he told me to keep writing no matter what. The only thing better than reading his poems was to hear him recite them in a noisy bar, or in a hushed room. "Beauty is everywhere, Baudelaire. Even a worm is beautiful," he said, and I was listening.

A collection of kind and generous readers took long hard looks at these stories, and gave me tireless and invaluable feedback. I hope to return the favor, someday—Martina Bergstrasse,

Alexis Burling, Maya Slobin, Ciaran Groarke, Susannah Harris, Rick Hochman, Ashley Iser, Lisa Montebello, and Jessica Treat.

I have nothing but gratitude for my brother Anatole, who gave me permission to include a story that is far too close to what really happened.

Last, but certainly not least—my wife Natasha and daughters Eve and Vera deserve a thank you as big as the sky. When I am a hot mess, you calm me. When we have something to celebrate, you raise the most perfect glasses. I would be completely lost without you.

About the Author

Marco North has been a circus welder, a short-order cook, and an instrument builder for the Blue Man Group. A Brooklyn native, he attended one of the country's first Montessori schools before the North family moved to Otego, New York, where they ran a pig farm.

His bittersweet stories about everyday people have been presented at Lincoln Center and La Mama, etc., and have been published in *Stray Dog*, *Red Wheelbarrow*, the *Black River Review*, *Poetry New York*, *On the Page*, *Colère*, *Lonesome Traveler*, *Vox Populi*, *Travel & Leisure*, and the *Raven Chronicles*.

In between writing and directing independent films (*Blackbetty*, *Whale*), he records alt. folk songs under the band name Martin Ruby and has released two studio albums, *Heaven Get Behind Me* and *Jacob and the Angel*. Marco spent fifteen years in Moscow, Russia, before moving to Tbilisi, Georgia. He publishes an award-winning blog, *Impressions of an Expat*, with readers from over 130 countries.

You can visit him online at www.marconorth.com.